HAPPINESS IS WASTED ON ME

KIRKLAND CICCONE

Cover illustration: Andrew Forteath
Front cover: image of child's face : © Frank Uyt den Bogaard

Published by:

Fledgling Press Ltd.
1 Milton Rd West
Edinburgh
EH15 1LA

www.fledglingpress.co.uk

ISBN 9781912280353
Printed and bound by:

Print on Demand Worldwide, Peterborough

What's it called?

Chapter 1

12th April 1992

Life would have been better if I hadn't looked inside that box, but not much better. The box itself wasn't particularly large. Neither was the baby inside. He was dead, of course. I found him by accident, because there's no such thing as fate. Everything that happened after that day only happened because I was forced to make a simple choice:

Do I go one way or the other?

I chose the other.

I looked inside the box.

I spent most of that day waiting for the sound of a bell. I couldn't concentrate on anything else. Not my teacher's voice, nor the sound of dogs yelping in the distance or pencil scraping roughly on paper. Just the bell. When it finally happened, I reacted immediately. Jumping up from my chair, I tore through the classroom, flinging myself straight out the door so fast I almost fell down the stairs. I sprinted as fast as possible (not very fast at all) to get away from Gary Dowds and his gang of cromags. If they wanted to get me, they had to catch me first. I'd spent all morning planning an escape route in my head. It took me along a field behind the football pitch, past the tall trees, thick grass and the sloping hill that caught a thousand empty crisp packets whenever the wind blew west.

The sky was bright, beautiful and blue.

It wouldn't last, of course.

It never did.

*

The mud beneath my feet squelched despite the summer heat. Deceptively slick, I found myself slipping down a slope, my arms flapping like a coyote falling off a cliff in a cartoon. It didn't help, of course, but anything seemed possible at that age, even flouting the laws of aerodynamics with my skinny arms.

I slid, tumbled, and finally came to rest at the edge of some bushes.

My school uniform (a pair of black trousers, a grey V-neck sweater, white shirt, and navy tie with the Langland's Primary School logo) were caked in thick wet muck. I shuddered. The uniform was brand new, paid for by a clothing grant. My mother had a habit of loudly announcing the cost of something, quickly following this with a complaint about price increases. I knew she'd explode when she saw the state of me, but I wasn't too concerned. Not yet. That was another few hours away, a lifetime really. My main priority was to hide from Gary Dowds and his gang. Their voices followed me, a warning they were still close by. There was still a chance they'd catch up with me.

So I ran and ran and ran and ran.

Eventually, I stopped running.

My first hiding place wasn't good enough. One of the lads found me and yelled for Gary. I had to run again. My legs took me outside the school grounds, at the far end near St. Joseph's Primary, a rival school built next to Langland's and dangerous territory for me. Desperate to get out of sight, I hid by some bushes, counting the seconds until they became minutes until they became hours. At one point I realised I'd been holding my breath too hard and too long. Releasing the stockpiled air in my lungs made the world bend slightly. I fell back, landing in some muck and old empty crisp packets. Sitting there in the muck, the stark reality of my situation was obvious: my uniform was more than just dirty, it was now ruined beyond the limit of anything Persil or Daz could do to fix it. What would I say? I couldn't tell my parents. Fishtank wouldn't be sympathetic, not one bit. I could imagine him saying something completely unhelpful, something like — If someone hits you, then you hit back harder. Okay?

Dark clouds seemed to come from nowhere, hanging above me, reflecting my mood. Eventually they burst and I found myself running for shelter under some thick trees, wishing my time away until the downpour stopped. In my rush to escape, I'd left my jacket in the school cloakroom. Shivering, I waited. The rain seemed to last forever. Worse, it was cold. Whistling, desolate wind parted the branches of the big trees, allowing the rain to get in at me. I felt submerged in my clothes. It was just me, all alone in the storm. However, the rain had an unexpected side-effect: it made Gary and his friends give up. We'd all been soaked under the same sky. Once again I was safe, until the next time Gary decided he had a problem with me. Moving quickly out of the rain, I headed towards a small expanse of trees, trying to find one perfect place to rest. Somehow, without realising it, I found myself behind a set of flats in Sandyknowes Road. It was a dingy little place. It seemed cut off, somehow. Distant from both the rest of the town and sunlight itself.

Just up ahead, there was a forest and a small grassy field.

I headed in that direction. I made that choice.

I wish I'd gone the other way.

I stood beneath the trees, wondering what to do next.

Something at the edge of my eye caught my attention.

Something in the muck.

It wasn't a badger hole. Not even badgers wanted to live here.

I peered closer at my discovery.

Half-buried in the soil was a recently dumped cardboard box.

There was a logo on it, washed-out by exposure to the rain. AMSUNG MICR WAV OV N, it said.

Bending down, I reached out and pushed aside a cardboard flap.

It disintegrated into watery mush and my hand went into the box itself. I felt something slimy smear itself across the top of my fingers, and an evil-smelling stink escaped, covering me completely. With a cry of fright, I pulled myself away from whatever I'd disturbed. Seconds later, after wiping my hand on the sleeve of my jumper, I went back for another look. I hadn't imagined it. There was a plump little hand with five perfectly formed fingers reaching out for me. The hand was connected to an arm that joined a torso. By the time I reached the face, I already knew what I'd found in the undergrowth.

A baby in a box.

A *dead* baby in a box.

Its skin was mottled grey, the colour of slick mushrooms.

I bit my knuckles to stifle a scream.

When I realised I'd used that same hand to open the box, I felt nauseous. I spat into the grass a few times, trying to get the feeling of dirt and vileness out of my mouth.

The longer I looked in the box, the more I learned about the baby.

It...he...was a boy. Possibly days old? I wasn't sure. The only experience I had had with a baby up until then was my little brother, Laddie. He was a few years younger than me. We both attended Langland's Primary, though I'd soon be leaving for high school. The baby still had skin on his tiny bones. I didn't want to touch that skin again. There was movement beneath the thin surface of the flesh, the start of the putrification cycle. As I peered into the box, I felt a strong sense of protectiveness. I didn't just want to leave the kid lying about in the mud, surrounded by trees and changeable weather. But what else could I do? I couldn't tell the police. My parents wouldn't want me to get involved. Never ever. If you went to the police, you were a grass. It was that simple. But…leaving the baby to rot seemed somehow monstrous. I had to keep myself out of it, but still help him.

I wanted the baby to have a bit of dignity in death.

That one pure thought helped me come to an important decision.

There used to be a phone box at Beechwood Road. It had holes on the side where glass windows used to be and the British Telecom logo above the door, the blue and red one with the man blowing a long thin horn. Keeping the phone box in one piece was a tireless, thankless task, one that BT had given up long ago. Glass panels in public phone boxes never lasted long in this town. Bored kids, breakable items. A logical conclusion.

The little shelf inside the phone box should have had a phone book on it, but it had been taken and slashed up, the sliced remains thrown into the wind. A nearby bush had caught some of the tattered pieces of paper. It didn't matter to me anyway: I already knew the number I needed to dial. Three digits. A triple tap of a button. Nine. Nine. Nine.

It should have been the easiest thing in the world to do.

The right thing to do.

But knowing the number and dialling it were two different things altogether.

Ten minutes passed as I stood in the box with the receiver propped against my chin. Finally, I gave in to the choice I'd already made: I jabbed the '9' button three times and waited patiently as the tone quavered in my ear. Suddenly, I had an unpleasant notion that it might be better for me in the long run if I disguised my voice. It was the sort of idea only a mistrustful child, one constantly hiding from bullies, would seriously contemplate.

Every accent I attempted sounded like a Dalek on the verge of a nervous breakdown.

—Operator, said the voice on the other end. —Could you please state your emergency?

It was a quiet voice, both calm and smooth. The opposite of my own voice.

—I found a dead body.

Her tone immediately shifted. Just a little. But enough for me to catch the variation.

—Where did you find the body?

—Down in the forest behind the flats at Sandyknowes Road.

—Okay, give me a second to find it.

A second passed. She was as good as her word.

—Cumbernauld?

—Yes.

—Have you touched or moved anything?

That seemed like an odd question, but actually it was the only question that mattered in that moment. I had to be honest. Honesty hadn't always served me well in the past, but on this occasion, it felt important to be as straightforward as possible.

—Yes. It's a dead body in a cardboard box. A dead baby actually. I opened the box.

She probably thought this was a crank call, but once the police headed down to the trees behind the flats, they'd see I wasn't a liar, that I'd been honest.

—Right. I need you to do something for me. I need your name. Are you okay with that?

A surge of paranoia suddenly made me reconsider being too honest. Primitive, sometimes destructive, but it was always there, the sense someone was taking notes on me.

There was only one way I could respond:

I put the phone down.

A shower started as I left the phone box. Rain was this town's default weather. But any attempt to wash away Cumbernauld was doomed to failure. A concrete kingdom, or an urban jungle, this town did everything to extremes, including the sudden changes in weather. As I shivered in the downpour, my first thought was for that poor baby, stuck inside a box, all alone in the cold.

Dead but not quite buried.

In the distance…sirens…

I call them sadness sirens, because that's how they've always sounded to me.

Mum went nuts at me when I got back home. She saw the state of my school uniform and literally screamed her anger in my face.

I told her everything.

Everything but the truth.

Chapter 2

Antenna

The reason Fishtank didn't work was because there were no jobs out there for him. Also, he was far too intelligent for menial labour. This meant Mum had to go out and work four jobs in order to feed and clothe her kids. Anytime someone asked her why she married him in the first place, Mum explained that when she first met Fishtank back in the 70s, he had a good career at Clyde Shipyard as a welder.

Except...

Fishtank later admitted he hadn't worked as a welder.

He'd worked as a cleaner.

For three weeks.

By then it was too late. Mum had already fallen pregnant.

Not having a job meant Fishtank could stay at home with his kids and indulge in his two favourite pastimes. We didn't understand these hobbies, but they kept him occupied and for that we were truly grateful. Anything that kept Fishtank's mercurial moods at bay was absolutely fine by us! His first hobby, his main passion, was spending the day (and a lot of the night) upstairs in his bedroom on his CB radio. That radio meant we could do whatever we wanted without fear that he'd beat the shit out of us with a belt, or in the case of Jake, my eldest brother, a piece of wood from the garden fence.

Fishtank seemed to have endless planks of wood from that fucking fence.

There was one large drawback to the CB radio. Literally. In order to use it, Fishtank had to fit a tall ugly antenna up on the roof. We all watched him put it up, a large metal middle-finger right at our neighbours, an extension of his power to do whatever he wanted without consequence.

—I hope the old bastard falls and breaks his neck, said Jake rebelliously.

Lorna, my eldest sister, shushed Jake.

—You hate him too, said Jake accusingly.

But Lorna said nothing.

She kept her hopes and horrors locked tightly inside her heart and head.

Only one person stood up to Fishtank and his ugly radio antenna. Mr. Moore, our neighbour four doors up, was a kind older man with a beard and moustache. He always seemed to wear a tweed hat and jacket, the sort with large patches on the elbows. It looked wonderfully out of place in Craigieburn Road, a grey area furnished by the council. We all knew Mr. Moore from The Boy's Brigade. I didn't care much for The Brigade, feeling eternally out of sync with the other kids, but it was one of my only ways out of the house at night during the summer and Mr. Moore never failed to ask if I was doing okay.

Instinctively, I knew he hated Fishtank and felt sorry for my mum.

The antenna was his opportunity to strike.

—That's a cancer rod, he yelled as Fishtank struggled on the roof.

Fishtank's response?

—Fuck off and mind your own business.

—Take it down, John, or I'll report you to the council.

If I'd known Fishtank needed planning permission to stick the aerial on our roof, I probably would have gone straight back to the phone box in Beechwood Road and reported him myself. But I had no idea about these things. It was all part of the mysterious adult world I dreaded, a world I expected to enter in the future.

—Go to the council, yelled Fishtank. —Fucking go! I don't

care. I'll just go to the police.

Any mention of the police spiked my anxiety above my usual level, especially since I knew Fishtank hated them. Mr. Moore, however, wasn't backing down to this threat.

—Go to the police? For what?

—To tell them you're a fucking pervert.

Mr. Moore (not a pervert in the slightest) looked absolutely sickened that Fishtank would stoop so low. Sounds that couldn't quite form words came from his throat. I wanted to tell him he was a good man, but he shouldn't have tried to take on my father.

He didn't stand a chance against Fishtank.

No-one did.

Fishtank's second passion was far more...niche...and a little bit difficult to understand. Sometimes, whenever he felt a certain way, he'd take me out and together we'd go for a walk up to Cumbernauld Town Centre, the ugliest building in the world. It looked like an experiment conducted by insane Lego enthusiasts on LSD. A rabbit warren on stilts, or a decapitated alien's head, the shopping centre evoked strong feelings from everyone. In fact, the only time the people of Cumbernauld could unite as one was whenever someone insulted the town. We didn't like that. And yet...we loved insulting it ourselves. Ugly or not, Cumbernauld Town Centre was the core of culture in our town – and the place Fishtank needed to go for his other favourite pastime.

It was always the same. We went to The Royal Bank of Scotland, where I'd wait as Fishtank popped into the Loans office for a quick bung. It didn't matter that he couldn't pay the money he owed back to the bank. Mum always ended up getting into more debt to pay off his debt. It was an endless circle of financial peaks and poverty.

Anyway, he'd emerge from the Loans office looking

triumphant. This familiar look of self-satisfaction was the same as all of his other facial expressions. Once he had his money (usually a grand, maybe a bit less) he would take me to the Cumbernauld branch of John Menzies. I pronounced it 'Men-zeez', but he always called it 'Ming-ez'. He had to be different, make himself stand out in some stupid way. In all honesty, I never liked John Menzies. All those toys on their shelves that I wasn't allowed to play with, that I'd never get at Christmas. It was a Greek tragedy that Homer didn't put in his *Iliad;* the tale about the boy who wanted toys so much he ended up trapped inside a shop full of toys he couldn't touch.

Fishtank would strut through the shop entrance and I'd tag along like a poor puppy.

—Walk properly, snarled Fishtank. —Like me!

So I changed my walk to make him happy. But it wasn't enough. It was never enough.

The first thing Fishtank always did after entering John Menzies was head over to the counter. It was part of his weird hobby. Once there, he'd select the cheapest product he could lay his hands on. I'd watched him do this a few times over the years. It was like a tired comedy routine. He never changed it, and the only applause he needed was in his own head.

On this particular occasion, he picked up a measuring tape that cost one quid.

—That'll be one pound exactly, said the girl at the checkout.

This was the bit of his routine Fishtank loved the most. He would put his hand deep into his rain jacket, then bring out one thousand quid. He'd drop that thick wad of notes onto the counter, take a few agonising seconds so that everyone could see the money. Then finally, always with a big arrogant smile on his face, he'd look up and say:

—Have you got any change?

Depending on how well the staff were trained (and John

11

Menzies usually trained its staff to a good standard), this would always end in one of two ways: the girl would either gasp and look at Fishtank like he was some sort of secret millionaire, or she would sullenly snatch a note from the roll sitting on the counter, go away, and return with almost too much change to carry, some of it slipping through nervous twitchy fingers.

Eventually, all the staff had to help. Tills were emptied. Safes were opened. Cloth bags crammed with clinking clanking coins were emptied just so Fishtank could get change owed from buying something cheaply at a quid.

He thought this was a hoot.

Like, the funniest thing ever.

Really, what chance did I have?

Chapter 3

Haircut of Revenge

It was my own fault. My folks sent me to Aff Yer Heid, Cumbernauld's premier barber, with only one thing to keep in mind. Get a short back and sides. It was right across from The Royal Bank of Scotland. I had a pair of headphones pressed hard in my ears, the thick wire from the headset trailing down to an old Walkman playing Shakespears Sister on cassette tape. It belonged to my second eldest sister, Donnie, (don't ever call her Danielle). I sat in the shop thinking everyone was staring at me, seeing something I couldn't see. Then finally, the time came.

I'd rehearsed it in my head on the way up to the shop.

—I want a short back and sides.

Actually, I didn't want a short back and sides. That's what I was told to get.

—Alright lad.

The barber grinned, revealing gaps in his smile. He was completely bald. The idea of a man who worked with hair having none of his own seemed funny to me, but I said nothing.

Instead, I sat down and waited for my haircut.

—You need to take those out your ears, he said.

Oh. My headphones. The music wasn't so loud that I couldn't hear what was going on around me, but I'd always thought life was better with a backing track. Sheepishly, I removed my headset, which played a blast of *You're History* to everyone else in the shop. Some people sniggered, though I didn't know why. Feeling self-conscious, I looked away.

Finally, the barber started on my hair. Halfway through, I

knew something was wrong. These days I speak up if I feel something isn't right. But back in 1992, when I was a quiet little kid, I would *never* have said anything out of turn. You were raised to trust in the supreme authority of the adult. Barbers knew what they were doing, didn't they? And I kept that in mind as huge tufts of hair dropped onto my lap.

By the time the cut was finished, I was completely bald.

I looked like a grumpy boiled egg.

—That's what you get for skipping the queue, laughed the barber.

I'd been so deep in my head, rehearsing what I needed to say, that I'd skipped the queue without realising it. When you lived inside your own head, you lived away from other people. I hadn't noticed they were before me. It hadn't crossed my mind.

Looking up at the barber, still in mid-laugh, I said:

—I'm bald....just like you.

He stopped laughing.

I ran out the shop and didn't stop until I got back home.

When I went back to school on Monday, it was with not a single hair on my head. People laughed, of course. Kids see wet eyes and sense weakness. My first tactic was to pass it off as a deliberate decision to do something different. I wasn't merely bald, but a pioneer! Yes! An icon of future fashion. Me, the glorious Walter! Besides, it would grow back.

My attempts at presenting myself as an innovator didn't go well.

—You look like that baldy from *The Crystal Maze*, shouted Gary Dowds as soon as he laid eyes on me. And when Gary said something, everyone agreed. Like they had a choice.

—Has anyone seen Walter Wedgeworth?

—Yeah, he got a job on Channel 4 presenting *The Crystal Maze*.

14

It didn't take long for the gossip to reach every nook and cranny of Langland's Primary School. Soon enough, I was a tourist attraction in the playground. People wanted to touch my scalp, feel the stubbly skin that had been thick with brown hair only a couple of days beforehand.

Teachers were especially interested. One of them asked if I was okay.

—I think so, I said.

Teachers always seemed concerned about me. It got a bit much at times.

By the end of the day, people stopped caring about my stupid new haircut. There was always something new happening in Cumbernauld to get excited over.

A week had passed since I'd called the police about the baby. I couldn't think about anything else except that mottled little face in the soggy old box. He'd been in the newspapers, of course. He even had a name. Not his real one, of course. No-one knew that. But in the absence of a real name, the papers christened him Baby C, which was how he would remain until his real parents were found and his actual name recovered. Naming the baby after a single letter seemed quietly terrifying to me. I couldn't help but think there was an entire alphabet full of letters for other dead babies. The whole ordeal soon got much worse. According to the report in *The Cumbernauld News*, Baby C had been asphyxiated, which was a nice way of saying someone stopped him breathing on purpose. Apparently, police were on the look-out for witnesses. They especially wanted to talk to an anonymous caller, someone who'd led police to the baby's body.

Apparently, the caller sounded like a 'little girl, possibly 8-12 years of age'.

—A little girl! I shrieked in the middle of Mr. Ali's cornershop.

Wounded, I put the newspaper back on the shelf and headed

off back home. Well…not home, as such. Just the house I lived in with my family and Fishtank.

Chapter 4

Entertainment

Fishtank always made sure we had the latest in-home entertainment technology. We must have been the only house in the entire town to have a Betamax video recorder in the living room and bare cupboards in the kitchen. We also had a fancy record player with lots of vinyl records, all of which were piled up on the cabinet shelf near our 32" Panasonic television set. Next to that cabinet was a fully-furnished fish tank that had unintentionally given Dad his nickname. It was full of bright tropical fish, plastic furniture, and pink neon lights that cast shimmering shadows across our living room. Oh, it couldn't just be a tank with some water like every other fish tank. It *had* to have a light show. Sometimes, during the dark winter nights, I felt like I lived in an aquarium. Yet, despite all these wonderful toys, we were completely at the mercy of a coin-operated television. We had BSB/Sky TV before everyone else in Craigieburn Road, but couldn't watch most of its scheduled programming because we had no money to fill the little box. I hated that fucker. If one of your few escapes in life was television, then a coin-operated TV was the bane of your existence. Worse, it gave Fishtank more power over everyone living under his roof. I could swear he deliberately timed when he'd top up that meter, just so it would cut out during *Going Live* on Saturday morning.

During the summer, I spent most of my spare time at Danny McDonald's house along with other friends. His TV was free and so was his Super Nintendo. Danny's bedroom was the closest thing me and my friends had to a club house. An only child, Danny got everything he asked for and everything he didn't. His mother worked the day shift at William Low's in Cumbernauld Town Centre, which meant she was out of the house for hours. No-one knew much about his father, not even Danny, but I suspected his dad was probably married – and not to Danny's mother. I didn't care. I was happy so long as I could play games and watch television. Danny was a laugh. He'd say random stuff, nonsense he'd rehearsed before I arrived at his front door, but he did it with such nonchalance that it looked spontaneous. Even if Danny's jokes weren't funny, I'd laugh anyway. Laughing kept me in his house, far away from Fishtank and his extortive television set.

There were certain special situations that would take Fishtank out of our house for a good few hours. A trip to the pub, a day out with his fishing rod, or football. Fishtank loved football so much he couldn't just sit and watch it at home. He had to see it live, be part of the crowd, wave his scarf around in front of everyone. He fancied himself as a football player. Actually, he just fancied himself. I loved football too, but not because I watched or played it. I wouldn't waste my time. No, whenever a big match happened (and they happened often), Fishtank would head out to Ibrox Stadium with my two brothers, giving me a break from his mercurial mood swings. My two sisters used this time wisely, invited all their friends to our house for a party. They wouldn't dare do that if Fishtank was around, but bravery thrived in his absence. Lorna, the most sensible of my sisters, always managed to balance out Donnie, the loud and brash show-off. They were perfectly matched as siblings, twins born three years apart. Deceptively resourceful, they pooled their meagre resources to buy Fishtank a season ticket to Ibrox. Birthdays, Christmas, and Father's Day were all opportunities to get Fishtank out the house so we could live our lives, if only for a while. Anything to let off a bit of steam. Anything for a bit of *fun*.

One night, after a day playing Nintendo with Danny, I returned to my house and a party in full swing. My sisters were using Fishtank's new CD player to blast Happy Mondays at full volume, giving their shindig a soundtrack to show off their moves. My initial instinct was to warn them that Fishtank would go nuts if he knew they'd touched his CD player, but my second instinct told me to ignore my first instinct. The lights of the fishtank had been switched on, bathing the room in lo-fi psychedelia. Lorna and Donnie had been to a lot of raves, always returning home in the early hours of the morning with big happy smiles and wide dark eyes. This seemed like one of those nights, except instead of a field with a DJ, it was my house and a CD player.

Donnie immediately acknowledged my arrival with hugs and kisses.

She didn't look drunk, so it had to be drugs.

—Come and dance with us, Walter!

—Leave me alone.

—Come on. Don't be boring! Just one dance.

One of my sister's friends, a freakishly tall girl named Steph (she later ended up in prison for stealing money from a food bank to fund a glam holiday in Turkey) yanked me across the room by my arm, throwing herself around while everyone laughed and cheered.

Not knowing how to rave, I simply stood around waiting for the song to end. I was relieved when it happened. Once everyone else headed outside into the garden for a cigarette, I took the opportunity to sneak out of the living room and tip-toe upstairs to the safety of my bedroom. I couldn't relax around my sisters when they were in this sort of mood. Their idea of fun might have been dancing like they'd dropped their hairdryer in the bath, but at the tender age of 11 and a half, my idea of fun was a mug of hot chocolate and a *Nancy Drew* novel – and we were all out of hot chocolate. Alone in my room, I relaxed with a book and got through the first chapter. Halfway through the second chapter, I realised I needed snacks and a drink. It was part of my special thing. We had plenty of biscuits (*Trio! Triiiiiooooo!*) in the cupboard downstairs, but I needed a mug or a cup in my hand. Something to sip for every turn of the page. Rolling off my bed, I fell onto my feet and headed out the door in the direction of the kitchen.

The first thing I did was raid the cupboards in a desperate search for a bottle of American Cream Soda. It was Fishtank's favourite. He loved it with scoops of ice-cream. Mum called it a *glass of diabetes*. We usually had at least one bottle of American Cream Soda.

Usually, but not this time.

Admitting defeat, I looked for something...*anything*...to drink that wasn't water.

No Irn-Bru. No Solripe. No Soda Stream.

No luck!

I returned to my room, opened my book and didn't stop reading until the last page. By the time Nancy cracked the case, Fishtank was back and my sisters had cleaned away all evidence that anyone but us had been in the house that night.

Beer cans. Wine bottles. Cigarette stubs. All gone.

Party? What party?

Chapter 5

A Miracle On Christmas Eve

It was obvious something was wrong with Mum on Christmas Eve. There were no presents under the tree which was odd, considering Mum always prepared in advance, buying presents as far back as April. Her theory was that Christmas shopping was cheaper at Easter, so buy the lot months in advance and avoid the stress of doing it in December.

Anyway, the house was empty when I got back from the library. Fishtank was off to see Granny. Lorna and Donnie were away to a rave with their friends, Tia and Maria. Jake was out at the Job Centre, or so he said. And my little brother had taken his bicycle (an old thing with bendy wheels passed down over the years) out for a ride.

That left just me and Mum.

I headed into the kitchen to make a cuppa. Tea had replaced hot chocolate as my favourite thing in the world. It was quick, easy, and most importantly...teabags were cheap.

It didn't take me long to hear a strange sort of snuffling sniffing sound.

Someone was taking drugs, suffering a bad bout of hay fever, or crying.

In my house, it could have been any one of the three.

The sniffing was so loud I heard it over the sound of a boiling kettle.

—Are you okay, Mum?

Mum looked up at me from behind the kitchen bench.

Her expression answered my question. Her face was streaked with tears, the sort that left incriminating evidence along the cheeks. Normally she'd hide the evidence. But today she didn't care. That's how I knew this was a bad situation.

—I can't afford to pay for this year's Christmas, she said.

—What?

—We've got no money, son.

—But…what about your jobs?

—My wages were frozen so debts could be paid off.

—At Christmas?

Mum laughed at that comment. My naïveté was good for something, at least.

—They don't give a shit, so long as they get their money back.

—Who?

—Creditors. They got permission from the banks, the cunts.

—Can't Fishtank get another loan?

—Don't call him that, said Mum sharply. —He's your dad, alright?

—Okay, can't Dad get another one of his loans?

Mum could have lied, but on this occasion she knew that wouldn't work on me. To her credit, she treated me not like a stupid little kid but as someone intelligent, whose opinions were worth hearing. That wasn't always the case. Mostly, I stood in the background, watching and listening to the world around me. In this instance, the truth wasn't pleasant. Unfiltered, the truth usually isn't. Yet no matter how unpleasant, I'd always found the truth to be beautiful in its own strange way.

—Your dad has never taken out a loan by himself.

—That isn't true. I've been with him when he went into the bank for his cash.

Mum said nothing. She wondered whether or not I'd get the hint.

It took a few seconds for my brain to crunch the data.

She'd said Dad had never taken out a loan *by himself*.

Finally, I understood.

—All his loans were joint loans.

22

She nodded up then down.

—And your dad can't pay his share of the debt because he doesn't have a job.

—Because he relies on you for all his money, I said.

It was a rare moment of bravery on my part. I never usually said these things aloud.

—Now do you understand why I can't afford Christmas?

Then and there, I noticed how *poor* my mother looked. Literally, she looked like poverty. Her clothes were old, with her pink and white striped blouse looking raggedy and shabby to my young eyes. She'd had that blouse for as long as I could remember. Likewise, her jeans were tattered and torn, worn to whiteness, though they used to be dark denim blue. I'd never considered her anything other than my mother, but ever since I found that baby, I couldn't help but see the world differently. And I saw my mother for what she really was: a downtrodden wife desperately trying to keep everything together against terrible odds.

I didn't know what to do. What would a normal person do? They'd comfort their mother, wouldn't they? I had to tell myself to move around the table and wrap my arms around her, give her a squeeze, try desperately to shift the sadness from her to me.

This didn't help. She burst into tears again.

—Christmas doesn't matter, I said quietly.

But that wasn't true, not really. Christmas *always* mattered at my age. Everyone at school would want to know what everyone else got 'from Santa' and all of us would silently loathe Danny as he rattled off a long list of stuff, because he always got the most. Perks of being his father's dirty little secret, I suppose. But for as long as I could remember (and I remembered everything) no-one had ever turned up at school having had nothing for Christmas. It was unthinkable! Maybe they'd laugh if I told them Santa didn't have time to deliver my presents because Rudolph caught pleurisy and his nose stopped glowing?

It didn't matter. I'd already become proficient at masking problems and telling lies. I'd learned from my mother, of course. No-one could know we were in debt because of Fishtank. Mum couldn't have coped with the shame. She didn't have much in her bank account, but she worked hard and held her head high. It wasn't her fault she couldn't pay the bills. And there were a lot of bills to pay. We had poll tax, rent arrears, bank and Provident loans. We owed the milkman. We owed Betty, two doors down, a tenner that Fishtank had tapped for cigarettes. The list was endless. We owed and owed and owed.

Getting money wasn't difficult, but paying it back always seemed impossible.

Mum was already cleaning up her face when Donnie got back from work. She'd managed to get a position at a local frozen food shop named Capital. There was a branch in Cumbernauld Town Centre and as a result our cupboards were now full, as was our freezer. Donnie had brought back a dozen bags of shopping to unload, which is how she got involved in my conversation with Mum. Immediately sensing something wasn't right, my sister put the bags down and blinked at the two of us, her eyes taking in everything, including her mother's swollen eyes.

She asked a simple question:

—What's wrong?

Mum gave a simple answer.

—Nothing.

Sensing a lie, my sister shifted her attention towards me.

—What's up with her?

—We've got no money for Christmas.

Mum glared at me, but I didn't care.

Donnie sighed slowly, then sat down on the wooden kitchen bench.

She immediately identified the cause of the problem.

—Is he at it again?

I nodded, but made sure only Donnie noticed. Mum could be unpredictable, giving praise, then taking it away with a slap to the back of the head. Donnie, however, was completely loyal to me. We were the same, in a lot of ways. Both of us looked more like Fishtank, with our thick brown curly hair and sullen expressions. Lorna, Jake and Laddie took more from Mum's side of the family with their blonde-to-ginger hair and good strong faces. When they smiled (which wasn't often) they glowed, if only for a moment.

I rarely smiled. Still don't.

The only time I smile is when I'm happy.

Christmas came a few days early for the Wedgeworth household. We were all busy doing our own thing. Lorna was upstairs in her room having a secret ciggie. Laddie was with me in our room, both of us playing our Sega MegaDrive on a small colour television. Sega was for people who couldn't afford a Super Nintendo. We didn't care. We loved our Sega. Donnie and Jake weren't in, having opted to spend the night getting drunk with their pals. Fishtank was out and we didn't question it, just hoped he'd be out for hours. Mum was apparently downstairs watching *EastEnders*.

The noise of Albert Square was too loud.

Until suddenly it wasn't.

Surely our TV hadn't run out of coins again?

I opened my mouth to shout downstairs when I heard... well, something unexpected.

—Ho! Ho! Ho!

For a moment, I thought I'd imagined it.

—What was that? Laddie asked with a frown on his little face.

—I don't know, I said.

—Ho! Ho! Ho!

—I heard it again, Walter!

I pressed the PAUSE button on the Sega game pad and listened intently.

—Ho! Ho! Ho!

—Do you think it's Dad? Laddie asked.

He was only seven-years-old and still in the mindset that a father automatically deserved to be called *Dad*. Really, the only time the rest of us called him *Dad* was when he was there in front of us. Laddie would grow out of it, of course. It would take a while though.

—It sounds like Santa.

—Walter, there's no such person as Santa.

—Ho! Ho! Ho!

—Then who's that? I asked in the full knowledge that it wasn't actually Santa.

Laddie leapt up and bolted for downstairs. I followed behind, not quite as enthusiastic, but intrigued nonetheless. Together, we barged into the living room to find Fishtank holding a large burlap sack around his shoulder, dressed head-to-toe in an ill-fitting Santa Claus costume. The bushy beard, however, was all his own.

—Hello boys! Santa's here with some very special presents for YOUUUUUU.

Laddie sparkled with excitement. He loved his father in that moment. Loved being treated like the most special kid in the world. Me? I watched balefully in the corner.

Fishtank seemed to enjoy this rare moment of benevolence. A consummate showman, he made his audience of two wait while he prepared the next part of his surprise. With a dramatic flourish, Fishtank swung the sack around his shoulder and emptied the contents onto the carpet at our feet. Laddie literally cried aloud in glee as parcels rolled over, landing in random piles. I couldn't believe my eyes. Yes, I was actually impressed. Not only had Fishtank gone out and found presents for us to unwrap on Christmas Day, he'd made sure we'd be able to unwrap them. I knew from bitter experience that Fishtank couldn't even fold a dishtowel properly, let alone wrap a present.

How the hell had he managed all this?

None of us questioned it. None of us except Mum.

Wisely, she kept quiet.

—Merry Christmas everybody, said Fishtank.

And just like that, I'd be able to show everybody at school what I got for Christmas.

Chapter 6

New Year

The fight between my parents on New Year's Eve happened because of a steak pie. Not just any steak pie, it was the *wrong* steak pie. Fishtank was brand loyal to the point of obstinance and wouldn't dream of having anything other than the famous Malcolm Allan Family Steak Pie, which sounded to me like a pie with a family in it. Eating a Malcolm Allan steak pie was one of our curious family traditions. We had to have one on New Year's Eve. It was every bit as essential as having a turkey on Christmas Day. Fishtank insisted on this above all else. Malcolm Allan pies had the fattest cuts of beef, the thickest gravy and the lightest pastry. It was always the same meal, just a different year. Steak pie, garden peas (not mushy under any circumstances), roasted potatoes, and – bizarrely – some mint!

The fight started as soon as Mum unloaded her shopping bags. She'd been to William Low (Willie Low's to everyone else) for the weekly shop, and was starting the long process of getting dinner sorted. Fishtank, in a bad mood for whatever reason, sauntered into the kitchen looking as miserable as a kicked cat.

I should know. I was there. I watched it happen.

—What's this? He asked.

—It's a steak pie.

—Don't get smart with me. I'll ask again. What's this?

—It's…a steak pie. What's wrong with you?

—I asked you to get a Malcolm Allen pie, you know, my favourite kind.

—It's the same pie, just a different box.

—That's a lot of shite.

—I got it from Willie Low's. It's as good as any other.

—BUT IT'S NOT THE ONE I WANTED.

As though to punctuate his point, Fishtank grabbed a cup from the sink and hurled it across the room. It hit the wall and detonated into shards, all of which rained down, scattering widely. Mum seemed startled, but kept herself calm and composed.

They still hadn't noticed me sitting on the kitchen bench with my book.

I wondered if invisibility was my secret superpower.

—You've fucked it up, hissed Fishtank. —You've fucked it up!

—It's just a steak pie.

—It's the wrong steak pie!

—You didn't mind last year.

—…

—I got you this one last year.

—You told me you got a Malcolm Allen Steak Pie.

—I know, but I didn't. And you ate it. You really liked it. This is a good steak pie.

Oh my God. All this over a sodding steak pie. A powerful urge to rampage across the kitchen and smash the steak pie with my fists nearly overwhelmed me, but I kept it at bay.

—How come you didn't go to the butcher?

—I didn't have time.

—You work at the chippie. It's a five-minute walk.

—I didn't have time!

—Why?

Mum suddenly seemed very scared and I immediately caught a change in the tone of Fishtank's voice. He wasn't shouting anymore. In fact, he seemed eerily calm, even gracious. Suddenly, I realised what was taking place in front of me wasn't about a steak pie. That was a mere focus for Fishtank's fears and frustrations, both of which would mix together and inevitably blow up into physical violence.

—I was running late with the shopping. There was too much to do, so I just got the pie from Willie Low's. That's it. No other reason.

Fishtank laughed in her face.

—You're seeing someone else, aren't you? Who is it? Where did you meet him?

I'd seen this happen before, many times in the past. But this fight would be different to the others. Something remarkable was about to take place. Something so shocking that I almost dropped my book. Mum spoke up. Softly, at first, but soon enough she was shouting at Fishtank. Mum was actually arguing back. I couldn't believe it.

She'd never, ever defended herself against Fishtank.

—I'm not seeing anyone. I don't have time! You're the one that sits on your arse all day chatting up tarts on that radio upstairs. You think I don't know? *I know*.

Before Mum could finish her statement, she was being slammed into the wall over and over again, bashed until she bled. Fishtank was punching and punching without a thought for anything other than his own anger. Mum was on the floor wailing, begging for mercy.

I screamed.

At that point, Fishtank finally noticed me.

—Hey, son, he said breezily. —Are you enjoying your book?

—It's okay, I said, completely and utterly shell-shocked.

A few hours later, once Mum had cleaned herself up, all my stuff was shoved into a large green holiday case that we never ever used for actual holidays. It was only filled when Mum had to escape to Aunt Edith's to recuperate from one of Fishtank's beatings. Aunt Edith wasn't my aunt by blood. She was one in an endless line of family friends we were encouraged to call 'Aunt'. Her house was large, but not so large that it could accommodate my older brother and two sisters. They had to be left behind while my little brother and I were whisked off in the night. Mum felt guilty. But what else could she do? Domestic abuse was a secret, silent shame, something many women endured, an unspoken part of their marriage vows.

What difference did a New Year make anyway?

It was just another flick of a page on a calendar.

My single vivid memory of that night wasn't the sight of my mother in a pool of her own blood, but of voices coming out of the houses as we left Craigieburn Road in a taxi. With Laddie leaning against me, half asleep, I heard voices from brightly-lit houses in the night singing joyfully…

Should auld acquaintance be forgot and never brought to mind?
Should auld acquaintance be forgot and Auld Lang Syne?

Then the bells came. I was thrown backwards in time to a few weeks earlier, the day I found a baby buried in a box in the dirt. As I sat in the taxi, watching the world zip past the window, my thoughts turned once more to that little boy left out in the rain.

To be honest, he was never far away from my thoughts.

Aunt Edith had dinner waiting for us when we arrived at her house in Pine Crescent. She was grateful to see Mum, though less happy at the state of her face. Quickly, we were bundled indoors to her home. And it was a home. Nice carpets, a big couch, a large TV by the standards of the time. Plates had already been set out on the small table in the kitchen, cutlery dumped in a little pile next to a half-empty bottle of tomato sauce. Mum gratefully embraced her friend, our 'aunt', who'd taken us in when we had nowhere else to go.

—When are you going to get a grip and leave that bastard?

To Aunt Edith, Fishtank would always be John 'Jacky'

Wedgeworth. She never bothered with his nickname. It humanised him in a way she disapproved of. He was that mean shit she hated when they were kids, living in The Gorbals. I knew she didn't approve. It was impossible for my Aunt Edith to say anything slightly polite about Fishtank. She couldn't. Her hatred of him was so strong she visibly vibrated it out of her body.

—Happy New Year, she said to me and Laddie.

—I'm hungry, Laddie moaned.

—Well, son. I've got just the thing.

I looked over at the table.

Aunt Edith had bought a steak pie.

—I went up to Malcolm Allan's this morning, she said proudly.

Mum uttered a sound that might have been laughter, but could easily have been a sob of pain. I knew her ribs were sore and the blood in her hair had dried to crust.

We pretended not to notice.

I was good at pretending.

I even pretended to enjoy the steak pie we had for dinner.

And just like that, 1992 reincarnated into 1993.

Chapter 7

Sticks, Stones, And Broken Homes

For two weeks I switched from Langland's Primary to Abronhill Primary. Laddie too. Despite being only a ten-minute trip on the bus from Cumbernauld Town Centre to Abronhill, it felt like another world. We had nothing in common. The pupils I shared a class with were very conscious that I didn't belong in their little world. We were escorted through the corridor from the main entrance by Mum and Aunt Edith. Posters of old movies were pinned up as far as the eye could see, and with my bad eyesight, that wasn't too far. *Aladdin. Batman Returns. The Mighty Ducks.* Goodness, even *Short Circuit* which I'd watched on videotape a few years previously.

It was a school stuck in a time warp.

—When are we going home? Laddie wanted to know.

—Soon, said Mum. —I promise.

Aunt Edith couldn't help but roll her eyes. She knew this was how Fishtank got what he wanted. Eventually one of us would break and want the comforts (such as they were) of our own home. We missed our friends. We missed our brother and sisters.

In order to keep our minds off our family back home, Mum wanted to keep us distracted in routine. She enrolled us into Abronhill Primary within a day of arriving at Aunt Edith's.

—Welcome to Abronhill Primary School, said a woman I presumed was the headmistress. She carried herself with some authority and Mum took her aside to talk in private.

Every now and then the woman looked at me and Laddie with something curious in her eyes, something she couldn't (or wouldn't) put into words.

Suddenly I realised it was *sympathy*.

She felt sorry for me.

A few minutes later I was introduced to my temporary new classmates. They seemed okay, at first. But as soon as they learned I was from the North Carbrain area of Cumbernauld, things moved in another direction completely. Apparently, there was a feud between these two areas of town. That made no sense to me. They were both part of Cumbernauld. It got worse. They recognised my surname. That was the first time I really understood how much power my brother Jake wielded. His reputation as a hard man was apparently quite severe. It was up to a girl with a dripping nose to break the bad news. Her name was Lesley and she almost ruined my new school jotter by dripping on it:

—You're Jake Wedgeworth's little brother?

—Yes, I mumbled.

—He's a nutter.

—Really?

—Aye. He robbed someone at a party last week.

I gasped. How did I not know any of this stuff? Fishtank wouldn't be happy. He always seemed to be in a bad mood with Jake, his oldest son, the one he took most of his aggression out on – and now it seemed Jake was returning the favour with other people.

Lesley continued telling me about my own brother.

—The guy he robbed? His little brother is at this school. He's in Primary 7. When Craig hears about you, he'll want to fight. Are you good at fighting?

No, I was a terrible fighter. But I could take beatings really well. For as long as I could remember, I refused to scream or cry when Fishtank belted me across the back with the front of his hand. Tears were a waste of time and effort. Of course that didn't mean I actually wanted to be hit by anyone. Who did?

The rest of my day was spent fretting and worrying about Craig from Primary 7. He was coming for me, it seemed. Everyone else revelled in the tension, the drama. Suddenly, being at the mercy of Gary Dowds and his gang of cromags didn't seem so bad. The sound of the old school bell burst through my thoughts, pulling me back to reality and the realisation that I was living the same life in a completely different school.

Everyone abandoned the classroom so they could go and get a good spot for the fight.

A fight they wanted me to lose.

Craig was waiting as I headed out the main doors of Abronhill Primary School with Laddie by my side. Incited by his group of friends, all of whom would probably grow up to join the Abronhill Stab Gang, Craig suddenly became ferociously loud as I headed towards him. He already knew I wasn't a threat to him, which meant he could show off.

—You're dead! He yelled.

—FIGHT! Voices screamed as one. —FIGHT! FIGHT! FIGHT!

Laddie held my hand and whimpered in fright.

We were all alone.

Until suddenly we weren't.

Someone appeared from behind Craig and his mates. A large hulking figure that scattered everyone aside in fear. Laddie cheered and released my hand, but I stayed completely, disconcertingly still. Maybe my brain was trying to process what just happened? Or perhaps I knew this moment would come, as it usually did. We could build a rocket and soar up, up, up into space and he'd still find us.

—Fuck off you little pricks, shouted Fishtank at the kids.

—My dad will take drugs and beat you up, retorted Craig.

35

Fishtank flexed his right bicep. He literally flexed it. I was mortified.

—This'll smash fuck out of your poofy dad.

Helplessly, I stood watching as Fishtank reached out and swiped at Craig, catching him behind his right ear. He wailed for his mum and turned away. A part of me, an atom, was impressed by what had just taken place. But I was completely aware that there'd be consequences to Fishtank's actions: I wouldn't be allowed back into Abronhill Primary.

—We're going to see your mum, said Fishtank cheerily.

—I thought you'd be on your CB radio at this time of the day, I replied.

That sort of comment would normally have resulted in a smack to the back of my neck, but Fishtank was trying to show us how he'd changed, that he was a reformed man. I could get away with a bit more backchat than the usual.

—Have you enjoyed your holiday to Aunt Edith's?

—Yeah! Laddie said enthusiastically. —We sat up to nine o'clock the other night.

Fishtank's face darkened slightly, but the smile didn't leave his face. Suddenly I remembered my brother and sisters back in Craigieburn Road. I hoped they were doing okay. The idea of them alone with Fishtank was too terrifying to contemplate and much easier to just…ignore. Forget about everyone else. Push them out of mind since they were out of sight. Selfish, but necessary for my sanity.

We walked down the street towards Pine Crescent, where Aunt Edith lived. Laddie clasped Fishtank's hand tight as they walked. Feeling that I was too old, I didn't want to hold his hand, but it found mine and gripped tight, so tight I nearly cried out in pain.

—I've got good news for the two of you, said Fishtank.

—A real *Tracy Island*? Laddie replied with excitement in his blue eyes.

36

—No! Something better than Tracy Island!

Laddie couldn't comprehend *anything* being better than *Tracy Island*.

—I'm going to get your mum back.

What was supposed to be a declaration of romantic intent sounded vaguely like a threat.

We led Fishtank to Aunt Edith's home, though we really didn't need to bother. He knew the way from all the other times he'd suddenly appeared, completely unwanted, heralding his arrival with hard chaps of the letterbox. It sounded like a police raid being announced, a sound we'd all learned to dread, especially Aunt Edith who wanted us to be safe.

Laddie made to open the door, but a large arm blocked him from doing so.

—We're allowed, he said, his eyes narrow with confusion.

—It isn't polite to walk into someone else's home.

Ah, really, that was a masterstroke of subtle manipulation on Fishtank's part. Not that I knew it at the time, but years later, when I got the chance to think over my life as a boy in Cumbernauld, recalling everything including the baby in the box, it all became clear.

By reminding my little brother that he couldn't just walk into Aunt Edith's home, he was in fact telling him that he didn't belong there, that it wasn't *his* house. And by saying *that*, he was reminding him he had his own house he *could* walk into. Right before my eyes and ears, the way of the manipulator laid bare.

Fishtank lifted the letterbox and hit it three times in succession: *bang, bang, bang*, and then leaned away from the door, waiting patiently, our hands held hard in his own.

Aunt Edith's expression when she opened the door could have curdled a carton of milk. She didn't bother to hide the boiling hatred she felt for this man in front of her; she knew more about him than we did at the time, to be fair. I suspect she would have slammed the door in his face if he hadn't brought us with him. But that was the point of meeting us at school, wasn't it?

—Morna, said Edith. —Your ex is here.

Fishtank looked like he wanted to let go of my hand and smash Edith down with one punch, but he knew better. She had brothers. Strong and powerful brothers. Mum told me this years ago, during one of our kitchen conversations. Without the threat of violence, Fishtank really was quite pathetic. Mum, sadly, had a younger brother in awe of Fishtank.

He always impressed stupid people, I suppose.

Aunt Edith moved aside and Mum popped her head around the door.

—I'm sorry, said Fishtank, his face wobbling.

(He wasn't.)

—It won't ever happen again.

(It happened again.)

—I've changed!

(He hadn't changed a bit.)

—Can we talk in private?

(They talked in private.)

I waited with Aunt Edith and Laddie as Mum went into the next room with Fishtank. Surprisingly, Edith let him into her home despite her skin crawling at the thought of looking at his beard and untrimmed nostril hair. She always noticed the things that we all saw but didn't really see. Maybe that's why her house was so clean? That was the sort of stuff I noticed. Nice clean floors and well-made beds. No-one knew it, but I'd taken to washing my hands over and over again, scrubbing away dirt that wasn't there, burning my skin with hot water to try and purge some hidden stain. It had been like that since I touched the soggy box with the little dead baby inside it, his crib of wet cardboard.

Water and soap took away the feeling of disgust.

If only all my other problems could be that easily washed away.

When Fishtank returned to the living room with Mum, he had a smug expression on his face that told us we were going back to the house. Truth is, I knew that would happen. While they'd been in the kitchen, I'd overheard Mum asking about my sisters and brother. She couldn't get it out of her head that she'd left them with him. He knew. He always knew.

—Get your stuff, kids, said Fishtank. —We're going home!

I stood up, headed over towards the door, stopped and said:

—I'm sure we'll see you again soon, Aunt Edith.

It wasn't much, but it made me feel better that maybe I could annoy Fishtank a little.

Small victories could sometimes feel gigantic.

Chapter 8

Family History

We were always told that Granny's real name was Frances, but years later, once I'd reached the age where I needed my birth certificate to get a student loan, I finally discovered the truth. Locked in the old battered brown leather suitcase we kept the old photos we didn't want to see, was a crumbling piece of paper held together by bits of tape. On it was a name that looked familiar, though different.

Fanny Wedgeworth.

Not Frances, as we'd been raised to believe.

Oddly enough, I wasn't surprised.

It didn't take long for Fishtank to revert back to his old ways. He'd managed to pretend for a whole two months; a record-breaking attempt for him. Money, however, was always a problem and Mum fell ill with a bout of depression (we called it 'not feeling herself'), which meant she had to take time off her four jobs.

—Fuck, said Fishtank when the electricity cut off during a lengthy radio session.

There he was, happily chatting up Miss Plastic Pussy from Portsmouth, before flatlining into literal radio silence. I was next door in my bedroom, one of the three bedrooms in our house on Craigieburn Road. I heard him muttering and whispering, but being nearly twelve, I didn't quite understand what was happening. Later, I'd realise it was the radio equivalent of phone sex, the seedy sort that Fishtank apparently enjoyed regularly with his 'friends'.

When the lights cut out, the little cries of ecstasy became loud shrieks of anger.

—Lights are out! Lorna shouted unhelpfully from her room.

—Okay, okay. Fishtank called back. —I'm sorting it out!

But I knew Mum had no money in her purse. Jake had already tried to empty it for spare change so that he and his mates could get a carry-out from The Vineyard. I'd caught him earlier that morning with the upside-down purse in his hands. If he wanted to get smashed, he'd need to do it another way, with someone else's cash. Worse, Fishtank desperately attempted to prise open the coin box connected to our television. He couldn't do it.

Afterwards, I overheard Fishtank ordering Donnie to head over to Granny's flat in Beechwood Road. Desperate times, it seemed, required desperate measures.

Granny Frances – let's *not* call her Granny Fanny – wasn't actually Fishtank's real mother. Just like all the other parts of my family history, there are a few nasty surprises waiting to be revealed. His so-called mother was actually his grandmother. Apparently, his real mother died giving birth to him. On the way out of her womb, Fishtank killed his mother.

With Fishtank's mother dead, his grandparents (*her* mother and father) decided to raise him as their own. Granny Frances doted on her evil grandson, lavishing him with all the love and attention he never bothered giving his own children. However, his father (really his grandfather) despised him, never ever forgiving him for the death of his daughter.

Complicated, crazy, cuckoo.

That's my family.

I never ever met my grandfather (actually, my great-grandfather). He died of a heart attack, though according to Mum he really died of a broken heart, because he missed his daughter so much.

—Oh, he was a gentleman! she said of Grandpa Jacky, whose real name of John was passed down to Fishtank by Granny Frances.

She shouldn't have bothered. They were nothing at all alike.

Years later, Fishtank confessed to my mum that the one person whose respect he wanted, whose admiration he craved more than anything else in the world, was that of his 'father'. And sometimes, when he dreamed, he would see his 'father' waiting for him outside the pearly gates of Heaven.

Those dreams always ended the same way.

With Jacky kicking his 'son' in the face so hard that he spun away to the depths of Hell.

—We've got good news for everyone, said Fishtank during one of our 'family meetings' no-one wanted to attend. This one was an improvised affair, held in candlelight, because the power still hadn't been restored. I enjoyed the candlelight, weirdly enough. Sitting in front of a flickering flame, reading *The Ringmaster's Secret*, I found the words danced on the page, with my focus completely on Nancy and her friends. Even the background hum of the refrigerator was absent. The whole wide world was inside a book.

Nothing else existed.

Nothing until this stupid family meeting.

Fishtank sat on the chair across from the couch where we all waited. The couch was a burst old thing, covered in a plaid patterned cloth with green/red/black stripes running through it. Mum hated it, desperately fantasising about owning a real leather couch.

We waited.

—There's been a power cut, said Fishtank grandly, though we only had to look out of the living room window to see every other house on our street still had their lights on.

Obviously, they'd paid their bill on time.

42

—So, what are we going to do? Lorna asked.

She was the favourite, his princess, but still on our side.

—It's being sorted. But there's something else we need to tell you.

The expression on Mum's face was desolate, even in the dark. This was going to be bad.

It was actually worse than bad.

—Granny Frances is coming here to stay with us for a little while.

He explained that Granny was feeling ill, that she struggled terribly with her elephantiasis-bloated feet. She desperately needed our help to look after her, but of course we were only happy to help our beloved granny, weren't we?

Mum said nothing. She was still not feeling herself. She probably wouldn't recover until Granny Frances went back home. It wasn't a secret that they didn't get along. In fact, Mum hated her.

—She's a complete hypo, said Mum during one of her unguarded moments in the kitchen. —Honestly, if you have a flu, she's got pneumonia.

And now her arch-nemesis was coming to stay with us for a short period.

But how would that help us get our electricity back on?

Fishtank, as usual, had prepared for every eventuality.

—Of course, while your Granny is here with us…she'll need to contribute to our bills. We can't just let her stay for nothing, even if that's what I'd love to do for my mum.

As he spoke, the refrigerator in the kitchen started to hum again.

Then the lights came back to life once again.

We all cheered, all of us except Mum.

—Let there be light, said Fishtank gleefully

Chapter 9

The Lodger

A little-known fact about my father was that he actually came from a wealthy family. You wouldn't know it to look at him. The fact I was raised in a council house also belied the reality of the situation. Yet it's true. Fishtank's grandparents had lots of cash stashed. His father/grandfather was a prudent man when it came to his finances. Granny Frances was…not as prudent, and given half a chance could bankrupt Britain with her obsession for buying useless tat from the catalogue. Grandpa Jacky kept her under control for years, but his death meant Frances suddenly had a bulging bank account and a lot of catalogues with UNBELIEVEABLE offers, crap you had to buy WHILE STOCKS LAST.

Fishtank might have been a bully and a fraudster, but he was smart, or at least he possessed the intelligence to know how to escape from bad situations. With huge unpaid debts, he'd quickly come to the conclusion that only one person could help.

The day after the lights came back on, that help arrived in a wheelchair.

—Granny! Donnie shouted, hugging Granny Frances though her arms didn't reach all the way around her enormous body. As a mark of respect we all gave her a little hug. She, in turn, gave us a peck on the cheek, her coarse hairy lip scraping against the skin of our faces. Not that we cared. She was Granny and we adored her regardless.

Mum finally got around to greeting her 'mother-in-law' in a

loose embrace. She didn't look happy in the slightest. But what could she do?

—This is nice, said Granny Frances. —It's lonely in that flat. Why don't you visit me more often? You're always saying how you need to come over and see me, but you don't.

This was aimed at Fishtank, who was leaning against a wall in our hallway, the same hallway that led to the back door and garden. He was shirtless, wearing a pair of jeans and ugly shoes that were falling to pieces. Those shoes had been used to stamp down on Jake's face many times in the past. To this day, a certain type of shoe, black patent leather ones just like Fishtank's shoes from Clarks, dredge up screams buried in the back of my brain.

—I know, Mother. But I'm making it up to you now, aren't I? You're coming here to live with us. We don't want you in that flat anymore. We want you here with us, your family.

Granny Frances shook her head in agreement. Her face was heavily lined, weathered as a result of her forty-a-day cigarette habit. Two twenty-packs did her for twenty-four hours. The smell of smoke made me gag, but in a family full of smokers, it was something to be accepted. Even Laddie would eventually take up the habit.

—Where am I sleeping? Granny asked eagerly.

—In the living room, where you've got the TV.

Mum rolled her eyes. She hated it when Fishtank sucked up to Granny Frances.

—You're sticking me in there with a coin-operated telly?

—We can't afford a TV otherwise, said Fishtank smoothly.

—It's a disgrace.

—It doesn't cost much though. Honestly, Mum. It's really reasonable. Pennies, really.

I caught Lorna and Donnie giving each other a glance loaded with meaning. Obviously, they were starting to comprehend why Granny Frances had been invited to stay.

—How much?

Fishtank took a deep breath, as though breaking terrible news to his mother.

—It's included in your weekly rent.

—WHAT?

Granny didn't realise she was a paying guest in our house. Clearly, this move had been sold to her as something else, something far more beneficial to her needs. Worse, her flat in Beechwood Road had already been given to another family. She had no choice but to live with us now. It wasn't as though she could return home and watch *Coronation Street*.

—Okay, Granny said, finally accepting her fate. —I want to go and watch TV.

Then she froze, apparently realising something else needed dealt with first.

—Can you help me up to the toilet? she asked.

Mum looked like she might tip Frances off the chair and onto the floor, but instead of doing what she wanted to do, she did what she *had* to do. I watched while Mum smiled graciously, then manoeuvred Frances to the bottom of the staircase that connected the hallway to the top of our house in Craigieburn Road. From there, things got complicated.

It was Lorna who asked the important question.

Sensible, thoughtful Lorna always asked the important questions.

—How are we going to get her upstairs, she asked.

Granny Frances didn't know what fruit looked like. To her, a Cadbury's Fruit and Nut chocolate bar counted as part of her five-a-day, though in her case it was five-a-month, if she was lucky. My grandmother's bulky body was a testament to her inability to put anything in her mouth that hadn't been deep fried in boiling fat. Most of my memories of Granny Frances were of her eating a fish supper or a tub of ice-cream.

Sometimes both at the same time.

46

*

—You'll need to hold her by her arms and go upstairs while your mum holds her ankles. That's the only way you're going to get her to the toilet, said Fishtank.

It didn't escape our notice that he used the words 'you'll' and 'you're'. I wasn't surprised. No way would he risk putting out his back, not even to help out his own mother/grandmother.

—Hurry up, Granny Frances whined. —I need to go soon. I have loose stools.

—For *fuck* sake, muttered Mum beneath her breath.

Lorna, who had been volunteered to help Mum shift Granny upstairs, struggled to keep hold of her wrists. There was a lot of loose skin, and we watched blankly as she pulled and heaved her old grandmother up the staircase. Likewise, Mum battled hard to get Granny upstairs. My Granny Frances was heavier than she looked, and she looked *really* heavy.

—You can do it, said Fishtank encouragingly.

They were halfway up the stairs when Granny shit herself. It came out in a torrent of brown spray and it hit the carpet, which happened to be a thick nylon, the sort that was tough to properly clean. Worse, our carpet was a lovely shade of blueberry. Not anymore!

I opened my mouth to say something.

Fishtank immediately quelled me with a terrifying stare.

Laddie pointed, but didn't get a chance to speak as I placed my hand over his mouth.

The smell from poor Granny's bowels was a sour beefy stink; it was strong enough to stain the carpet, stay in the air and cling to my memories decades after it happened. However, the worst part of Granny's accident wasn't the smell. It was a curious fleeting thought I experienced while standing at the bottom of the stairs.

The mess reminded me of the inside of a steak pie.

I almost screamed at the thought of it.

Chapter 10

Swimming

I hated swimming. It wasn't fun. I hated sharing my water with weirdoes and the changing rooms terrified me. But in a town like Cumbernauld, there was nothing else to do during the summer and so I always found myself at the pool with my friends. Unlike me, they loved dive-bombing into the water. They literally threw themselves down the chutes and slides. They always found me at the shallow end, watching from a safe distance.

Everyone in Cumbernauld went swimming.

Unfortunately, that also included Billy The Squid.

Every town in the world has someone like Billy The Squid. More myth than man, he was the urban legend we whispered about in the playground. No-one was sure what he looked like, because he looked different in each sighting. Sometimes he was tall, other times small. He had a moustache. He was clean shaven. His hair was dark. Or was it dirty blonde?

Turned out, the truth was far stranger than any playground story.

My best friend Moo knew everything about The Squid. He loved to freak everyone out with stories about how The Squid once tried to lure him into his house so they could watch WWF wrestling together. We were shocked and scandalised. Moo, being brave and resourceful, fought The Squid off and escaped with his life. Every time Moo told that story, we listened attentively, a perfect audience. He was the keeper of knowledge and we listened to everything he had to say on anything that mattered. We all looked up to Moo. We had no choice: he was obscenely tall. Seriously, Moo looked like Worzel Gummidge with NHS spectacles. We called him Moo because his name was Keith Moon, but Moo sounded much cooler, didn't it? Not that Moo was cool, of course. He'd been named after a famous drummer, apparently. That was the one cool thing about him. He was obsessed with *Neighbours*, for goodness sake. None of us were cool though. We were lanky, speccy geeks. But we got on because we made each other laugh.

My other best friend was Poppy, who happened to be Moo's cousin. Really, they were twins under the skin. Poppy was small and feisty, but ultimately deferred to her cousin in every debate, which meant I often lost even when I was right. For instance, I knew implicitly that James Bond was the code name for a ring of spies, which explained why he had so many different faces. Moo stubbornly refused to even consider this theory, telling me he was one man played by different actors. It was the battle of 1993.

—Clearly, Bond is a squad of men with the same codename.

—No, Walter! No! He's the same man.

—How can he be the same man when Roger Moore and Timothy Dalton are so different? They're two different people with the same codename.

—No, they're two different actors interpreting the role.

In the end we both managed to agree that James Bond was a raging alkie.

The open changing rooms at the swimming pool frightened me and I hid in the farthest cubicle, covering up with a towel. Mum would never have allowed me to go out swimming without a good quality towel, so anything ragged or frayed was definitely not allowed in my backpack. Mum was very conscientious about her bath towels.

—Hurry up, Walter!

Moo sounded impatient.

—Gimme a minute, I snapped, trying to undress with a towel wrapped around me.

—Poppy'll be pissed off if we don't hurry up.

—Poppy's always pissed off! I grumbled.

—I'm telling her you said that.

—NO!

I barrelled out of the cubicle, shoved my stuff securely in a locker, and headed out to the pool. With spectacles awkwardly perched on my nose, I sped out past the gross naked people towards the water, my baggy green shorts making me look like half boy/half Hulk.

—Don't run, growled a lifeguard as I sped by.

Immediately my sprint slowed to a leisurely walk.

My sudden change of speed made Moo cackle like Bette Midler in *Hocus Pocus*.

We met Poppy and I stood back as the cousins leapt into the water together.

There were two main swimming pools at The Tryst fitness centre, one for beginners and another for serious competitive swimming. Unfortunately, I swam like a brick. With that in mind, I always chose the smaller pool. The water was warmer, not as severe or sharp as the grown-up pool. My swimming technique was to swing my arms clockwise and thrash my feet, which worked for me but not for anyone else at The Tryst.

It was Moo who noticed him first and didn't hesitate to point in his direction.

—Is that who I think it is?

I looked across the pool, but my vision was blurry due to water pouring down the lenses of my spectacles. My spectacles were a necessary evil, if only because I was practically blind without them; however, they didn't do well in the water, which was another reason to hate going swimming with my friends.

—Who is it? Poppy asked from halfway beneath the water.

—It's Billy The Squid

—No, I gasped.

—Let's stay together, said Poppy nervously.

—Goddam perv! Moo yelled in the direction of a man at the other side of the pool. He glided through the water, his legs and arms working in perfect synchronicity. We didn't move. Somehow, we felt moving might draw attention to ourselves. There were other kids in the water too. Didn't they realise who was nearby?

—If that perv so much as looks in my direction, I'll kick him in his balls.

I was impressed by Moo's vow. He was normally quite a docile character.

—Can you kick someone if you're under water?

Why I asked that question I do not know, but it suddenly seemed important.

Poppy attempted to answer my question by kicking outwards, but the water made everything move in slow motion. We waited to see what would happen next. Billy The Squid was still moving in our direction, seemingly unaware that we were in his way.

He got closer and closer...

Nearer and clearer in my vision.

Our collective nerve broke.

—Run! Moo yelled.

—Swim! I corrected.

Poppy was already blasting through the water away from me and Moo. She was the best swimmer by far, always had been, and it served her well in situations such as That Time We Met Billy The Squid At The Swimming Pool.

—He wants our arses, squealed Poppy hysterically as we fled The Tryst.

—Why? I asked.

—We're safe, Moo said once we'd reached Stonylee Road, a safe distance from The Squid. My lungs felt ready to burst, so we stopped and gathered ourselves before deciding to go and watch *Neighbours* at Moo's house. It started at half one, so we still had enough time to get to the telly and switch on BBC1. I *knew* we'd end up watching *Neighbours*. Moo loved it passionately. He enjoyed the bright smiles, bouncy perms, and sunny scenery.

Me? I found it all relentlessly depressing.

Years later, during a casual conversation between old friends, Moo admitted it wasn't Billy The Squid at the pool that day, just some random dad teaching his daughter how to swim. Moo had made the whole thing up so he could head home and watch *Neighbours*.

Actually, I'm not sure Billy The Squid really existed.

Chapter 11

Nightclubbing

I woke up one night to find Lorna in my bedroom getting ready to go out. She'd apparently stashed her clothes and bag underneath my bed. A savvy move, because Fishtank never searched through my stuff. He'd only find *Batman* comics and old *Doctor Who* books anyway. Lorna and Donnie's room was constantly under investigation for signs of anything that didn't meet Fishtank's lofty standards. This included love letters, cigarettes, drugs or contraception. Wisely, my eldest and most sensible sister had decided the best way to outmanoeuvre was with a bit of careful planning.

Unfortunately, she hadn't counted on waking me up.

I'd always been a light sleeper. I still am. The lightest footsteps can pull me out of my dreams, which were never that exciting to begin with, so waking up made no difference. I opened my eyes at the sound of a creaking floorboard to find Lorna shimmying into the tightest jeans in her wardrobe. Her clothes were terribly impractical, or so I thought. Fashion conscious to the extreme, my sister's dedication to looking trendy meant she could only wear clothes shoplifted from Flip (her favourite clothes shop) or bought out of the Littlewoods catalogue. Her peroxide perm was the height of style, the tight curls a nightmare to get right, but worthwhile in the end. But where on earth was she going at such a late hour? I shifted my weight in bed, trying to make sure I didn't wake Laddie up. The sky outside my window was a limitless void without stars. The only light in my room came from a broken streetlight beyond the garden.

It flickered at an erratic pace, an unintelligible Morse code.

—What are you doing? I whispered.

—Shit, muttered Lorna.

She'd evidently got a bit of a fright.

—Sorry, I whispered.

—Go back to sleep, she implored whilst adjusting her curls.

—Are you going out? I asked.

—Go back to sleep, she repeated.

—Where are you going?

—Never mind. Go back to sleep!

—Do Mum and Dad know you're going out?

—No. And I'd like you to keep it that way.

—Where are you going?

—I'm going to Papa Docs.

—Oh no! I gasped.

Papa Docs was the most popular nightclub in Cumbernauld for teenagers, because it was the *only* nightclub in town for teenagers. Reflections (the other major nightspot in town) didn't count, because it was full of grey growlers. That's what Lorna called them. To her, a grey growler was anyone in their mid-twenties. Likewise, she avoided the grizzled old Red Triangle Snooker Club, which she referred to as The Hooker Snooker. For Lorna, there was only Papa Docs. She made it sound like a magical place full of music, dancing, laughter and joy. She forgot to mention the screams, vomit and flying pint-tumblers.

—I'm not coming back, said Lorna solemnly.

—You're…not coming back?

—Never.

Laddie stirred beside me, but didn't wake up. He slept deeply, which made me jealous. He didn't hear a single part of my talk with Lorna. We kept our voices down to the quietest whisper, making it difficult for the two of us to hear each other. Part of me was terrified Fishtank would have his ear to the wall, just

54

as I did whenever he spent his day chatting next door on his CB radio. Not that I understood half of what he said. —Oscar, Bravo, Tango! This is Oscar, Bravo, Tango! Are you scared of the beard Oscar, Bravo, Tango?

I pleaded with my sister to change her mind.

—You can't leave. You've got to stay here with us.

—No. I don't like it here. I'm going to Papa Docs.

Tying her pristine Reebok trainers tightly, Lorna was almost ready to leave. I became aware of the fact that this might be the last time I ever saw my eldest sister.

Suddenly, I had a notion that perhaps she wasn't being totally serious.

—Are you really leaving forever? I asked.

—Nah, she said, stifling a wicked grin.

What a bitch, I thought. Aloud, however, I said:

—I hate you!

—You love me.

—Be careful, okay?

—Don't worry, she said. —I'm only going out to meet Declan.

Declan was my sister's new boyfriend. He loomed large in her life. I'd heard things about him, dark rumours I was worried might be true.

—Be careful, I repeated.

Chapter 12

November 17th 1993

England failed to qualify for the World Cup (despite winning their game) and parties were held all over Scotland to celebrate their failure. Fishtank threw a party in our garden and invited all his freaky friends over, but only if they came with a bottle of Buckfast or two. One of them, an enormous fat bald man with a homemade tattoo of Sham 69 on his left forearm, blocked our toilet with a huge shit and broke the seat for good measure. Fishtank blamed his mother/grandmother and nothing else was said about it, much to the fury of Granny Frances. I paced around the garden silently, a little ghost, watching from a safe distance the way David Attenborough might if he were in the jungle observing some wild animals. Our garden wasn't a nice place: broken fences made it look rundown and nasty, our large wooden shed was a rotting spider's nest. The grass was thick and intrusive. It needed cut badly, just like my hair, which was now thick and dark and curly. Obviously, I didn't want to return to Aff Yer Heid.

Laddie came over with a sausage roll in his mouth. This was known everywhere as the 'Cumbernauld dummy' because of the amount of kids in our town you saw with sausage rolls stuck in their gobs. Chewing his food, Laddie sensed something was troubling me.

—You okay?
—I don't get football, I replied.
—That's because you're weird.
—Am I?
—Totally.

I thought about it and agreed.

—I am a bit weird.

—You're mega mega weird.

—Mega mega weird? In a good way? Tell me it's in a good way?

My voice sounded imploring and probably just a little pathetic.

—I don't care if you're weird.

—Thanks Laddie.

—Or mega mega weird.

—*Thanks* Laddie.

Laddie chewed the rest of his sausage roll into oblivion, then sat with me on the steps. They were small steps, two actually, and they led to the back door of our house. It wasn't sunny, in fact the clouds looked ready to split open. We sat together but said nothing as the garden party happened around us. We simply listened to all the noise and music, observed strangers singing offensive songs about England and Ireland and whatever country wasn't Scotland. Even at 12-years-old, I knew none of this was for me.

—Walter, said Laddie quietly.

—Yes?

—Happy Birthday.

I smiled, but said nothing. At least someone remembered.

Chapter 13

Money Problems

It didn't take long for Granny's bank account to run dry, which was incredibly inconvenient for everyone, but mostly Fishtank, who relied on her money to fund his extravagant lifestyle. The albums he bought on vinyl and CD. The high-tech equipment he needed to operate his CB radio. His season tickets for various football teams. His snazzy new clothes he wore while we went with whatever Mum could make on her Brother sewing machine. That money was all but gone. Granny, meanwhile, had made the most of her stay. We literally did everything for her. When we took Granny in, we'd given her permission to treat us all like slaves. She barked the order and we obeyed without question. We desperately tried to medicate (or cure) her endless array of diseases and illnesses, all of which seemed to come out of nowhere. It was a tough situation, especially for Mum.

That's why she had to call in a nurse to help out.

The nurse, a lovely lady named Patricia, popped in twice a week.

She was the first to tell us the truth about Granny Frances.

Mum had used peeling the potatoes for dinner as an excuse to get away from Granny. I was at the table, reading (what else?) a new *Nancy Drew* book the librarian up at the library had requested in especially for me. Laddie was at the other side of the table, eating a Fiendish Feet yoghurt. Slightly bitter that he'd eaten more than his fair share and left me with bugger all, I had to be content with a packet of KP nuts I'd found at the back of the cupboard. A good source of fibre, apparently. I had no idea what fibre actually did.

—You shouldn't be eating before your dinner, said Mum.

It could have been aimed at Laddie, myself, or most likely the two of us.

Laddie made a performance of licking the yoghurt off his spoon.

—I love yoghurt!

—I didn't get a chance to love it, I said bitterly.

Laddie stuck out his tongue.

I kicked him under the table.

Mum had officially *had it*.

—If both of you don't act your age, I'll take this slipper and tan your arses.

That's when I realised Granny's nurse was blocking the kitchen door. To her credit, she looked sheepish at the intrusion, but she was…waiting…wanting something that none of us quite understood. Mum finally mumbled an apology for losing her temper. The nurse, dressed in a mint-green NHS uniform and white badge with the name *Patricia* engraved into the plastic in black bold font, waved a hand dismissively.

—Don't worry, she laughed. I've got three little terrors and they're always at it. But what would I do if they behaved themselves?

Mum smiled, but it wasn't a real smile.

Like me, she didn't smile much back then.

—Look, started Patricia. —I need to speak with you.

My ears immediately perked up, waiting to hear something exciting.

Nurse Patricia noticed my interest and reacted accordingly:

—In private, she added.

Damn, I thought. She's smart.

Mum didn't go far though. She couldn't, because there was a pot of bubbling hot water on the front left ring of the cooker. The peeled potatoes were meant to be dropped in, just so Fishtank could get what he wanted for dinner: mince 'n' tatties. I hated mince 'n' tatties as much as I hated steak pie. A few years ago I'd mixed HP Brown Sauce into the mince and the result was so revolting that I became vegetarian overnight. Really, I only wanted chips. I'd ask for a plate of something and chips, but chips were always my main target.

In the hallway, the two grown-ups were having a conversation.

—What's wrong?

Mum sounded concerned. I craned over the table slightly, holding my book tight, pretending to be reading it while actually earie-wigging into the conversation. My little brother was playing with his yoghurt tub, pretending it was trying to kill his spoon.

—It's about your mother-in-law.

—How bad is it? Mum asked, her voice sounding somewhat detached.

—What?

—Her illness. Is there anything we can do?

—You can stop buying her chocolate and crisps, for a start.

I frowned. This wasn't going the way I'd expected.

Nurse Patricia didn't look remotely ashamed at her outburst.

—There's no easy way to tell you this, Mrs. Wedgeworth, but there's nothing wrong with your mother-in-law. She's perfectly healthy for her age.

—But…she can't walk properly.

—That's because she's morbidly obese. I would say 'fat', but the nurses at the health centre have been told to mind what we say. So 'morbidly obese' it is.

Mum gasped loudly. I turned a page in the book I wasn't actually reading.

—What?

—If she stopped eating all the time, she'd feel a lot better. The reason she needs to use the toilet so much is because she's cramming all that crap down her gullet. Apart from that, she's perfectly capable of movement. But you need to make her get up and move around.

That revelation nearly made me ignore another few pages of *Nancy Drew And The Witch Tree Symbol*, but I managed to keep it in a tight grip. Any noise would have alerted my mum to the fact I was listening to her private conversation with Nurse Patricia.

Mum said exactly what I'd been thinking:

—You really mean to tell me she can walk?

—Yes. If she can get up off that wheelchair, she's able to move around freely.

The water in the pot was boiling over, and it wasn't alone.

Mum took a step back, her brow furrowed, fringe falling across her eyes.

—That lying old cow!

—Don't do anything you'll regret, said the nurse. —The only reason I told you is because I don't think it's right that you're running about after her, doing everything.

—We had to carry her upstairs, said Mum in astonishment. She was clearly having flashbacks to her and Lorna's abortive attempt to heave Granny up the staircase to the toilet. The hall carpet was ruined and Fishtank regularly made digs at Mum for being neglectful, which only had the effect of making Mum slave herself harder to be helpful.

—She doesn't have elephantiasis?

—No.

—She doesn't have scarlet fever?

—No.

—She doesn't have diabetes?

—No. She's fat, Mrs. Wedgeworth. Just fat. Sorry, *morbidly obese.*

Without saying another word, Mum came back into the kitchen. She headed to the cooker, where she proceeded to

61

drop the peeled potatoes into the pot. Then, once that was sorted, Mum turned the heat down and saw the nurse out.

—Eleanor, a voice from the living room wailed. —I need help! I need help!

—You need help alright, said Mum viciously.

I immediately knew Granny Frances wouldn't be living with us for much longer.

Chapter 14

Out In The Street

My favourite teacher at Langlands Primary School was Mrs. Robertson. Tall, bohemian, with thick curly brown hair and lots of simple dresses made from tartan of every conceivable colour, she was a stable presence in the lives of her students. Every Friday she turned Classroom 7B into a church and got everyone in Primary 7 to sing hymns and pray to God. We all did it, though not all of us believed in God. Something about a powerful deity watching us every moment of every second of every day of our lives absolutely *terrified* me. He knew what we were thinking. Every thought was His to see and judge. He took notes. And if you weren't His sort of person, He cast you from the holiest heights of Heaven into the forever-burning fires of Hell.

While praying in Classroom 7B I had a sudden revelation of my own.

Hell wasn't somewhere we potentially went when we died.

We were already in Hell.

This world. Our lives. Cumbernauld.

Everything was Hell.

Proud of my minor theological moment, I found myself laughing out loud.

—Walter, said Mrs. Robertson mildly yet firmly. —This isn't a classroom. Right now, it's our church. You don't laugh at church.

I was torn between telling Mrs. Robertson that I felt we *should* laugh at church, that we should laugh at the whole stupid thing. Torn between that and keeping her happy, I opted for Mrs. Robertson's happiness. She was very dear to me. Her disapproval would have been too savage to bear. Everyone at our school adored Mrs. Robertson. We really did. She cared even though she didn't need to care. And that made us care about her in return.

After telling me off, Mrs. Robertson smiled and made her way to the bulky old-fashioned tape-deck that was half-metal, half brown wood. A museum piece, really. Instead of rewinding the tape, Mrs. Robertson paused it and asked me a question in front of my classmates. It was a question I hadn't expected to be asked.

—Do you believe in God, Walter?

Everyone in Classroom 7B looked at each other, their eyes meeting, leaving, finding and sending messages in silence. They sensed something was about to happen. Drama!

I looked away, my thoughts suddenly drifting towards a child in a box.

—No, I don't believe in God.

Mrs. Robertson smiled a big genuine smile, the sort that our hearts danced to.

She didn't judge me.

I hoped perhaps she understood me.

Perhaps.

Hours later, shortly after the final bell, a group of us headed up the bumpy cobbled ground that surrounded Langlands Primary School. Walking alongside me were Moo and Poppy. We saw Danny split off from a group of people and he came our way. Though I got along well with Danny, bonded by his Super Nintendo, Moo didn't care for him.

—Hey, Danny, I said.

—Fuck off, Danny!

I shot Moo a sharp look, but clearly it hadn't been sharp enough. He ignored it and walked past Danny. Where Moo walked, Poppy followed. My two friends were moving away from me, striding past garden fences opposite the school. I shrugged. What else could I do? Danny was still my friend. But Moo and Poppy were friends too.

—I'm okay, said Danny, even though he looked ready to burst into tears.

—Come on, I told him. We walked together towards St. Joseph's Primary School. The pupils there were strictly Catholic, though none of that stuff mattered to me. Every now and again they'd fight with Langlands. Again, none of that stuff mattered to me.

—You better go and catch up with Moo, otherwise he'll be pissed off.

—Me, Poppy and Moo have other friends.

—Poppy, Moo and I, corrected Danny.

—Nah. I always put myself first.

We both laughed. It was a good comeback and I felt very proud of my burgeoning wit.

Danny started humming the tune to East 17's *Stay Another Day*.

Battle lines were suddenly drawn. This stuff was important to me.

—Don't sing East 17, I begged. —They're crap!

—I like them.

—They're manufactured! They're made to steal pocket money from daft girls.

Back then, I was precious about music and bands. They weren't just bands to me; they were tribes you lived and died for. Their iconography wasn't just a t-shirt in State of Independence. It meant something. I didn't believe in God, but I believed in Kurt Cobain. I worshipped at the altar of Nirvana. I'd accidentally taped over Donnie's old Terence Trent D'Arby tape with the BBC Radio 1 broadcast of *Smells Like Teen Spirit*. One song was all I had, because we couldn't afford to buy albums unless Fishtank wanted them.

But it didn't matter.

I had that one song, and it had me.

We would be there for each other forever.

—East 17 suck, I insisted.

—Well *I* like them.

So intent in winning against Danny that I hadn't noticed how quickly time had passed, I was nearly home. Wrapped up in our debate, we'd walked off our usual route. Danny would get home late, but me? I was just about there. My house literally a few minutes away. I split off in that direction and waved goodbye to Danny for the day. He headed towards his flat, in the same block Granny Frances used to live at before she moved into 145 Craigieburn Road with the rest of the family.

I walked back slowly, trying to delay the inevitable. It was only as I reached the road that curved towards my house that I saw Moo and Poppy running in my direction. Evidently, they'd made it back before me. With Poppy living up the street from me, she had to pass my house on the way to her own.

Immediately, I knew something was wrong.

—There's a bloody riot going on outside your front door, gasped Poppy.

—What?

Moo looked exasperated.

—Don't just stand about. Get your arse in gear and move.

We ran together until the commotion outside my door came into focus. They weren't wrong. There was a fierce battle taking place at my house. The voices came first, then the faces, then finally an explanation.

It was Fishtank, Granny Frances, Lorna, Donnie, Jake, and Mum.

Laddie, thankfully, had decided to have dinner at his friend's house.

—Please, wailed Lorna. —You can't do it.

Fishtank gave her his most disdainful expression.

—I can do what the fuck I want!

As if to prove a point, Fishtank reached over and grabbed the handles of Granny's wheelchair. Violently, he pushed, lifting it up off the ground a few inches. Granny screamed but didn't fall. When she screamed, my sisters and Jake cried out in panic. Mum seemed stunned, rooted to the pavement in disbelief.

She often looked that way when Fishtank went off on a rampage.

—Look. It's simple. You can't stay unless you pay, said Fishtank in an ever-so-reasonable voice.

—But…but…I've no money left.

Oh dear. Granny had spent it all on her son, his house, and his bills.

—What about the lump sum dad left you when he died?

—You've spent it all on your radio thingy. There's nothing left!

—She's a fat lying bitch, said Fishtank to his little audience.

My friends decided to back off and get home as quickly as possible. This was far too much for either of them. Obviously they knew what my house was like. I'd spent many hours complaining to them about my lot in life. But hearing it all from me versus seeing it with their own eyes, hearing it with their own ears…well, it didn't seem quite so funny anymore.

—Tell us what happens next time we see each other, said Poppy.

At least they weren't angry that I chose to walk with Danny instead of them.

That was the least of my problems.

Before I could say anything, a nearby door opened and a friendly face popped out.

It belonged to Mr. Moore, our neighbour whose last fight with Fishtank over the antenna up on our roof had ended in name-calling and defamatory slurs. I tried to make Mr. Moore go back inside, but he didn't pick up on my little gesture, the slight nodding of my head that said *please don't get involved or you'll make it worse*.

—What is all this noise about?

—Fuck off, snarled Fishtank. —This is none of your business.

—My own son is making me homeless, wailed Granny Frances.

The scene in front of me suddenly made sense. There was a suitcase on the kerb with clothes scattered across the ground. The suitcase itself was sitting at an odd angle and it looked as though someone had kicked it out of the door, where it had burst in mid-air. The various items of clothing included nightgowns, knickers, tights and some old misshapen bras. Horribly, a rather hefty pair of pink bloomers lay on the ground, partly covering Fishtank's left foot. He didn't notice. I did, and shuddered.

—You're always causing problems in this street, Mr. Moore stated calmly. —Enough is enough. You better start treating your family right, or they'll end up being taken away. Is that what you want, John?

Suddenly I believed in God, if only for a short while.

By the look of his face, Fishtank couldn't believe someone had dared stand up to him. His skin was red hot, the colour spreading across the surface, even his ears burned.

—What's going on? I asked.

I'd suddenly made myself a target. Normally passive, I now had all eyes on me.

—Nothing's going on, replied Mum hastily. She looked terribly sad. Everyone had been crying, except Fishtank. Lorna and Donnie were by Granny's wheelchair, holding onto it protectively. Jake, however, seemed to stand close to Fishtank. He stood by him in fear, of course. We all did. As much as we despised our father, we feared him more.

—Let's go inside.

With that command uttered, we all followed Fishtank through the front door.

Granny Frances was in tears, real ones, not the fake kind she usually deployed.

—Please. You can't do this to your own mother.

—You aren't my mother, said Fishtank, before finally slamming the door shut.

Chapter 15

High At High School

My brother Jake committed his first robbery on the same day the IRA launched their five-day assault against Heathrow Airport. It happened in March of 1994. These events aren't connected, except in my memory, where everything meets the other, inextricably linked together in the story of my life. The robbery happened like this: Jake and his mates were outside at the swing park in Craigieburn Road, all of them sitting about with bottles of Buckfast. My brother can't remember who said it, but someone came up with the bright idea of robbing the corner shop (not actually on a corner) at Stonylee Road. Pulling his t-shirt across his face, my brother walked into the shop with his usual swagger. According to witnesses, the shopkeeper *laughed* at my brother, whose shirt covered his face so effectively that he couldn't actually see properly. Worse. Not only did my brother walk into the shop, but he also walked into the counter by the till. Furious at being laughed at, my brother promptly lifted a bottle of Barr's American Cream Soda from the rack – and swung it around in random directions.

The bottle struck the shopkeeper on top of his head.

Both bottle and head cracked wide open.

Luckily, the shopkeeper survived and eventually recovered from his assault.

And my brother?

Fine. Hunky Dory. Lucky as fuck. Why? Because no witnesses came forward. The shop had no CCTV, which meant there was no actual evidence to prosecute Jake.

No-one could quite believe it.

In the end, it was Jake's word against that of the poor shopkeeper.

And it *couldn't* have been Jake, because he was out with Fishtank all day, apparently.

One of the perks of being twelve-years-old at Langland's Primary School was the common room. It was full of broken desks and old blackboards, the sort with chalky smudge marks that no amount of wiping could erase. While my friends played outside in the rain, I enjoyed nothing more than hiding out in the common room with a book. Boring, maybe. But I liked what I liked. So after eating my free school meal (always something with chips), I headed to my little sanctuary. The peace and quiet made me sigh gratefully. I'd spent the whole morning being asked by my classmates about Jake and the robbery.

—What really happened?

—Did he really skelp someone across the head with a bottle?

Moo, in particular, wanted to know the gory and grisly details. I suspected he was planning to repackage my story as a Billy The Squid epic, a tall tale to be told to everyone in the playground. The last thing I wanted to do, however, was go to school and talk about my family.

Halfway through reading a *Doctor Who* book, I realised someone else was in the room with me. When I looked up, it was to the sight of a welcome face.

Mrs. Robertson had taken some time out of her lunch break to come and visit me.

—Are you okay, Walter?

The question affected me in a way I didn't quite understand. No-one had ever asked me about my thoughts and feelings. Was I okay? Confronted by a simple question, I found that I didn't know what to say. So I simply gave the easy, maybe untrue answer:

—Yes, I'm fine. Thank you for asking.

—You'll be okay, said Mrs. Robertson thoughtfully.

—I will?

—You're strong, Walter. You just don't realise it yet.

Mrs. Robertson turned to leave, but not before I had a chance to get one last thing out:

—I'll miss this place.

Really, that was about as much emotion as I could muster in public. What I'd actually wanted to say was —*I'll miss you, Mrs. Robertson.* But I couldn't. I was twelve-years-old. So there I sat with my *Doctor Who* book while everyone else ran around the playground making noise and having fun and telling stories about Billy The Squid and my brother.

Mrs. Robertson seemed to understand my mood:

—Not long to go before you start high school, eh?

—High school is ages away, I blurted. —Three whole months!

—Walter, time moves faster when you're my age. Or at least it feels faster. One day, you'll understand. You'll look back and wonder where it all went. Then you'll remember this moment, this talk we've just had.

She was right.

The best teachers usually are.

Two weeks later, I got my first taste of what the future held at high school when I attended a special two-day visit. I'd already selected Cumbernauld High as my school of choice. It was the same school Jake had been to a few years previously. My sisters, however, attended Greenfaulds High at the other end of town. They delighted in spending hours terrifying me with horror stories about kids snorting glue on the staircases and that one time a teacher slapped a pupil for pointing out her moustache in front of the other students. Okay, they were probably trying to freak me out for laughs and giggles, but it didn't really matter. I never considered Greenfaulds High in my future plans for the simple reason, all of my friends were going to Cumbernauld High. It made sense to join them. Poppy and Moo were going to Cumbernauld High. Danny was going to Cumbernauld High. Maria. Gary. Barry. Lola too. We were the Langland's Primary School posse. We weren't much in the grand scheme of things, but we had an advantage over everyone else. A hidden bluff that I could use under the direst of circumstances, a weapon of massive destruction to be used against bullies. And this secret weapon?

My brother Jake, actually. The robbery at Stonylee Road cornershop had increased both his reputation and ego. He was now known and feared by people in Cumbernauld.

—Don't fuck with Jake Wedgeworth, they said in hushed voices.

—He's a crazy bastard.

As much as my own brother frightened me, I also understood the value in sharing his surname. It prevented me from having my head baptised down the bog.

We all walked together through the school's forbidding iron gates, both rusted so badly that that a well-aimed sneeze might have ripped them from their hinges, hurled them through the air, over the playground. But it wasn't a playground. It was a *schoolyard*. A playground was something for little kids, not a manly high school student like me whose voice hadn't yet broken and whose chin-stubble was actually a spattering of blackheads.

Dress code for high school back in the 90s wasn't as strictly enforced as it is these days. We were told in our official enrolment letter to dress smart, which for me meant looking like a poverty-stricken pimp. Poor (but crafty), I was able to turn trash into class. Me, who once tried to sell a revenge haircut as a statement of high fashion! Now I had Granny's old fur coat, which for me was the epitome of pure glamour. I wore it on my first day without a shred of shame or embarrassment.

WORLD, my clothes screamed. LOOK AT ME! My clothes also screamed I LOOK LIKE A TIT, WHAT THE HELL WAS I THINKING, and WHY DID MY PARENTS LET ME WALK OUT THE FRONT DOOR DRESSED LIKE THIS?

We passed by a group of glowering girls with cigarettes hanging out of their mouths.

—This is amazing, whispered Poppy in admiration. —I can't *wait* to start high school. I wanna smoke fags every day. I'll look totally trendy with a fag in my hand, I just know it.

Moo seemed less confident, which (for him) was rare. Though I seemed the most assertive, if only because of how I dressed, Moo was by far the most self-assured of everyone in our little group. Our de facto leader, though not for much longer.

—Welcome to Cumbernauld High School, muttered Moo quietly.

He had a new haircut. It didn't suit him. His fringe was a curtain, two long parts that flopped over his eyes. But at least he didn't have a bowl-cut like Danny did. According to Gary Dowds, girls didn't fancy boys with bowl-cuts. But girls didn't fancy Gary and he had dyed blonde spikes and a line shaved through his eyebrow.

We got closer to the smokers, ready to pass by, when one of them snarled:

—Got any fags?

—No, I'm sorry. I…I don't smoke.

That's when they noticed my fur coat. How could they not? It was big, black and fluffy.

—What the fuck are you wearing? Is that your granny's coat?

Startled by her insight, I blurted out the truth.

—How did you know?

They burst out laughing. It wasn't nice laughter, the sort I let out whenever I watched *Beavis and Butthead* or *Absolutely Fabulous*. Their laughter robbed me of whatever confidence

I'd convinced myself I had. The result? I immediately went to take off my jacket, so no-one else would see me, so no-one else would laugh.

—Keep that on, hissed Poppy, bravely eye-balling the bitchy smokers. Or maybe she was thinking of asking them for a cigarette?

Anyway, I did as she ordered, but passed the school gates quaking and shaking, pining for the safety and security of the little common room at Langland's Primary School.

Chapter 16

Near Death At The Dinner Table

I nearly choked to death on a Findus Crispy Pancake because of Fishtank. It wasn't attempted murder like what happened between him, Mum and the steak pie. He simply wanted to surprise everyone. I just happened to be eating my dinner when he stood up and uttered the words that would change all of our lives. We didn't know that at the time, of course. I've come to learn that momentous events start with stupid white men standing up to make speeches no-one wants to hear.

We were facing each other at the kitchen table, eating in silence, all of us apart from Donnie and Lorna, when Fishtank suddenly decided to make his Very Important Announcement. Nothing leading up to Fishtank's speech suggested everything was about to change with a few words. Not a clue. I'd been so distracted by my brief visit to Cumbernauld High that I hadn't picked up on any signs of impending change. I hadn't noticed Mum's sewing machine sitting on the kitchen counter, the one she only brought out when money was tight enough to snap. Sewing wasn't a pleasure for my mother, it was pure necessity. If she couldn't afford to buy us clothes, then the sewing machine was required. Mum literally turned cloth into clothes, which we all wore, whether we liked it or not. Also, Mum and Fishtank had started fighting again and my books weren't enough to blot out the noise. Money problems had put a strain on all our lives. Mum had lost two out of her four jobs. With Granny's bank account bled dry and Mum earning far less, we were in dire straits, and I don't mean the band. Fishtank seemed a bit nervous, though he was probably terrified the electricity would be cut off again. In his mind, it was a simple equation: no money plus no electricity equals no CB radio.

And *that*, above all other things, was absolutely unacceptable.

Dinner was always a struggle. Fishtank insisted on making us all eat cabbage, which I hated. Laddie would burst into tears though, which I refused to do out of principle. Emotions, I'd decided, were pointless. My tactic to win the dinnertime wars was simple but effective. If I chewed my food…very…very… slowly…I'd still be at the table eating long after Fishtank had finished. Then, once he'd upped and left the table, my plate would be quietly scraped into the bin, the leftovers covered up with whatever rubbish was at hand. Usually the remains of torn up envelopes, the tell-tale signs of unanswered debt letters.

Not that day.

Fishtank seemed to have lost his appetite, casually forking his food in an uncharacteristically absentminded manner. Not even his beloved cabbage or carrots went into his mouth. Mum kept giving him meaningful looks, though their meaning didn't mean anything to me. Yet. I had a *Nancy Drew* book to my left, on the edge of the table.

—Aren't you too old for that? Fishtank said all of a sudden.

It took me a few seconds to realise he was talking to me.

—Too old for what?

—*Nancy Drew* books. Why are you reading a girl's book anyway?

I knew what he was getting at, of course. But Nancy Drew had the life I wanted. She was middle-class, her father was a lawyer, she had a fabulous car and the adoration of her upwardly mobile friends. Plus, she solved mysteries that no-one else could crack. If she ever discovered a baby inside a mouldy old box, she'd have taken up the quest and tracked down the culprit. Not like me, awkwardly phoning the police from a box in Beechwood Road. In all seriousness, I wanted to be like Nancy Drew, and I had no problem in admitting that to anyone. Anyone, that is, but him.

—He can read whatever he wants, snapped Mum.

—*Nancy Drew* is for girls, whined Fishtank.

—At least he's reading books. That's a *good* thing.

—He wore granny's fur coat to high school, blurted Jake, trying to curry favour with Fishtank, even though he despised him more than anything else in the universe.

—What?

—My pals saw him with a woman's jacket on!

—You don't have any pals! I snapped at Jake, angered by this betrayal.

He raised his table knife menacingly at me, but the effect was ruined by the stray bit of cabbage hanging off the blade. Mum reached over and gave him a slap on his head. A stray whack, but it was enough to quieten him. For now, at least.

Fishtank shook his head in disappointment. I'd already spotted a particularly large vein in his forehead. Fascinated, I looked, watching it pulse, ready to burst through the skin's surface. I had a vision of blood spraying all over me. I'd become a bit morbid of late.

Locked in an inner monologue about death and cabbage, I almost missed the moment Fishtank took to his feet to deliver his Very Important Announcement. Mum looked on eagerly, her eyes large with excitement. Whatever her husband was about to tell everyone, she already knew. More so, she seemed happy with it.

I put a piece of Crispy Pancake in my mouth.

—I'm going to look for a job, said Fishtank.

I spluttered. Then I choked.

—Oh my God, yelled Mum. —He can't breathe! He can't breathe!

Laddie slapped me on my back, but it didn't dislodge the

food. Sensing an opportunity for revenge, Jake punched me hard, under the guise of trying to help clear my windpipe. He punched once, nearly sending my lungs out of my mouth permanently.

Mum reached over and clouted him on the forehead with the back of her hand, again.

Finally, after nearly dying at the dinner table, I spat out the gloopy gooey mess that used to be my Findus Crispy Pancake. It plopped onto the table, giving me the opportunity to suck in huge gulps of oxygen. My lungs full up, I slumped on the bench, mindful not to fall onto the table with the plates and cutlery. Besides, I was wearing a white tracksuit Mum had made for me on the sewing machine. The last thing I needed to do was stain it.

—I'm applying for jobs today, continued Fishtank, as though I hadn't nearly died.

—Where? Jake asked.

—One of the factories, replied Mum.

—They're okay taking on people with no qualifications, added Fishtank.

Admitting he had no qualifications was rare for Fishtank. He always presented himself as the smartest man in the room. He was always better than you, no matter what you did. Back when Mum first met Fishtank all those years ago in the Gorbals, he was GOING PLACES. She once told me how charismatic he was and praised his good patter. Mum had been particularly proud to tell all her friends that she was dating a welder (actually a cleaner for three weeks) who was GOING PLACES in life. Qualifications? She assumed he had some. They married and then Mum discovered the truth about her new man. Really, despite her disappointment, she was GOING PLACES with Fishtank.

Cumbernauld, the so-called ugliest town in Scotland, wasn't quite what she had in mind.

*

Later, after making his shocking announcement, Fishtank suddenly became adamant that I eat *everything* on my plate. It didn't surprise me. He was clearly in a bad mood at the prospect of being forced to work for a living. He wanted to lash out in some small way, so he sat and watched me eat every forkful of food, every bite and every swallow. I ate everything that had been set out in front of me, including the cabbage I'd always hated.

Weirdly, for that one single dinner, even my cabbage tasted great.

Chapter 17

Kurt Cobain

My last day at Langland's Primary School filled my thoughts with fear of the future. Mrs. Robertson gave me a hug as I left her class for the last time, then waved me off. I'd never been hugged before, so I froze as she took me in her arms. One lasting regret is that I didn't hug her back, tell her how grateful I was to have her in my life.

But I didn't.

And now she'll never know.

Mum successfully scored a job for Fishtank at a plastics factory in Cumbernauld. He headed off every day to a big tall blue building with a large white sign with red letters which read ISOLA. The factory looked terribly menacing, putting me in mind of a prison. Apt, really, because that was where Fishtank belonged. He wore a blue uniform with a badge he proudly showed off to the girls at the checkouts in various different shops around the town centre. He couldn't take out loans and flash the cash anymore, so he let them see his badge. He seemed taken by the novelty of working.

I saw him with my own eyes, heard him with my own ears.

—It's one of those days.

—Yes, the check-out girl would say politely.

—I'm absolutely shattered.

—Long day?

—I've been working since seven this morning! But it's good to have a job, isn't it? Not like those lazy bastards down at the Unemployed Workers' Centre, eh?

—Okay…

—They're not like us. We're workers, not shirkers.

And so on, much to my embarrassment. But everyone in 145 Craigieburn Road loved the fact Fishtank was working long hours, because it meant we had the house to ourselves. With Mum out working too, it left Lorna in charge. Unfortunately for her, Lorna was in the throes of first love with her arsehole boyfriend Declan and couldn't be bothered to babysit. That suited me fine. Jake was upstairs, locked away in his bedroom with some friends, emerging with large red eyes and a serious case of the munchies. Laddie, meanwhile, bounced on the couch, screaming and wailing joyfully. I listened to CDs, enjoying Nirvana's music the way it should be enjoyed: loud, loud, LOUD. My entire family knew of my very pure devotion to Kurt Cobain. His voice was a scream that tore through bullshit, his songs guided messages that I received gratefully. He made music as tuneful and poppy as Abba or Erasure, yet ferocious enough to feel like a baseball bat bopping me on my brain. I lived for Kurt Cobain. He was my Yoda.

My friends and family didn't understand him.

They didn't care.

But everyone suddenly cared on April 8th 1994 when a story broke on ITV's *News At Ten*. Fishtank was back home from a long day at work (and didn't he let us know it) when a familiar face suddenly popped up on our television. I wasn't used to seeing Kurt Cobain on TV. He'd been on an episode of *Rapido* and Nirvana had appeared on *Top of the Pops* as well. Normally, every appearance of Nirvana was special and exciting for me.

But not this one.

—The lead singer of Nirvana, one of the world's most popular rock bands, has been found dead at his home in Seattle. Police said Kurt Cobain had apparently shot himself and a suicide note found nearby…

—Look, shouted Jake excitedly. —He topped himself!

—He probably listened to his own music, said Lorna dryly.

—Drugs, said Mum.

—What? Fishtank asked.

—I bet it's drugs.

—No! He shot himself. That's what the news said.

—He shot himself up?

—No. He *shot* himself. Bang! Bang!

I stood up and walked out the living room and didn't stop until I was upstairs in bed, with headphones and his voice in my ears. As I lay on my bed thinking about the death of my idol, I tried to analyse how I felt, what the news meant to me. He was gone. But really, I could always call his voice back any time I wanted to hear him again, just by pressing PLAY on my cassette player. Slowly, I took inventory of my feelings; Kurt Cobain was dead. He committed suicide. He'd taken the choice to end his life. He looked at the world around him, saw how shit it was, and made a logical conclusion to end his existence.

I felt sadness, of course.

But more than sadness, I felt *jealousy*.

Chapter 18

Lies

It didn't take long for all of us to realise something wasn't quite right. Fishtank had spent our lives at home while Mum worked various jobs. That he got his first proper job in his late thirties was shocking enough. That he spent all his time at the factory, clawing in all the overtime he could, well...that was virtually unbelievable. He seemed happy to go to work. I heard him whistling one morning as Mum ironed his uniform. His jolly (and tone deaf) tune pulled me out of my light sleep. That's when I realised Fishtank was up to something. I knew my father only too well: he was too lazy to be successful in the workplace. There had to be something in Isola he wanted to see or do every day.

Something.

Or someone.

Eventually, my suspicions seemed to spread. I never told anyone, but they were smart enough to come to the same conclusion I'd reached weeks earlier. It was Lorna who put it into words: thoughtful, calm, insightful Lorna who spent all her time with her boyfriend – and the rest of it trying to hide the bruises on her body.

—Mum, she said while waiting for the toaster to jump. — Dad seems to be enjoying his new job, doesn't he?

Mum was at the table with her two best friends, Mr. Benson and Mr. Hedges. Lost in her own thoughts, as well as a cloud of thick grey smoke, she looked over and said:

—It gets him out of the house, doesn't it?

—He's never in the house though.

—I'm glad, muttered Donnie.

The others hadn't caught her comment, but I was close enough to receive it loud and clear. We smiled, bonded in our own private little moment of rebelliousness. I agreed with Donnie, but that didn't change the fact Fishtank was never in the house anymore. Something was wrong. But before I'd open my mouth to say anything, I needed to know what Lorna was thinking. It was likely she had the same suspicion I had.

—I don't want toast, moaned Laddie from the living room.

—What do you want? Lorna asked.

—I'm hungry for a bowl of Ricicles!

—Jake ate the last of the Ricicles last night.

—He's eating *everything*, I moaned. But that wasn't quite true. He was only eating everything I liked. The chocolate, the cereal, the crisps and the biscuits. He left all the rubbish foods that none of us liked or wanted. Even when high, Jake knew to avoid the microwavable kebabs from Farmfoods and the terrible fake pancakes from Capital.

Donnie understood the context of my catty comment and sniggered.

Mum quelled us into silence with a pointed glare.

We went back to the main topic of discussion *i.e.* Fishtank and his sudden absence.

Lorna drove her point across with one damning statement:

—He dyed his hair, Mum.

—*I* dyed his hair, came her response.

—For a job in the factory? It's just…

—You think he's seeing someone else?

The kitchen went deathly silent.

Mum had literally just said what we were all thinking.

No. What we were all *hoping*.

—If that's what you're thinking, you're right. Your father's seeing a tart from the factory.

—What? Donnie snarled.

—She's a dinner lady, continued Mum, whilst puffing on her fast-disappearing ciggie.

—A dinner lady, gasped Lorna.

—A dog's dinner, more like.

They were talking about this as though I wasn't there in the same room as them, but my power to remain hidden in the background had always proved useful. No-one seemed to care if I was there, often talking about stuff that adults normally wouldn't talk about in front of their children. In this instance, I was grateful to be dressed in quiet clothes, rather than Granny's old fur coat. That way I could listen to everything. Possibly even contribute.

—When did he tell you? I asked,

—He hasn't. He doesn't know I know.

Mum sucked away the final bit of her cigarette.

—Yet, she added.

The kitchen fell into uneasy silence.

When the toaster jumped, I did likewise.

Chapter 19

The Surprise Party

We threw a surprise party for Fishtank, the surprise being that Mum was divorcing him. He didn't know that, though. There we stood, together as a family in the living room, waiting for him to get back in from another long day at the factory. We couldn't wait for him to see the banners announcing the end of his marriage. Yes, we actually made banners. There was a strange nervous tension in the room, one that caused a tightness behind my eyes. Yet I couldn't deny my feeling of anticipation. Years of misery were coming to a final end. A lifetime of abuse, of measuring Fishtank's moods in order to survive his explosive outbursts…none of it would happen ever again. We would be free. Mum had finally taken the necessary steps to purge the cause of our problems once and for all. She'd been working in secret with us, her children. For weeks, she'd diligently travelled into Glasgow with Lorna, the two of them sharing their plots and plans.

—What's going to happen? I asked.

—Just wait until your dad gets back home, said Mum.

—You can tell me. I won't tell anyone else. I can keep a secret!

—Yeah right, said Lorna with a disdainful expression.

They never knew that I had a secret and it was rotting away in a cardboard box somewhere, probably inside an evidence locker at Cumbernauld Police Station. Or perhaps he'd been burned into dust, scattered in the wind? The newspapers didn't really talk about Baby C anymore, so I had no idea about his fate. Sometimes I thought about the baby, but remembering meant reliving and I didn't want to feel that way again. In order to make it through life, I had to push all thoughts of Baby C deeper into my brain, locking him permanently in the past. Life found other problems to keep me occupied.

And one of them eventually returned home from work.

—Where's everybody?

His voice made me feel ill. Could we go through with this? Would we survive it?

—We're in here, called Mum.

We caught a glimpse of his shape through the glass door of the living room, which meant he probably saw us huddled together with banners draped above our heads. The door opened and there he stood, quizzical and unsure. His eyes swept through the room looking for an explanation. We stood there together as a family; Mum, Lorna, Donnie, Jake, Laddie and me. I was terrified. His moods were unpredictable. I'd once watched Fishtank hack Jake's skateboard into splintered wood with a hatchet because Jake had dared collect rent off him during a game of Monopoly. Thankfully, there were no hatchets nearby.

Mum waited. Fishtank reacted.

Our party finally started.

—What the fuck's going on?

—What do you think?

—You're having a party?

—Is that what you think?

—What are these fucking things up on the wall for?

—What? My HAPPY DIVORCE banners?

—I know what they are. What are they doing on my wall?

—I'm divorcing you. My lawyer will be in contact soon.

During this exchange, Lorna took an opportunity to edge away from us, slowly past Fishtank, out into the hall. She made it look very casual, but I sensed she didn't want to draw attention to her sudden exit. I opened my mouth to ask where she was going, but Donnie gave a slight tilt of her head. It said

NO. That told me to say absolutely nothing.

Besides, Fishtank was saying more than enough for everyone.

—You can't divorce me, he yelled.

—I can. I *am*.

—Did you know about this?

All of us felt the full force of Fishtank's fury. It was in his eyes, transferred through his stare, but none of us broke. I withstood it, but more than that...I served it back at him.

—This is *my* house, said Fishtank, drawing himself to his full height.

He suddenly seemed smaller. Or maybe I felt taller?

—No, said Mum. —It's my house. You never put your name on the lease, so you could get out of paying your debts. So if I tell you to get out, you get the fuck out. Right?

Fishtank was many things: malevolent, sadistic, selfish, childish, vain and bratty. But he wasn't stupid. I could see his brain bursting at the realisation that Mum had outmanoeuvred him. He decided emotional blackmail might succeed where intimidation had failed.

—You can't throw me out, he whined.

—Why not?

—Because I'll be homeless.

—You won't be homeless, replied Mum smoothly. —You can go and live with *her*.

Fishtank didn't quite get it.

—I can't live with Mum. Her bedsit isn't big enough for the two of us!

That officially solved the mystery of Granny's whereabouts.

—I'm not talking about your mother. I'm talking about your dinner lady.

Fishtank feigned confusion

—But she's just a friend!

—I hope she roasts your potatoes, you rotten cheating bastard!

The expression of horror on Fishtank's face gave me everything I needed in life.

—I don't know what you're talking about.

—Yes, you do.

—You fucking cunt! Fishtank roared.

He stepped forward, but something stopped him in his stride, a noise that saved us all from being bashed by his fists/a piece of the garden fence/a dog lead/whatever weapon he could lay his hands on. At first, I struggled to place the sound, because my heart was pounding so hard, the blood rushing through my body, racing past my ears.

Then I heard it again. Loud and familiar, it was now utterly undeniable.

BANG! BANG! BANG!

Three hard slams of the letterbox. It was either the TV Licence inspector or...

—They're here, said Mum with relief.

—Who the fuck?

—I've invited some guests to our party...

We waited. I felt Laddie's hand wrap around my own. He was frightened, of course. I gave him a little smile, which seemed to embolden him a little bit. My interest was now completely engaged in the two newcomers to Fishtank's surprise divorce party. Mum walked past her soon-to-be ex-husband, out into the hall, where she opened the front door. She invited her guests into the house. Clearly, it wasn't the TV licence people.

The uniforms confirmed everything.

Two policemen stood behind Fishtank.

Jake looked away, trying not to make eye contact.

—I called them, admitted Lorna.

That explained her sudden absence. What she'd done wasn't something to dismiss easily. It was a matter of principle in our household that no matter what happened, regardless of the situation, the police were **never** called. If you phoned the police, you were a grass – and grasses were the lowest form of scum. Lorna had weighed up the odds and decided it was worth it, if only to save her family from one of Fishtank's legendary rages.

—I want this animal out of here, Mum told the two officers.

—Think about what you're doing, screamed Fishtank. He couldn't hide his rage.

—I mean it, Mum continued. —I want him gone forever.

—Is he refusing to leave?

Fishtank turned his frustration on the two policemen.

—Stay out of this you nosy fuckers.

—He's violent, shouted Lorna. —We don't want him here anymore!

The policemen calmly led Fishtank away.

Out of the front door...

Out of the street...

Out of our lives.

Chapter 20

A Cup Of Tea For Mrs Coffee

Though it seemed like the final end of Fishtank, I also knew from bitter past experience that he could expertly work his way back into our lives using his tried and trusted techniques of greasy charm and emotional extortion. The first week without him was fraught with an underlying tension I felt more than the others. We were deliriously happy, but it all felt too good to be true. Could this be it? Could he finally be gone, at last?

I asked myself those questions over and over again.

Another week passed and still he was gone.

And another week after that.

Eventually, we all realised Fishtank was gone for good.

That's when everyone went crazy.

It started when Donnie redecorated her bedroom. She didn't want to go through the hassle of buying new wallpaper, nor did she want to exert herself with the burden of scraping away her old wallpaper. Instead she took a can of blue spray-paint to the walls and decorated all four with slogans and graffiti. She particularly liked to spray big happy faces and Union Jacks on the wallpaper. Not to be outdone, Lorna joined in with a lovely shade of red paint, which was used to spray dicks of varying shapes and sizes. The choking stink of paint fumes made me feel light-headed, but Jake found the smell oddly satisfying, and spent a lot of time outside Lorna and Donnie's room, just standing there...inhaling it.

I had to get outside and fill my lungs with fresh air. Whenever

I needed to escape my house, there was one place I knew I could rely on. It was my home away from my house, a place without fights or boxes with nasty surprises. Whenever I felt anxious or upset (quite often throughout my childhood), a few hours in this place restored me, bringing stability even in the most unstable of situations.

I headed to Cumbernauld Central Library.

Everyone at the library knew me as a diligent and loyal customer and greeted me with a smile and a wave. I always felt welcome at the library. The main library was for adults and I wasn't quite there yet, so off I headed into the Children's Library. My routine was always the same: look at the new books, see if there were any *Point Horrors* or *Doctor Who New Adventures* I hadn't read. Grab a few *Nancy Drew* novels. Maybe a *Three Investigators* book. A *Theresa Breslin*, maybe? Then I'd go and sit at the table near the back of the room. I could sit for hours reading, sometimes starting and finishing more than one book. The Library also shut at eight, which gave me a lot of time away from my family.

With a trashy horror novel in my hand, I sat down and started on the first page, not stopping until I reached the last page. By the time I'd finished, it was dark outside. Natalie, one of the library assistants, said in passing:

—I can't believe I'm going to say this, but I think you read too much.

—What?

Her comment came out of nowhere, startling me with its bluntness.

—Are you trying to avoid someone?

Suddenly, perhaps realising she'd said too much, Natalie smiled and headed away to shelve some of the returned books that had accumulated throughout the day. But her words remained in the air between us. I considered her comment;

was she shaming me for reading too much? Was reading too many books such a bad thing?

Soon enough, I came to the conclusion that Natalie talked shit. Books were full of stories and stories had the power to save lives. How many times had I found my way out of misery through a book? Stories on a page, stories spoken aloud, other places, other worlds.

Without stories we have no substance.

Defiantly, I lifted another book from my pile and started reading it.

Doctor Who and The Pyramids Of Mars by Terrance Dicks.

I was on Chapter Ten when Natalie announced it was nearly eight o'clock.

By the time I got back to the house, things were really out of control. I returned to discover 145 Craigieburn Road had been transformed into the street equivalent of Papa Docs. Lorna was nowhere to be seen. Donnie and Jake were about, along with their friends. The walls throbbed with music I recognised as being from Bjork's debut album. Jake hated Bjork, so the fact he was bopping along to *Big Time Sensuality* was the clearest sign he wasn't quite here with us on Planet Earth.

Also, he had a mug of tea in his hand as he danced.

—You're gonna spill that, I said.

—There's nothing in it! Jake laughed, his eyeballs glowing bright red.

When had Jake graduated from sniffing paint fumes to... drinking tea?

—Be a good wee bro and refill my cup.

—That's not a cup, Jake. That's a mug.

—You're a mug. Go make me another cuppa.

Then he grabbed me, almost causing my hand to let go of his precious mug.

—Use the teabag in the cup!

Tentatively, I sniffed the teabag and recoiled in distaste. It smelled of boiled socks.

—Hash tea, I muttered as I pulled myself away from Jake's grip.

The music suddenly cut out and I breathed a sigh of relief that I was able to hear.

—Mum's coming, shouted Donnie.

The back door was opened and everyone in our house was swiftly ushered outside, but the evidence of their presence was all around: bottles, ashtrays brimming with smoked stubs, the stink of marijuana, the mugs of unfinished 'tea' on the floor. Mum would immediately know a party had been thrown while she was at work. Usually, all the evidence was gone by now. But Fishtank was also gone – and that changed everything.

When Mum opened the door and wiped her feet on the mat, I held my breath for a few seconds. Obviously, I had nothing to worry about, but none of us wanted to see our mother in a bad mood. Worse, she was wearing her lettuce-green cleaning overalls, which meant she'd spent the night cleaning out the Farmfoods factory; it was the least favourite of her various jobs. Mum closed the door behind her and frowned. She knew something wasn't right. She felt it. Without saying a word, she barged into the living room. She almost kicked over a stray glass, but her foot missed it by inches.

—Where's Lorna?

—I don't know, I said.

—She went out for a few minutes, said Donnie.

Her lie wasn't very convincing, which only served to enrage Mum even more. Jake, meanwhile, seemed oblivious to everything. He passed by, his movements jerky and uncoordinated. The kettle was still boiling, but that didn't seem to matter to my brother. He lifted it up off the counter and poured it into his mug.

Then, with a blazed-out blissful smile, he asked Mum a stupid question.

—Do you want a cup of tea, Mrs. Coffee?

Mum replied by clouting Jake across the back of his head with a frying pan.

He dropped his mug and staggered backwards.

—Where's Lorna? Get her in here right now.

But Lorna wasn't in and she wouldn't be in any time soon. Apparently, she'd decided to go out and see her boyfriend, leaving Donnie in charge of Laddie. Instead, Donnie decided to invite her friends around, which meant Jake invited his friends around, which meant everyone got high.

Mum was halfway upstairs when she froze in mid-step.

—Can anyone smell paint?

Then she barged into Donnie and Lorna's room.

A second passed, just a second.

It felt like an hour.

Mum screamed.

—Oh my God! What the hell have you done to your room?

Donnie looked down at her paint-stained hands, then held them up in surrender.

—Where's Laddie? I asked.

—He's playing the Sega.

—He doesn't have a Sega, I whined. —It's *my* Sega!

The front door opened and in crept Lorna, completely oblivious to everything. She looked loved-up, a girl with a guy she adored. Nothing else was as important.

I told her she was busted.

—Mum's upstairs.

—Fuck, she must have got back early.

—Evidently, I added.

—Evidently, mocked Jake in a high-pitched approximation of my voice.

—Shut up and drink your tea!

He swung for me, but I was too fast. His fist missed. Before Jake could throw another punch, Mum rapidly descended the stairs and caught sight of Lorna, which then ignited an argument about irresponsible behaviour. Lorna gave as good as she got, yelling at Mum for staying with a monster for years. I'd never witnessed anything like it. No-one would have dared speak out this way had Fishtank still been around. Fear of violence had always kept my family in line, but that line had been completely erased by Fishtank's departure. Many things were better without him, most things actually. But without his malevolent presence to back her up, Mum was powerless. As Mum and Lorna yelled in each other's faces, I found myself searching my bedroom for a book to read, something to take me away to another place far away from Cumbernauld. Eventually, I found myself in *Willy Wonka's Chocolate Factory*, but I only stayed there for an hour.

Then I was back at home.

Back in the middle of a mess.

Chapter 21

An Unwelcome Visitor

The TV License man surprised us because he didn't park his detector van outside our front door. Fishtank had always warned us never to answer the door if there was a van nearby. Truthfully, The TV License man looked like a Mormon, or how I imagined a Mormon to look: clean-cut, with a bow-tie, a white shirt, black trousers and sensible shoes. He smiled when I opened the door, speaking ever-so-politely as I stood before him.

—Is your mum or dad there?

—No.

Actually, Mum was upstairs having a bath before her next shift.

—Neither of them is in?

—No, I repeated.

Laddie poked his head from behind me and said, —Mum's upstairs!

And that's how we were busted for not paying our TV License.

Mum seethed in the living room for a few minutes before she lit and sucked a cigarette to life. It was her fifth in an hour. She didn't know I kept count, but she was struggling and needed as much nicotine in her body as humanly possible. The smell made me sick, but I knew better than to cross my mother during a five-ciggie marathon.

In the background, our TV broadcast the worst television show in history.

—Ugh, I moaned. —I hate *Going For Gold*. Can't we turn this over?

The topic of television was still firmly in Mum's thoughts.

—Isn't it funny that the moment we get rid of that bastard, I get done for not paying the license fee? I bet he stuck us in. Well, if he thinks I'm going to take that shit from him and that beast of a dinner lady, he'd better think again.

—You reckon Fishtank grassed on us?

—Your *dad*, Walter. Not Fishtank. I always hated that name.

Without missing a beat, I repeated:

—You reckon Fishtank grassed on us?

—It would be a big coincidence if he hadn't, said Donnie.

Donnie was perched on the single chair at the far end of the living room listening to KD Lang on her CD Walkman. The music blaring out of the headphones was loud, though not loud enough to drown out the surrounding conversation, allowing Donnie the best of both worlds: the music she loved and the conversation she wanted to hear. My sister worshipped KD Lang. She was likewise obsessed with the likes of Melissa Etheridge, Tracy Chapman, Ani DiFranco and Michelle Shocked. A keen lover of music, Donnie was always on the hunt for The Next Big Thing. She'd spend hours in Our Price looking for ideas and music, which was miraculous considering the Cumbernauld branch of Our Price was the size of a coffin. My sister loved music so much that one Christmas, Fishtank bought her an acoustic guitar so she could learn to play all her favourite songs. He later smashed that same guitar over her head because she came home five minutes after her assigned curfew.

—Thanks to your tosser of a dad, I have no money to buy new uniforms for you and Laddie. You need schoolbags too. I'll need to get another loan to pay for it all.

—I've already got stuff I can wear.

Donnie squashed a scream before it had a chance to escape her throat.

—You can't let him go to his new school in granny's fur coat. Please Mum! You don't know how embarrassing it is to be related to him. He's a weirdo.

—I'm not a weirdo. I'm alternative.

Mum was allowed to call us names, which she did quite often. She considered it her maternal duty to stop us getting too egotistical. But she never allowed anyone else to make fun of us. She didn't even let us make fun of each other! Fixing my sister with her one-of-a-kind patented eyeball rolls, Mum let her have it.

—He can wear whatever he bloody well wants! What does it matter to you anyway? You aren't at Walter's school.

—I graduated from a better school, Donnie shot back.

—Did you hell! You were kicked out with how many O Grades to your name?

—None, I suggested wickedly.

—Three, cried Donnie.

—Little good they're doing you now that you're working at Capital.

Instead of bursting into tears or getting upset, Donnie seemed to actively consider her mother's words. Then, in typical headstrong manner, she found herself in agreement. She *was* wasting her time at Capital. The frozen food industry didn't interest her in the slightest, it was just the first job she landed after getting kicked out of high school.

A few days later, my sister handed in her notice.

Three weeks after *that*, she got a job at a fancy insurance company.

It was her way of saying FUCK YOU to Mum without actually saying the words aloud.

Mum, however, got revenge on her daughter.

She increased Donnie's rent by a tenner and blamed the TV license.

Chapter 22

Jake Explains It All

My first proper day at Cumbernauld High School started off disastrously when my registration teacher read my name out to my classmates. Her name was Mrs. Dawson. She was an old raisin with glasses, a shock of white curly hair, and bourbon breath so strong it could rot the gold plating from a Ratner's ring. Mrs. Dawson rattled through the list of names until she got to mine.

—Walter Wedgeworth, she called.

Someone snickered.

Apparently, I had a funny name.

—Here, I replied.

Mrs. Dawson looked over at me, tell-tale traces of surprise reaching her face.

Finally, she said what everyone in the room knew she wanted to say.

—Are you Jake Wedgeworth's younger brother?

—Yes.

—Jesus Almighty, she muttered, loud enough for everyone in her classroom to hear.

Another voice from nearby whispered:

—*That's* Jake Wedgeworth's brother?

If the ground could have opened up and swallowed me, I would have gladly gone headfirst into the hole. I hadn't come to school dressed in Granny's fur coat, but that didn't mean I wanted to blend into the background either. I wore a blue Teddy Smith jumper, a green shirt, a pair of red denim jeans, and my blue Kickers trainers. I liked my style, preferring it to what my Kappa-clad classmates wore. Kappa (or Krappa as I called it) seemed to be the popular brand now that Fruit of the Loom had rotted out of fashion.

—Your brother tried to kill me, said Mrs. Dawson calmly.

—What?

—Four years ago in this very room.

—He tried to kill you?

—Yes. He was eating a packet of cheese 'n' onion crisps during a lesson. And he had his feet up on the table too. I told him to take his feet off the table and stick his crisps in the bin. Do you know what he said to me?

—No, I'm sorry I don't.

—He said piss off.

—That sounds like my brother.

—I took a heart attack. He got up and helped.

At last, a nice comment about my brother.

—He helped?

—Yes. He helped himself to my purse and the packet of 20 Club King Size out of my handbag. He smoked all of them as I lay on the floor just by this cupboard behind me.

When the bell went ring-a-ding-a-ding in the background, I barely heard it.

I couldn't believe what I'd just been told, until I remembered it was about Jake.

Suddenly it all seemed believable.

Later that night, I asked Jake to tell me what happened, so I could hear it explained in his own words. I found him on his bed, an old futon in the downstairs cupboard. Propping himself up against the wall, he told me his version of Mrs. Dawson's story.

—You can't trust a lying old alkie, he laughed.

—Which part of the story isn't true? I asked.

—The most important bit.

—She's lying about the heart attack and the robbery?

—What? No, that all happened for real.

I felt my jaw slacken in amazement. I was related to Rosemary's Baby.

—Then how is she lying?

—Did she really say I was eating a packet of cheese 'n' onion?

—Yes.

—Then she lied. I was actually eating a packet of smoky bacon.

He paused to let me consider what he'd just said.

—I don't like cheese 'n' onion crisps.

Chapter 23

19th November 1994

Fishtank made his first (and last) attempt at returning home on the 19th of November 1994. He came with flowers, a smile, an apology, and…a gift. The house was mostly empty because it was the weekend. My sisters and brother were out at a rave somewhere in Falkirk. Laddie was upstairs playing videogames and eating chocolate raisins, his favourite. Mum was dressed in her blue velour pyjamas, which she referred to as her 'lazy gear', sprawled out on the couch watching a rented videotape of *Death Becomes Her*.

Me? I spent the night reading an Agatha Christie novel.

By page 107, I'd already worked out the identity of the killer.

If only I could apply my skills to the real world, but truth is never as easy as fiction.

A sudden sound at the front door made me lower my paperback.

—That isn't Lorna, Donnie, or Jake.

Mum didn't speak. She lay very still. Then adjusted her weight in order to better receive sound. There wasn't much to hear, just some footsteps that didn't stop until they reached the living room door. As soon as the shape appeared behind the glass, I knew it.

—It's Fishtank!

—Fuck, hissed Mum. —Fuckkk!

A fearful flutter passed through my chest and I had to breathe slowly in order to steady myself. Fishtank was back and we were defenceless. But I wouldn't go down without a fight. Immediately I started looking around the room for blunt objects, items I could use to hit hard if I had to. Yet when Fishtank poked his head out from behind the door, it was almost sheepishly. He looked nervous, even worried. It was strange seeing that side of him.

Things had definitely changed since the fateful day Fishtank left Craigieburn Road.

Mum looked on furiously.

—What are you doing here?

—I've come back.

—You aren't coming back.

—I can't go back to her. We've fallen out. I told her I still love you.

—But I don't love you.

—You don't mean that.

—That's how I feel. You have to leave, John.

Fishtank let out a long, theatrical sigh. He wasn't quite ready to surrender.

—I've got something that might change your mind.

Mum sat up, not quite knowing what to expect.

—A surprise, continued Fishtank.

—What are you up to?

—Wait a second.

He left the room and went back out into the hall like the last time he was with us, before the police led him away. Mum looked at me and I shrugged. We waited anxiously. Laddie was still upstairs, completely oblivious, thankfully.

When Fishtank returned, he wasn't alone.

Mum's mouth opened. I laughed in disbelief.

There was a little girl with him. She had to be about five-years-old. The girl wore a timid expression on her face, but remained silent and close to Fishtank.

—Don't worry, he whispered. —You'll be fine. They're your family.

I didn't know what to do. It was too ridiculous to process.

Then I noticed something interesting.

The little girl had frizzy, difficult hair.

I knew that hair. I had the same hair. So did Donnie.

We'd inherited it from him.

—We'll raise her as our own, said Fishtank softly.

Mum opened her mouth to say something, but the words didn't make it.

I spoke for the two of us. My voice trembled, much to my annoyance.

—She looks like you, I said.

Mum agreed.

—Is she yours?

—Yes.

—And…hers?

—No, she's yours if you take me back. Yours and mine. You always wanted another daughter, didn't you?

Did she? Fishtank had a whole lifetime of private moments with Mum. Maybe during some private pillow talk, they'd discussed having another child. If he felt bringing this girl to the house might sway Mum into taking him back, there had to be a reason for it. I looked at my mother and waited for a reaction. Her feelings were all in her face: shock, anger, devastation, and finally…understanding. Mum leaned down and smiled at the little girl cowering behind Fishtank.

—Hello, said Mum gently.

—Hello, replied the kid, shy but defiant.

—What's your name?

—Rosie.

—And what age are you, Rosie?

—I'm four and a half, she said proudly.

Mum redirected her attention to Fishtank.

She finally had exactly what she needed.

—So, it's been going on for five years at least?

It took me a few seconds to comprehend Mum's thread

of thought, but once I got it, I followed until it took me to a logical conclusion. She was insinuating Fishtank knew the dinner lady years before he started working at the factory, that this affair had been going on far longer than anyone suspected. Maybe she'd got a job at the factory to be close to him? Or had Fishtank suggested it during his job hunt? Regardless, this affair had started long before Fishtank was forced into the factory. It had started long enough ago for them to make a baby that was now the little girl in front of me.

We'd all been played for fools and none of us had suspected a thing.

Fishtank frowned. He'd been so excited by his batshit plan to win Mum back that he hadn't considered the consequences of his actions. It was already too late. Mum finally understood the full extent of Fishtank's betrayal. Any remaining doubts or worries about starting a new life without her husband were completely destroyed.

—Can I at least get my radio stuff?

Mum tutted, because it wasn't really what she'd wanted to hear.

Before she could spit in his face, I spoke up.

—I smashed your radio to pieces.

Fishtank gnashed his teeth like a dog ready to leap and bite.

—You smashed up my CB apparatus? Why?

He said CB *apparatus* rather than radio. It made his equipment sound valuable.

—I smashed it because it reminded me of you.

Fishtank spun around and stormed out of the house.

—Daddy, said the little girl.

Fishtank returned, grabbed her by her right arm, and led her out of the house.

The door slammed so hard the cabinets juddered.

—He nearly forgot about her, said Mum in astonishment.

She went out and locked the door behind him, then faced me with a smile on her lips.

—You told him you smashed up his radio.

—I did.

—Why did you say that?

—So we could go upstairs and smash it for real?

Armed with a rolling pin and a hammer (guess who had which) we both headed upstairs. Mum warned Laddie that we were going to dismantle the CB radio and it might be a bit noisy. Oh, we dismantled it alright. We attacked every single part of it until it lay at our feet in a billion little bits. Then, sweating with exertion, Mum looked at me and said:

—I feel much better now.

Chapter 24

Becca

Becca Boglin was Godzilla in fake Gucci, a rampaging force to be admired from a distance. Any closer and you risked being zapped by her fiery breath. Yet, somehow, I knew she would become very important to me, if only for a while. She had the biggest hair, the highest heels, the driest wit, and she hated the world with a ferociousness that I found captivating. Becca enjoyed shocking people with outrageous comments, all of which she practiced in front of a mirror whilst posing like Kate Moss in *The Face*.

She said stuff like:

—In a past life I was a French nun.

—Cockroaches ate my wig last night.

—My dad fucked Belinda Carlisle.

—God is a girl and she looks like me.

In life, certain friendships have to happen.

For me, that was Becca Boglin.

We found each other in the school canteen, a grimy place with blue-tiled floors and old windows that looked like they might topple out of their frames. I'd previously overheard people in Computing Studies bitching about Becca, which was great because it stopped them talking about me. Becca was infamous at Cumbernauld High School, not because she had a crazy family like I did, but because of her unpredictable behaviour. These days, she probably would have been diagnosed as having Attention Deficit Disorder, but no-one cared back in the 90s. Becca was someone who couldn't behave herself in a way expected of girls. Eventually, in a queue in the canteen, I got the opportunity to see Becca as a person and not just as a topic of bitchy conversation.

I'd spent most of my lunch hour waiting for food, or what passed for food at Cumbernauld High School's canteen. But I was bored. So bored that I started playing around with the little Free Lunch ticket. After creating a graceful swan out of my ticket, a crazy girl suddenly stomped through the queue, passing me and my tiny paper swan, until she came to a halt at the front of the line. My first instinct was to tell her to rotate towards the back and stay there, but I never ever went with my first instinct. Only hotheads did that. I forever battled the urge to lash out verbally or physically, preferring to contemplate myself out of anger. I'd literally hold entire conversations only I could hear, interior debates that would go on ad infinitum until *finally* I settled on taking the least offensive course of action. My life up until high school had been a series of unspoken opinions and quiet introspection. Becca, however, could never be that way.

She had no filter, no control, and no shits to give.

We were fated to be friends. Somehow, against all odds, we were going to meet. There was no way I could hide from Becca. Literally. I was wearing a multi-coloured 90s shirt and neon green jeans. In due course, we realised we were staring at each other.

She shouted down the line at me, much to the annoyance of everyone between us.

—What the hell are you wearing?

—Clothes, I called back.

She burst out laughing. It wasn't a dainty girlish laugh, but a loud raucous ear-splitter howl, a laugh so big it bent her body over. No-one could ignore that laugh. In fact, everyone in the canteen stopped eating just so they could look in our direction.

—What are you fucking staring at? Becca yelled at everyone.

—Do you have Tourette's or something? I asked.

She didn't hear me, or chose to ignore my comment.

—You're all a bunch of nosy bastards! Stop staring. Fuck off!

The pupils in the canteen, some of whom I knew from various classes we shared, looked away awkwardly. With that said and done, Becca moved down the queue, giving her space up at the front, weaving past people until we were together. She didn't speak at first. Instead, she took in everything I had to offer with the sort of analytical gaze that might make others uncomfortable. Instead, I did the same back.

My eyes hurt after ten seconds of relentless glaring.

—Are you Jake Wedgeworth's brother?

—Is it that obvious?

—No, actually.

—Well, fuck you, I said, much to her delight.

We shared a similar sense of humour, which boded well for our future as friends.

Then she asked a question.

Not just any ordinary question.

An unexpected question!

—Is all this for real?

I didn't understand. All what? Fortunately, she explained.

—Do you go into clothes shops and buy the ugly stuff nobody else wants to wear?

—My aesthetic is my aesthetic, I told her pompously.

—I think it's a performance.

—What do you mean?

—I think you want people to see you, but you don't want them to *know* you.

Clearly, I'd been too quick to judge Becca. She was obviously a very smart girl, more than anyone had probably realised. Perceptive but likely unhinged. Unpredictable. Chaotic.

—Proceed with caution, I told myself.

But it was far too late.

I'd already been pulled into the vortex.

We ended up sitting together at one of the tables in the canteen. It was treason, because Moo and Poppy were waiting outside. They didn't need free lunch tickets because their families were well-off, at least in comparison to the Wedgeworth clan. However, I soon forgot about my two friends, banishing them from my thoughts, albeit for a short time.

By the time the bell went, I knew they'd make me suffer for spending my free time with a stranger. But Becca wasn't a stranger. It felt like I'd known her forever. We flung ourselves into each other's respective orbits and now we couldn't be apart.

—Let's meet up at some point, she said whilst adjusting her giant hairdo.

—Is it real, I asked slyly.

—Everything about me is real, she purred.

A third (and unwanted) voice cut into the conversation.

—WALTER.

I shifted my weight on the hard-plastic seat and found Moo and Poppy waiting by the canteen's entrance, scowling-faced, folded arms; the familiar body language of the scornful.

—This is Becca, I said, trying my best to bridge the chasm between everybody.

—You'll be late for class, said Poppy in a voice cold enough to kill Eskimos.

Becca smiled thinly, but she already knew what was going to happen.

By the end of the week, I'd ditched Moo and Poppy.

Yes, certain friendships have to happen. Sometimes at the expense of other friendships.

Chapter 25

Sister, Sister

Donnie moved out and headed down to London to start work in a fancy insurance firm whose details seemed suspiciously nebulous. This meant Lorna got a room to herself. She was delighted, of course, because that meant she could invite Declan over and they could head upstairs and make a lot of noise for twenty-minutes. I didn't like Declan very much. He was handsome in a swarthy way, with thick brown hair, a gleaming smile that could be put on a Colgate box, and he always had the nicest clothes and most expensive Nike trainers. But…something about him seemed a little greasy to me. Whenever he chose to speak to me (and that was only when he wanted something) I came away feeling like someone had dumped a tub of Lurpak over my head. Without Fishtank in the house, Declan suddenly felt he could do whatever he wanted. There came a point when Lorna's room wasn't enough for him. He wanted to be in the living room, sprawled out on the couch, with the television on in the background. He enjoyed walking about in his underwear, which bothered me because I'd never do that in anyone else's house.

I didn't even do that in my own house.

But the one thing I hated most about Declan was that he smacked my sister about. He didn't do it all the time, of course. He was far too savvy to be a common thug. In many ways, he reminded me of Fishtank. Just like Fishtank, he knew how to emotionally manipulate my sister. Just like Fishtank, he had to go.

But how?

He was a scab that refused to be flicked after being picked.

Worse, he had already arranged via Lorna to spend New Year at our house.

It was to be our first New Year without Fishtank and Mum wanted to make it special. The only negative was that Donnie was down in London. She couldn't make it up to Scotland for New Year, but assured us she was working hard. As a compromise, she granted us a phone call. Answering it was a competition between Laddie and me, but I managed to get there first, lifting it off the cradle within three rings.

—Wedgeworth residence, Walter speaking. How may I help you?

—You can help me by speaking normal, she said gruffly.

—This is my phone voice, I explained.

—I wouldn't know. You never answer the phone.

—I'm worried I'll pick it up and get into a debate with a debt collector.

—Where's Mum?

—She's at the VG buying booze for tonight.

'The VG' was what we called the local cornershop owned by Mr. Ali. It was short for Vegetables and Groceries. Mum used to send me there to buy cigarettes and tampons, which wasn't an experience I enjoyed. If I hadn't accidentally discovered a dead baby in a box, shopping for Mum's tampons alone would probably have put me into therapy.

—Okay, I won't be on the phone for long. It eats my coins. How are you doing?

—Fine.

Without meaning to, I went very quiet. Donnie suddenly seemed concerned.

—What's wrong?

—I think you're the only one in our family that ever asks me how I'm doing.

—Don't take it personal. They care, but they're not good with that sort of stuff.

—I'm not good with that sort of stuff either.

—We are who we are, Walter.

Donnie went quiet for a few fading seconds and I heard the slight sound of coins being dropped into a metal slot. When Donnie spoke again, it was to enquire about Lorna, which led me to mention her insufferable boyfriend.

—Declan's never away from here, I said irritably.

—Lorna told me they broke up. I take it they're back together?

—They were never apart!

—Are they still fighting?

—Do you mean is he still kicking her about? Take a guess.

—He's a shitebag, muttered Donnie viciously.

Aware that our time was as limited as the coins in Donnie's pocket, I attempted to steer the conversation in another direction. I asked Donnie about life in London.

—It's okay. I'm a bit bored.

I didn't believe her for a second.

—You'll be fine, I said positively.

—Yeah. I know. I miss everyone. It's a bit quiet here.

—In London?

I couldn't help but sound incredulous.

—In my flat. I think I've been so used to the drama that I miss it.

—I wouldn't miss it. I'd give anything for peace and quiet.

—So you can read more books without being interrupted?

She was right and I wasn't bothered in the slightest. It was one of my fantasies in life to live in a nice flat with stacks of books on the floor, a kettle forever filled with water, and an endless supply of Typhoo teabags. Wherever the bedsit of my dreams existed, I wanted to go there. I'd go anywhere, any place, so long as it was far away from Cumbernauld.

—Okay, I'm running out of coins. I have to get going. When

Mum gets back from the shop, tell her Happy New Year from me.

Ah. New Year was fast approaching. I hated it, despised saying the words Happy New Year as though it meant anything. All that fake jolliness: the hugging, the laughter, the bad Hogmanay TV, the hangovers everyone suffered. Everyone, that is, except me, because everyone except me got steaming.

—I promise to tell her. Have a good time down there.

—Happy New Year, said Donnie.

—With luck, I replied.

Chapter 26

Punk Rock

Mum ended up falling in love with an ex-punk from Paisley named Davy Death. He used to be in a band, back in the 80s, called Savage Wank. They never quite made it onto *Top of the Pops*, but they played a legendary gig at Paisley Town Hall in 1982 that helped score them a record deal with Fast Product alongside labelmates like the Fire Engines and Scars. Davy had real punk cred. I actually took time to listen to his records; they were mostly quite good, though the last album was a bit too slick for my tastes.

According to Davy Death, that was the band trying to 'cross over'.

Clearly, it hadn't worked otherwise he wouldn't need to work as a college lecturer.

Mum and Davy made an odd couple. With the exception of the Patsy Cline cassette she played every Sunday whilst hoovering the house, Mum had never been much of a music fan, yet there she was with her new boyfriend, going out to see bands, or as she referred to them, 'gigs'. But love has a way of making its presence felt. Love joins the dots. From Lorna's destructive relationship with Declan to Mum's blossoming romance with Davy, I watched from a safe distance as love took members of my family and turned them into strangers. From level-headed Lorna pretending her boyfriend wasn't a scumbag to Mum forgoing Patsy for punk rock, nothing made sense to me. I stood in the distance, watching dispassionately, a face at the window peering in from the outside. However, it wasn't all bad. Mum definitely seemed happier at home. She'd also started smiling a lot, something she did rarely during her marriage. While she fell in love with a punk, I lived in the library, looking for a book to get lost in. Yet somehow the real world always found me again.

Not everyone liked the idea of Mum dating a new man.

Jake didn't appreciate the interloper, and said as much.

—He's not her type.

—Because he doesn't hit her?

Jake looked as though he wanted to hit *me* when I said that. It was the truth though. Where Fishtank resorted to violence and control tactics, Davy Death was placid, though he liked a drink or two. But essentially, he seemed like a decent person.

—How can he be a punk when he's bald?

—Not every punk wears a mohawk, I suppose.

—How do you know? Did a book tell you?

He meant it to be spiteful, a small but petty victory. It didn't matter. Nothing he said could touch me. We had history and blood in common, but it wasn't enough to matter.

Here's how I met Davy Death. One morning, whilst watching *The Big Breakfast* on Channel 4 with a bowl of Ricicles, I turned to see a stranger standing by the living room door. He was dressed in white boxers and a vest. My first instinct was to looked away, blink a few times, then look back again. I did. But he was still there.

He seemed...lost, or unsure what to say.

Our eyes locked on each other. He spoke first.

—Hey, he said waving his hand at me.

I didn't know what to say, so I simply waved back.

He retreated into the kitchen. I heard the sound of running water.

Davy Death returned from the kitchen, a glass of water in hand.

—Bye, I said.

—See you soon, Walter.

He knew my name. That caused a burst of anxiety, because it meant Mum had talked to him about me. She'd probably told him all about Lorna, Donnie and Laddie too. She'd possibly omit a lot of details about Jake though, which was for the best. She wouldn't want to frighten any potential boyfriends and I already knew Davy Death was in that category.

Alone again, I returned to *The Big Breakfast*.

A few days later, I met Davy again. He was dressed in a black Ramones t-shirt and blue denim jeans. Grateful he had more clothes on this time, I actually said hello. Besides, I'd suffered a particularly dreary day at school. Poppy and Moo had made a point of trying to upset me, possibly in retaliation for my perceived slight against them. I'd moved on, preferring to avoid drama. Becca helped a lot. She would make jokes about Moo's walk. She claimed he walked like a constipated ostrich, which made no sense but kept things light, making me laugh so much I almost forgot there was a new man at home with Mum.

When I met Davy again, it was in passing. He was coming down the stairs in my house as I walked up them in the direction of my room.

—How was school? Davy asked politely.

—Fine, I replied casually.

—Good. I'm glad.

There was silence between us, the kind that you can almost feel, the worst sort of silence.

He spoke again. I didn't have it in my heart to be nasty. I knew he'd get a tough time from Jake, so I decided to be nice. Being nice didn't always come easy to me.

—Your mum said you like reading books.

—It's better than reading tea leaves, I suppose.

Davy Death laughed, which was strange for someone who wore black and wrote morbid love songs. I found myself smiling slightly. Whether he found it funny or just wanted to give us something in common, I didn't know. But I appreciated his efforts. We'd only met two times by that point and he was already far more agreeable than Fishtank.

—Do you have a favourite?

—*Bleak House* by Charles Dickens.

My actual favourite was *Mystery of the Tolling Bell* by Carolyn Keene.

—Sounds good.

—What's your favourite book?

Davy seemed to think it over. He hadn't expected the question, but took it well. After a good ten seconds (long enough to feel awkward but short enough to bear) he said:

—*Fantastic Mr. Fox.*

With those words, I knew we were going to get along just fine.

Chapter 27

Shopping Without Paying

When Becca suggested we take the day off school, I agreed. Then again, I agreed with most things Becca suggested. Not that I was a follower, but I usually chose the easiest option. Mum wouldn't have cared, because she kept me off school from time to time, usually when she had a parcel from Littlewoods on the way. Besides, it was a lovely day, bright and airy, not too hot. The perfect day to dog school with a friend. But if I thought we were just going to sit about doing nothing, I clearly didn't know Becca.

We were sitting on the stone steps next to The Twa Corbies, a pub that had been in Cumbernauld for decades. It was closed, which meant we were able to loiter without being harassed. We talked about how much we despised Mariah Carey, our mutual loathing of her vocal cartwheels. When I suggested she sounded like a cat being strangled by its own whiskers, Becca laughed. I liked making her laugh. It made me feel special.

Finally, I shifted the topic of conversation towards a question.

—What are we going to do today? I asked.

—Let's go shoplifting.

—But what if the shop's too heavy and I can't lift it.

—Terrible pun detected. Slap mode activated.

—I always knew you were a slapper, I quipped.

It was too easy. Becca rewarded me with a playful swipe, but it never landed. Honed by years of avoiding the random rages of both Fishtank and Jake, I successfully ducked away then came back up. We were laughing together, two friends taking a day off while our classmates toiled away in the stuffy classrooms of Cumbernauld High School.

—Where shall we go first?

—Let's try What Everyone Wants.

Becca always wanted to go to What Everyone Wants. I couldn't understand the appeal. It was all cheap shite, or so I'd assumed. But Becca loved it and whatever she loved, she stole. It wasn't just crap from shops. She'd already been in fights at school over boyfriends she'd pinched from her own pals. Poppy and Moo claimed she'd stolen me from them, though that didn't actually count as theft as I went willingly with Becca.

—Come on then, I said.

We got up and made the journey towards Cumbernauld Town Centre. It didn't take long, just a walk up a path that took us past the large flats in Stonylee Road, near the shop my brother robbed, up through Craigieburn Road's 'doll's houses' (named for their similarity to a vintage doll house), until we finally got close to our destination.

—What a shit hole, declared Becca.

—You're being too kind, I said.

We linked arms and skipped the rest of the way to What Everyone Wants.

Our shoplifting spree started minutes later.

Becca had her own special technique for distracting unwary security guards and pushy sales assistants. It was genius and never ever failed. Becca had a real understanding of human nature and would have made a remarkable psychiatrist in later life if she hadn't turned to crime. In hindsight, her propensity for lies and deception were obvious.

I just didn't care.

—Hello, she said to the nearest sales assistant.

I stood back, keeping out of sight near the clothes racks, and watched.

—May I help you?

—I'm embarrassed to admit this...

The way Becca pitched her voice, the performance and the drama, all of it was perfect. If I didn't know her, I'd completely believe she needed help. She did. Just not the kind the poor sales assistant wanted to offer.

—I've lost my contact lenses. They just popped out of my eye.

—Oh dear! Can you see anything at all?

— Very little. I'm blind without them!

That was Becca's cue to wave her arms around helplessly, doing her best impression of Velma from *Scooby-Doo* sans glasses. It worked, of course. It always worked. The lady in the What Everyone Wants uniform tilted her head in sympathy, then summoned two other sales assistants. They got down onto their hands and knees, noses almost pressed against the floor, doing their best to look for the missing contact lenses.

—I can't see them, said one of the sales assistants.

—Please keep looking, begged Becca.

She was already stuffing a fabulous pink sweater into her jacket, hiding it in a way that prevented any unsightly bulges. This was part of her flawless shoplifting technique. There was more to do, though. Becca had elevated stealing to an artform. The second phase of her spree would take place in one of the changing rooms kindly provided by the shop she was robbing. Being male (despite what people assumed), I wasn't there with her for that part of her operation. From past experience, I knew that Becca had a very large magnet in her schoolbag – the sort that could pull your fillings out if you aimed it properly.

Soon enough, it came time for me to play my part in proceedings.

—Are you okay? I asked.

—I've lost my contact lenses, said Becca weepily.

—Don't worry. I'll help you get back home.

Our routine was well-rehearsed. We'd done this a dozen times in a dozen different shops. None the wiser, the sales assistants climbed to their feet, only too eager to help a partially-sighted girl. Luckily, they didn't need to. I'd arrived to escort her back home. I took Becca's arm and led her away gently towards the changing rooms. Becca opened the door to a spare cubicle, disappeared inside, then pushed her head to the edge of the door to say one last thing:

—This'll only take a few seconds. I'll zap these tags and we can get the fuck out of here.

—Hurry up. They'll be suspicious if we stay too long.

—Oh Walter, you worry too much.

It was true. I worried about everything. I worried about growing up, being forced to pay council tax, large groups, electric shocks, light switches being left on accidentally, unplugged devices, background gamma radiation, and people that buried babies in cardboard boxes. All of these things worried me. The world was a worrying place.

—Hurry up, I hissed into the cubicle.

—I'm nearly ready.

—What are you doing?

—I'm trying to get these tags off.

A sales assistant walked by, giving me a wide smile.

My face froze into a crazy grin. I probably looked like Jack Nicholson in *Batman*.

Suddenly, Becca was done.

—Okay, let's go.

I gasped. Not only had she removed the tags from the clothes she'd nicked, she was already *wearing* the clothes she'd nicked. My uneasiness immediately went supernova.

—You can't be serious, I said.

—Come on, let's go.

—Really? You can't do it.

—Why not?

124

—Because you're wearing the clothes you just stole in the shop you stole them from!

Becca laughed, but said nothing. She was fearless and I admired that quality in her, but it also frightened me. No-one could be that lucky forever. Not even Becca.

—Please, I begged.

—What? You want me to be naked in public?

As if to prove her point, she started pulling at the zip of the pink jumper she was wearing. I waved my hands in terror, trying to stop her. She relented, but took the time to savour my panic. Eventually, we hurried out of What Everyone Wants, along past Mackays, up the stairs of the plaza into the main section of the town centre. The crippling feeling of panic that made me dizzy wouldn't stop until we'd put some distance between us and the shop. It didn't take long. I walked fast, my long legs powering me forward, Becca run-walking to keep up.

Sometime later, I suddenly remembered something important.

—What happened to the clothes you were already wearing?

—That old shit? I stuck the lot in my snazzy new bag.

Becca waved a white faux-leather tote bag at me.

A price tag dangled loosely from its handle.

Chapter 28

25th December 1995

As far as Mum was concerned, the worst Christmas present she ever received came in the form of a phone call made by her daughter on Christmas Day 1995. It happened while I ate dinner in the kitchen. At this point I was trying to be vegetarian again, so each piece of my fake turkey took approximately ten minutes to chew. Even the brussels sprouts tasted better in comparison. Surrounded by the rest of my family, we ate and laughed. I even managed to fake some cheer. Davy Death was dressed as Santa's evil twin brother, Atnas. Apparently, instead of giving presents to kids, Atnas took them. While Santa wore red and white, Atnas wore black and red.

(It took me years to realise that Atnas was Santa backwards. Well done, Davy).

The phone in the hall went off, giving me an excuse to stop eating. Darting up from my dinner plate, I shot into the hall towards the phone, which I deftly lifted off the cradle.

Donnie spoke first, her voice crackling through the bad connection.

—Merry Christmas!

It was good to hear her voice again. We hadn't really talked since New Year, which had been nearly a year past. Christmas has a way of making people feel guilty for not being close to their family. I wondered how Donnie felt about being so far away.

—Merry Christmas, sis. According to Mum, you couldn't make it home.

—Nah, I'm busy down here in the office. I don't have long. Where's Mum anyway?

Mum came out of the kitchen wearing an apron that used to be white, but looked a bit washed-out and grey. She looked weary, as she always did on Christmas Day. Mum made a big fuss about Christmas. She didn't spare any expense, slaving away at the oven, making sure everything was right with dinner. Oh, I felt really middle-class on Christmas Day.

It seemed like a lifetime ago that I found Mum crying in the kitchen because she couldn't afford to buy us presents. Now, thanks to Davy Death's lecturing job at Cumbernauld College, we had plenty of presents. Unless Atnas took them away. Oh, Davy was a panto villain, but I appreciated it. He was stability, kindness, money, bad jokes, silly costumes, mild manic depression, and old stories about his time on the road with Savage Wank.

—Is that Donnie? Mum asked.

Reluctantly, I handed the phone to her, then retreated into the kitchen to finish off my dinner. I'd kept the brussels sprouts to one side of the plate, where I hoped to win a war against them. The only time I ever ate sprouts was on Christmas Day. It felt like a necessary part of the ritual, something just as essential as pulling crackers, wearing hats.

Mum continued a conversation with Donnie, though I only heard Mum's part of it. She later went into detail, revealing more in each retelling. Mum didn't stop talking about her infamous Christmas phone call for weeks. I felt like I'd overheard the phone call.

Here is how it went:

—How are you, love?

—Merry Christmas, Mum.

—Merry Christmas, Danielle.

—I'm Donnie, Mum.

—Okay, Danielle.

In hindsight, this seemed unkinder than Mum had probably meant it to sound. Sometimes the cruellest cuts are the ones you barely notice at the time.

—It's a shame you aren't here with your brothers and sister.

—I know, but I've got a life down in London.

—We're your family, said Mum curtly.

—It's…difficult.

Yes. Apparently, my sister used the word 'difficult' to describe our family. 'Difficult' was a word I might use too, if only I'd been brave enough to form it in my throat and speak it into existence. But I couldn't. Not at that point in my life. Donnie, however, was the bravest woman I ever knew. She didn't care what anyone thought of her. The only exception to this was her mother. Donnie cared about her opinion above all else.

—I've got something to tell you, Mum.

—What?

—A secret.

Yes, my sister had lots of secrets. She told me some of them in confidence, secrets I've never told anyone else. She felt close enough to me to tell them. I'd often wondered why me? Did she see me as a safe presence? A background character in her life story?

Now she was about to tell one of her biggest secrets to Mum.

—You're pregnant?

Donnie cackled. I overheard her laughter from London as I struggled to swallow a mouthful of sprout.

—No, Mum.

—You're married?

—No, Mum.

—What is it?

—Mum, I'm gay.

—What?

—I'm **gay**, Mum.

—Oh my God, you're a rug muncher?

Yes. Those words were uttered by my mother on Christmas Day. —Oh my God, you're a rug muncher. She actually said that while we were around the table eating our dinner. If I hadn't learned my lesson after choking on a Crispy Pancake a few years ago, I'd have choked on my sprout for sure.

—Mum…please…I need to tell you…

Mum slammed the phone down.

She returned to the kitchen dazed, but still in 'Christmas mode'.

—Who wants dessert? I've got some Vienetta in the freezer.

Always the first to get dessert, I threw my hand up into the air and waved it around.

—What happened? Davy Death asked, concerned at Mum's rather pained expression.

—I'll tell you later, she replied.

She did. I listened by the door to their bedroom as she explained what Donnie had told her over the phone. Jake came out of the living room and caught me eavesdropping, but I didn't react. He'd heard what Mum had said on the phone, so he had to suspect what was happening behind the scenes. No doubt Jake would have a bad reaction to my sister coming out. He had a bad reaction to anything that might interfere with his reputation as Cumbernauld's nastiest bastard. I could only guess how he'd react to the news.

I went to my room and found Laddie playing his Sega Saturn, which had been left to him by Santa and ignored by the dastardly Atnas. He gave me a cursory glance, then turned his attention back to his game. He seemed to be riding a dragon in the sky.

—Donnie called earlier, I said quietly.

—Yeah, I saw you talking on the phone.

—It was just to wish us all a Merry Christmas.

—Mum didn't seem happy, did she?

My response to that was as vague and mysterious as I could possibly manage.

—They were probably talking about Donnie's job.

—Really? I thought they were talking about Donnie being gay.

—You knew?

—Aye. It's obvious, said Laddie.

—Really? How did you know?

—I knew because I've got eyes and she's clearly a lesbian, Walter.

—But...but...how can she be gay when she fancies George Michael?

(In my defence, this discussion happened years before George took a trip to a toilet in LA. Back in 1995, George Michael was the epitome of a safe hetero icon. Okay, so his beard looked a bit camp, but I didn't see past it.)

—She didn't fancy George Michael. He doesn't have boobs, Walter.

—I can't believe you knew about Donnie and I didn't.

—You notice these things when you have the life experience I do, big bro.

—Life experience? You can't even shave!

—That's true, but as soon as I hit puberty, I'm growing a beard.

—Just like George Michael?

Laddie laughed at the comparison. Oh, he knew all about him too.

—Why do you want a grow a beard anyway? I asked, my curiosity piqued.

—If I have a beard, I'll look older and my fake ID will work better.

—For what?

—So I can buy a carry-out at The VG.

—That's it? You want a beard so you can get ID to buy booze and get blitzed?

130

—What can I say? I'm a wee guy with wee ambitions.

—There must be something else you want out of life?

—I want to play video games without being interrupted.

I didn't say anything. Instead I just…thought about life. Laddie was growing up fast, just like me. Maybe too fast. At his age, I'd already found a dead body in a box. And there in front of me was my little brother, playing videogames without the slightest care. He was, as he said, a 'wee guy with wee ambitions'. But me? I wanted to do everything. I wanted to touch the moon with my toes, tell stories for everyone to hear and find a cure for people with bad taste in music. I wanted to run away and keep running until I found somewhere better than Cumbernauld. Where that was, I didn't know. But I needed out of this town.

Finally granting Laddie's wish, I left him to his game and headed downstairs.

—Shut the door, he shouted behind me.

I didn't. Instead, I went into the kitchen and stood by the sink.

My hands felt filthy. It was something I battled against every now and again.

There was only one way to make me feel better. Slowly, very slowly, I turned the hot tap on and thrust both hands underneath the stream of boiling water. Condensation quickly fogged up the window in front of the sink. I didn't care. All that mattered was getting the dirt off my hands. I couldn't see it, but I knew it was there because I felt the germs moving under the membrane of my skin. This happened because I opened that damn box.

My hands burned in the water, but they still felt unclean.

That's when I decided to scrub them with a wire brush.

Chapter 29

Cult TV

Davy Death loved punk, loud music, tacky costumes, celebrity deaths, the colour black and my mum. He also loved old TV shows. Once he moved into our home in Craigieburn Road, he started buying a huge collection of videotapes he'd use to record rubbish reruns from the 80s. From having virtually no television because of the coin box, we now had too much television. As far as Davy Death was concerned, there was no such thing as 'too much television'. My rampant insomnia kept me up, which gave him a bit of company into the early hours of the morning. To keep me happy, he bought cheap boil-in-a-bag curries from Farmfoods. If I could sum up my childhood in one smell, it would be the bubbling spicy scent of a Maharani quick cook curry. God bless the humble boil-in-a-bag.

One Saturday night, we sat up to watch some of Davy's favourite TV shows. I was grateful to do something other than struggle with my sleep. Together, we watched cop shows from the 70s, all of which were repeated on STV late at night. Davy's favourite was *The Sweeney*. We watched *Prisoner: Cell Block H* too. The theme tune reduced Mum to tears for some reason. Davy only watched *Prisoner* because I enjoyed it. He even recorded over one of his tapes for me. He also made me watch *Kojak*, which didn't appeal. I'd always imagined New York City as a place of glamour, full of art and artists, poetry and performance. If I could sleep, I would have dreamt of New York. Paradoxically, Kojak committed the crime of making New York look dirty and unpleasant. I wanted glamour and excitement. Dirty concrete streets reminded me too much of home.

Another favourite TV show Davy had on tape was *V*.

I became obsessed with *V*. It told the story of a friendly alien invasion, motherships controlled by models, all of whom were secretly meat-eating lizards. My favourite was Diana, a complete bitch with fabulous hair. No-one could defeat Diana. She was armed with a superior knowledge of science, a laser gun for killing scum humans and an endless supply of L'Oréal. Jane Badler, the actress who portrayed Diana, chewed the scenery just as much as Diana chewed on human bones.

—I love her, I uttered aloud one late night.

We'd just witnessed Diana shooting down a journalist for daring to tell the truth.

—She's an alien from outer space, said Davy.

—I don't care. I think she's amazing.

In the background, Mum shuffled about the kitchen. She had come downstairs quietly, so quietly we hadn't heard her. She poked her head into the living room. We were probably being too loud and she was about to give us a telling off. Instead, she said:

—What are you two watching now?

—We're watching *V*.

—The one with the alien baby?

—That doesn't happen until the next episode, said Davy.

—Thanks for spoiling it, I seethed.

Revenge accomplished, Mum smirked and headed back upstairs to bed. As we sat in the dark, enveloped by a cloud of curry, we watched another episode of *V* then moved onto something current. I suggested *The New Adventures of Superman*. Davy Death wasn't keen. He thought superheroes were stupid, regarding them as little more than figureheads for a 'conservative agenda'. For some reason, I thought he was taking the piss.

He was, in fact, being deadly serious.

—They're fascists in capes, he patiently explained.

—I don't know, I murmured. —I think it would be nice if we had people like Superman in the world. Someone doing stuff to help people for the sake of it.

—In theory, that's nice. But if Superman was a real person, he'd charge for his services.

The thought of Superman with a price list was absurd enough to make me laugh.

—I saved your life. That's forty pounds, please.

—If you want me to use my x-ray vision, you need to pay twenty pounds.

—I can leap tall buildings in a single bound for ten pounds.

A few minutes later, after rifling through some old tapes, Davy found something he knew I'd love. An old TV classic, he claimed. Something everyone liked, because if you didn't like it, you had NO TASTE. My interest piqued, I craned my neck down at the tape cassette box. My nosiness was in vain. Part of the fun was being surprised by whatever showed up on our TV screen.

The theme song started with the animated title sequence.

Who do you think you are kidding Mr. Hitler...?

Yes, it was *Dad's Army*.

—What the hell is this?

—A complete iconic classic of British television, enthused Davy.

Dad's Army was the hilarious (so Davy claimed) weekly story of a gang of pensioners who refused to die before Hitler. They kept Britain going whilst war was happening, but were too incompetent/inadequate/pompous to be successful soldiers.

Davy, a punk in a band named Savage Wank, absolutely *roared* with laughter at the least punk TV show in the history of television (with the exception of *Men Behaving Badly*, which was just shit). Loud laughter always cut through me. Loud guitar chords I enjoyed. But loud laughter, screams or cries shut me down. I cringed, hoping the neighbours wouldn't complain. Nearby, I heard birdsong outside the window, the familiar tell-tale sound that let insomniacs know they'd managed to stay awake until the early hours of the morning. Weirdly, after two more episodes of *Dad's Army*, I stopped caring about the neighbours and joined in with Davy.

By the time the credits rolled, Davy was snoring on the couch.

I switched the TV off and peeked out the window to watch birds digging for worms.

Chapter 30

Controversy

Becca decided the answer to our boredom could be found on the front of a t-shirt.

—How so? I asked.

—We write something really horrible and shocking on our t-shirts and wear them in public. It'll be really cool. I'll steal some plain white t-shirts and we'll write on them.

We were taking another day off school, exploring Cumbernauld without trying. It was almost symbiotic how we walked in unison, moving through town, no-one taking the lead, both of us simply turning a corner at the same time without directing the other.

Where she lost me, however, was with her idea to annoy people with t-shirts.

—What do we write on them?

—I dunno. How about…?

Becca ransacked her creativity until she finally came up with something suitably shocking.

—I shagged your husband and he was shit.

—You'll definitely be able to fit all that on your t-shirt.

Becca looked scandalised.

—I'm not a fat cow, you know!

It was a gradual change in her demeanour, but Becca had started to become slightly precious about her weight. It made sense. We were living in the decade of supermodels, where heroin chic was The Look, and anything else didn't matter. It never occurred to me that Becca would care about such things. I didn't. Instead of wolfing down boxes of Maryland

Cookies as I regularly did with great gusto, Becca would turn crisp packets and cookie boxes around in order to scrutinise their calorie content. I could almost see her working it out in her brain, trying to figure out how many bites were too many.

I couldn't be bothered thinking about food. Simply eating it was good enough for me.

Shortly after 'losing her contact lenses' in Asda (and not for the first time), Becca tore open the packet of white t-shirts she'd pinched from the nearest shelf and hurled one at me. Thinking fast, I caught it in mid-air, feeling pleased with my quick reflexes. We sat in the sunshine on a stone bench in an overgrown area of the town centre, just outside Cumbernauld College's canteen. It was a private little cubby, a place that used to look nice when Cumbernauld and Kilsyth District Council still looked after the building.

—What are you writing? Becca asked.

—I don't know. I'm trying to come up with something offensive.

—For our t-shirts to do anything, we need to upset people. We need something really shocking. I want the works. I want pensioners fainting. Kiddies crying. Mummies wailing.

—Okay, I said after thinking it over. —I've got another one.

—Tell me.

—How about 'Sean Connery Is The Worst Bond?'

—No! That's not shocking enough. Anyway, everyone knows that's George Lazenby.

—I thought he was very underrated, actually.

Becca gave me a filthy look, but wisely kept quiet. She knew all about my endless debates with Moo on the topic of *James Bond*.

Swiftly, I reconsidered my options for an offensive slogan. Truthfully, there weren't many. But I'd always been able to think quick, hit fast and win out against the odds. Surely I could dream up the perfect one-liner to decorate my t-shirt with?

It had to be something twisted enough to piss off the world, or my neighbours at least.

—I've got it!

—You tell me yours and I'll tell you mine, said Becca slyly.

—Okay, my t-shirt says...

Becca waited patiently.

—Get ready for it...

Becca was already running out of patience.

—Your Dad Is My Boyfriend.

As soon as my friend let out a loud gasp, I knew it was the one.

—Walter...

She wanted to ask a question. I just knew it. But I was too busy trying to write neatly on my t-shirt. My penmanship was something of a source of pride to me. If I had to go out in public with a shocking slogan on my chest, it had to be in neat writing.

—Yes?

—Can I ask you a question?

—Yes.

—You're writing 'Your Dad Is My Boyfriend' on your t-shirt.

—Yes.

—It just occurred to me that I've never asked you if you like girls or boys.

—You're right. You've never asked me.

—Well...do you like girls or boys?

Her face flushed brightly, a pink rash scattering around her skin. She seemed embarrassed about her question. I wasn't embarrassed. I answered as best as I could:

—I don't like anyone that way.

As an answer to Becca's query, it made *complete* sense to me. But to her, it was an evasive response.

—That isn't normal, Walter.

—I used to be normal, but it was just a phase.

Becca chuckled. She still didn't understand. But because she didn't comprehend my lack of sexual spark, absence of thrust and distance from emotion…she simply accepted it.

What other choice did she have? I couldn't imagine fancying someone. Anyone. It seemed like the strangest thing in the world to me. Why would anyone be like that?

—Done! I exclaimed with a flourish of my purple felt tip pen.

—Let me see, said Becca.

I showed her my t-shirt and she smiled appreciatively.

—What do you think of mine?

She presented me her t-shirt so I could *in theory* marvel at her handiwork.

It read Eric Cantona Karate Kicked My Baby.

—No, I said. Not that one.

—What? Why?

—I don't like it.

—How about I Hate Oasis AND Blur?

—That isn't shocking though. As you said, it has to be something really outrageous!

Reluctantly, Becca settled on Margaret Thatcher Was The Best Prime Minister Ever.

We put on our t-shirts and held hands, a modern-day John and Yoko. Together, we strode through Cumbernauld Town Centre in full view of shoppers, our faces impassive, our messages loud and clear. Every now and again, we'd stand completely still, our chests puffed out so people could get a good look at the words we'd taken so much care to craft. At one point, I pretended to be a hitchhiker, much to Becca's amusement. We posed, pouted and pretended to be the most amazing people in the universe. And for a few seconds, maybe we were. At least in our own minds. We stood in the midst of crowds, pushed ourselves in front of shoppers and their trolleys, we asked for help and directions from strangers. No matter what happened, we'd make sure everyone looked at us.

Oh, they saw us alright.

They just didn't care.

I couldn't believe it. What the hell was wrong with people? There we were with the obscenest statements emblazoned on our chests, yet nobody reacted. Not even a blink.

—What a waste of time, I said sadly.

—All that effort for nothing.

We'd spent nearly two hours trying to shake up the residents of Cumbernauld, only to discover they were completely unshakeable. A Richter-scale-busting earthquake couldn't shake them out of their collective complacency. To them, we were just a pair of stupid kids with stupid t-shirts. Maybe they were right.

—It's political correctness gone mad, said Becca.

That was her favourite one-liner. She said it often, uttering it at the worst moments, times where something went wrong. It was funny at first, but like all overworked jokes, it stopped making me laugh the more she used it.

—I need to get out of this town, I said.

—Nobody escapes Cumbernauld, replied Becca.

—I will. I'm getting on the first bus out of this dump.

—Will you take me with you?

—Of course I will.

And I meant it at the time.

Chapter 31

Discipline

Even though my headmaster's real name wasn't Adolf Shitler (his actual name was Mr. Boyd), it was what we all knew him by, the name we used in whispered voices. Small and vicious, he more than lived up to his namesake. Okay, so he didn't have a moustache nor was he particularly charismatic when he held us all hostage in the Assembly Hall. But there wasn't a single teenager at Cumbernauld High brave enough to take him on. He was the supreme leader, a complete and utter bastard, the dictator who behaved like a dick. We all hated him. But more importantly, we all feared him. It was an unlikely terror. Despite him being a four-foot streak of piss with a cheap grey suit, if his wrath crashed down on anyone, they inevitably begged for his forgiveness. Parents were equally as frightened of him and his watery eyes; he could drown people in a glance.

I came face to face with Herr Shitler during one of my rare days at school.

Worse, he wasn't alone.

In his office, seated at the other side of his desk, was *my mother*.

—Hello, Walter, she said coldly.

She was dressed in a cleaner's overall, so I figured she'd taken time off one of her jobs to be at school to talk with the headmaster. That alone would be enough to put her in a bleak mood. No matter what happened, I wouldn't get out of this unscathed or unslapped.

—Shit, I muttered.

—What was that? Mr. Shitler asked, knowing full well what I'd said.

—Nothing, I said hastily.

—It sounded like a curse word, young man.

—I wouldn't curse anyone, I quipped, hoping humour would take the edge off the situation. Not that it mattered. It was obvious why I'd been summoned to see the headmaster. He wanted to discuss my attendance, of course. Rather, my lack thereof.

Shuffling some papers and files on his desk, Shitler made a production out of our talk. Maybe he wanted to intimidate me into submission? Did he do this to everyone else?

Mum, however, looked unimpressed. Worse, she looked bored.

—Look, I don't have all day. Would you get on with it? Why am I here?

Looking slightly irked at Mum's harsh comment, Shitler got on with it:

—Your son's records show he's been absent ninety-nine times in total.

—Ninety-nine!

I covered my ears with both hands as Mum screeched the number in my ear.

—Yes, said Mr. Shitler calmly. Your son has been off school for ninety-nine days.

—What *have* you been doing?

—I know it sounds bad, Mum, but school is boring...

—School's meant to be boring, snapped Mum.

Mr. Shitler raised a bushy grey eyebrow up his fleshy furrowed forehead.

—Well, Mrs. Wedgeworth, actually...

Mum swerved on the headmaster and took aim with her forefinger.

—Keep out of this, she warned him.

He kept out of it. For now.

—What do you do when you aren't at school?

—Me and…

I stopped. Yet I already knew it was too late.

—You and who?

—You and *whom*, corrected Mr. Shitler in that snide voice all students knew and loathed.

—Fuck off, Mum said angrily.

—I would ask you to calm down and…

—And I would ask *you* to fuck off. I'm talking to my son. Right?

—Me and Becca. We just hang about.

—I don't like her.

—You don't like any of my friends, Mum!

—She's sleekit. I can tell by looking at her.

—That's paranoia on your part.

—Don't use long words, son. I'm not stupid, okay?

—Yes, Mum.

Herr Shitler decided this would be a good time to creep back into the conversation. He was the headmaster and needed to take control again. There was another reason he'd invited my mother to my school. Things were about to take an awkward turn for me.

—Teachers are also reporting that your son tends to go to the bathroom a lot, Mrs. Wedgeworth. In some lessons, he'll ask to leave the classroom up to three times in an hour.

—It's all that tea he drinks!

—No, I'm just washing my hands.

—There. He's just washing his hands.

Shitler wasn't convinced. He tried to get my mother on side.

—Three times per lesson? We have six classes per day. That's…

—Look, Mr. Boyd, I might not be great with long words, but I can count. Okay?

143

—The point I'm trying to make, Mrs. Wedgeworth, is that it isn't healthy that your son spends so much time washing his hands. Look at them. They're scrubbed red raw.

Self-consciously, I hid my hands away from view.

—Do you want him to be a smelly bastard? He washes his hands. So what?

—It's obsessive, Mrs. Wedgeworth.

—I just…like washing my hands.

In fact, I didn't like washing them. It was a necessary ritual to be observed at certain times during the day. I'd reached a point where I turned the hot water tap, waited until the water became boiling hot – then shoved my hands underneath, screaming in pain until something in my brain told me it was okay to stop; I heard a sound without any sound; it gave me permission to remove my hands from the stream of steaming water.

Mum faced Herr Shitler with the sort of steely resolve I'd come to know and love.

Sadly, my headmaster didn't know it and he certainly didn't love it.

—I'm considering suspending your son due to his bad attendance…

—I'll go to the *Cumbernauld News* and complain.

Shitler laughed. That wasn't his smartest move. He had no idea what he was up against. It was like a kid using knuckledusters to beat a nuclear bomb into submission. Mum had been toughened after years of living with Fishtank. She wasn't about to be humbled by my small and petty headmaster. She said once again that she'd go to the *Cumbernauld News*.

Shitler wasn't having it.

—And how is going to the *Cumbernauld News* going to help?

—My son has mental health problems.

Mortified, I rounded on my mother.

—I bloody well do not!

—Yes, you do. Shut up.

144

—I appreciate that Walter suffers from issues regarding his mental health…

—His father tried to beat his ADHD out of him.

—Mum! I gasped, absolutely scandalised.

—ADHD?

—Attention Deficit Hyperactivity Disorder. My son suffers from it.

I marvelled at my mum's ability to improvise nonsense in order to get whatever she wanted. This was the sort of crap they talked about on *Kilroy* every morning, which meant Mum knew exactly what to say with confidence; which current illnesses she could use to bamboozle headmasters and other officials into doing her bidding.

—If you kick my son out of Cumbernauld High, I'll tell the paper you discriminated against his condition. I swear I'll do it. And I'll win.

Herr Shitler no longer seemed confident with his pronouncement. He drummed his fingers together, keeping quiet as he considered Mum's ultimatum. His lips were a tight line above his chin, a bloodless slit. Honestly, I'd never seen him this quiet before.

It was an unnerving experience.

Finally, he spoke.

—Your son's attendance must improve and he needs to limit his hand washing to certain times of the day. He can't be allowed to disrupt lessons. Okay?

He spoke in the manner of a man who had won his argument.

He'd won nothing.

Ten minutes later, I was outside in the schoolyard with my mum. It was cold and rainy, she looked small in her large pink puffa jacket. Lighting up a cigarette, she gave me a hug, pulling me into the smoky cloud surrounding her head.

—Thanks, Mum.

—He's a little tit, she said dismissively.

—I've learned my lesson. No more extra days off.

—Except Monday next week, said Mum.

—Why Monday?

—I've got a delivery coming from Kay's catalogue. A new rug for the living room.

On Monday, I took another day off school.

The rug didn't show up.

I took another day off on the Tuesday.

It came.

Mum didn't like it.

Chapter 32

The Ice-Cream Van Man

Jake moved out of Craigieburn Road without telling anyone. One night he came back to collect Betty (his machete), then we didn't see him again for weeks on end. The only time he popped back into our lives was when he needed money. He was never alone. His friends were never far away. Worried for her oldest son, Mum warned Jake of the consequences of hanging out with the wrong crowd. Not caring about her opinion, Jake shrugged and assured her everything was fine in his life. I heard everything, of course.

They ignored me as I sat reading a library copy of *Great Expectations* by Kathy Acker.

—I've got a job, said Jake casually.

His announcement was just as astonishing as the time his dad wanted a job.

Thank goodness I wasn't eating at the time.

Mum looked surprised, but was absolutely supportive.

—You've got a job? Where?

—Aye. I'm working in Marky's Ice-Cream Van.

—Oh no, I gasped.

Marky's Ice-Cream Van was a busted old coffin on four wheels with a scary clown face painted on the side. The Scottish weather had worn away the image so the clown's smile looked vaguely bloody. Worse, the jingle didn't work properly. Whenever the van came within distance of Craigieburn Road, its arrival was heralded by a funereal tune, a slowed down, chewed-up version of the *Blue Peter* theme tune.

The only people happy to hear that jingle were chain-smoking housewives.

Satisfied her son now had a career selling 99 cones, cigarettes and ten pence mixtures, Mum hugged Jake and let him raid the freezer for old microwave meals. He took all the frozen kebabs, which suited me fine because I hated them. He also took the ice-lollies, which upset Davy Death slightly. Since moving into our house, he'd filled one of the drawers in our freezer with ice-lollies. Yes, we actually had an ice-lolly drawer.

After emptying the contents of our freezer into a blue plastic bag, Jake made to leave.

—Where are you staying? Mum asked, more out of nosiness than concern.

—I'm at Eddie's.

Eddie Moore was my brother's partner-in-crime. Literally. Tall, rakish, skin-headed and utterly without scruples if you crossed him, he was more of a brother to Jake than I could ever manage. They had more in common; both of them loved drugs, weapons, armed robbery, getting drunk and Mario Kart.

—Is Eddie working at the ice-cream van too?

—Nah, he wants to be a security guard.

In the background, from behind the cover of my book, I sniggered.

—Are you not meant to be at school today? Jake said, unable to mask his irritation.

—In-Service Day.

A complete and utter lie!

Though Jake said nothing, he didn't need to. My brother's expression said everything it needed to say; it was contemptuous, unreservedly so. But it meant nothing to me.

Mum lit a cigarette and took a seat as soon as Jake left.

—He's got a job, she said.

—Marky's Ice-Cream Van.

—It's a job, she snapped defensively.

—Yes, I agreed.

The next few weeks passed uneventfully until the sudden start of a police investigation into a strange spate of food poisonings. The weird twist in this investigation, however, was that the poisonings only seemed to affect children. Even weirder, it only seemed to affect *chubby* children. Something was happening to make these kids terribly ill. According to the *Cumbernauld News* reports, they would scream and shout, fight invisible aliens, froth at the mouth, scratch their faces to bloody ribbons and stomp on their pets.

Parents of chubby children lived in terror of what their bairns would do next.

It took one very clever parent to make a troubling connection.

This smart lady looked at the one thing the victims had in common.

Each child had been to Marky's Ice-Cream Van shortly before their symptoms occurred.

It didn't take long for the police to come for Jake. I'm surprised it didn't happen sooner, to be honest. The trial itself was a fiasco. I should know. I watched it unfold from the comfort of the spectator stall. Mum asked me earlier that week if I wanted another day off school. One day? She was optimistic. In fact, the trial lasted four days. After my confrontation with Herr Shitler, I was reluctant to take more time off school. However, Mum talked me round using a combination of persuasive charm and emotional blackmail.

—It'll be company for me, she explained whilst puffing on a ciggie.

—I don't need to be there, I told her.

—I'll buy you a pair of Dr. Martens.

—Okay, I'll come with you.

If the way to a man's heart is through his stomach, then the way to my heart is through my feet. I'd do anything for nice new Docs. I had no shame and my mother knew it.

Marky, the owner of the ice-cream van, unexpectedly passed away two days before the trial started. He took a heart-attack *and* the full blame for everything that happened. After all, it was now Jake's word against that of a man whose testimony had been rendered inadmissible thanks to his death. Worse, Jake seemed like a credible witness. How could he not be? He was their *only* witness. Even I had to admit that he looked the part in his nice black suit, the same suit he'd wear regularly to funerals of dead junkies, his fallen comrades. None of that mattered to Marky's family. They clearly regarded Jake as the personification of evil, the devil in Diadora trainers. Me? I knew better. Jake wasn't evil personified, far from it. He did evil things, but he was more misguided than he was actually evil. He'd been raised at the mercy of Fishtank's mercurial moods, beaten and battered into the kind of person who dropped LSD tabs into ice-cream and fed it to fat children for a laugh. Mum, in her infinite capacity for getting it wrong, blamed Jake's friends. She looked down on them as a gang leading her son astray, rather than the other way about.

I didn't have the heart to tell her that Jake was in charge of the local gang.

On the fourth day of the trial, the jury finally came to a decision.

It took them five minutes.

Five minutes out of four days.

—NOT GUILTY.

The riot started with an unidentified flying shoe. I screamed as the shoe (not a Dr. Marten) came at me, shooting through the air towards my face. Mum managed to shove me onto the floor, effectively saving me from the impact. The shoe looked vaguely like a Marc Jacobs heel, though it had to be fake. I lay on the floor, watching from a good vantage point, listening as the courtroom got smashed up. That's when I noticed Jake had been whisked out the room. The police pulled my brother and the judge to safety, but left his mother and I at the mercy of all the parents whose children had been poisoned.

Mum wasn't ready to go down without a fight though.

—Don't touch my hair, she snapped.

—Oh God, don't touch her hair, I wailed.

They didn't know it, but Fishtank used to drag Mum across our house by her hair, always getting a good handful so he could yank it violently enough to tear it out. Luckily, it always grew back. However, as a result of this abuse, Mum went into full-on psycho mode when someone touched her hair.

Where the heck were the police? We'd been left at the mercy of a mob.

I looked up to see Mum smacking a stranger with her handbag.

All this because of Jake behaving like an arsehole.

—We hate him too, I howled.

Finally (thankfully) the police arrived and pulled me up off the floor.

Ten minutes later, I was in a taxi with Mum.

Jake was there with us.

—I missed the game today, he moaned.

—Game?

My voice sounded exactly how I felt:

Weary.

—Aye, the match.

—Football, said Mum with a look of disgust.

Jake leaned over to the glass partition so he could ask the driver a question.

—What's the Rangers and Celtic score?

The driver was jovial. Clearly, he didn't realise The Cumbernauld Poisoner was in his back seat. If he did realise, he didn't let it show.

—Two nil, he said.

Jake threw his head back and laughed.

Mum suddenly looked very frightened.

Chapter 33

Boxes

It became necessary to leave 145 Craigieburn Road after the ice-cream van scandal. Not only did we have reporters from the *Daily Record* chapping our door at all hours of the morning, but we had to endure the anger of parents whose kids had been spiked by The Cumbernauld Poisoner. Clearly, no-one believed the verdict. And why should they? It was a load of crap. I was grateful to leave Craigieburn. It was a haunted house, full of ghosts from the past. Better still, it was our last link to Fishtank. A new house, a new start. We were leaving without Jake, which suited me fine. Lorna and Declan lived together a few streets away in Glenacre Road, not that we ever saw them. Bruises couldn't heal fast enough, I suppose. Donnie, meanwhile, was still living it large with lesbians in London.

It was just me, Laddie, Mum and Davy.

For now.

—It's a three-bedroom house, said Davy Death after giving us the good news.

—Does that mean…we'll get our own rooms?

Laddie really, desperately wanted his own room. I understood, of course. We were getting older and I needed my own space too, if only because I wanted peace and quiet to read without the bleepy-bloopy sounds of video games being played into the early hours.

—Both of you will have your own rooms, said Mum coolly.

—Where are we going?

—You can decide when you see the rooms.

—Not the rooms, I said irritably. —Where are we *moving* to?

Anywhere but Cumbernauld, I thought desperately. I'd already packed in readiness to leave. My boxes were crammed with clothes and books and junk and more books. Honestly, I just wanted to escape to a better place with a brighter future.

—We're going to Darroch Way, said Davy, hoping for my happiness.

It was a vain hope. Darroch Way was a twenty-minute walk from Craigieburn Road. Or four minutes in a car. That meant we were easily reachable by anyone. I'd still have to go to Cumbernauld High School, still need to walk the same streets, forever trapped.

Poor Davy. He'd expected (or hoped for) my approval and couldn't mask his disappointment at *my* disappointment. To take the sting away, I smiled.

It was too late. He'd already turned away from me.

Our new house in Darroch Way was a concrete villa. It was bigger than our old house, befitting the salary of a college lecturer. There wasn't an eyesore radio antenna grafted on top of the roof, like a botched nose job on a tired face. Our garden would be bigger. We'd have a patio and – OHMYGOD – we were getting actual Venetian blinds too. Mum had already assured us that she'd ordered them from her catalogue and they'd be arriving any day now. She'd started to receive mail under different surnames. *Wadgeworth* was a popular one. *Wedgewoorth* was another. My favourite was the hitherto yet incredible *Wedgeworthless*, which I almost adopted as my official surname. Mum wouldn't allow something as insignificant as a bad credit rating to put an end to her dream for Venetian blinds. To her, Venetian blinds weren't just for letting in the light, or blocking out random debt collectors. They were a status symbol of her ascent into middle-class society! It was as though erasing her past depended solely on whether or not her blinds were horizontal or vertical.

We got out the car, which had its own parking space near the house. It was an overcast day, the promise of rain hanging in the air above our heads, fat clouds ready to deliver. I had a large golf umbrella, which made me look ever-so-sophisticated, or so I reckoned.

—Close that stupid umbrella, said Mum harshly.

Davy Death waited for me to close my umbrella so he could make a speech. It sounded like the sort of speech he would probably make to his students on graduation day.

—Today is a special day, because this is a day for a new start. We're here at our new home. It's your home (he pointed at Mum), it's your home (he pointed at Laddie), and it's your home (he pointed at me). Welcome to your new home!

It was a nice sentiment. For the first time ever we had a home, not a house.

Davy went to open the door, only to find it was locked.

—Shit, he muttered. —I don't have the key.

—I don't have it.

Laddie didn't even bother to say anything. He wouldn't have been trusted with the key to our new home. The rest of us started searching our pockets for the missing key.

—Calm down… said Mum, as though sensing Davy's panic.

—Where's the key? How will we get in without the key!

Someone two doors down came out from their house to point and laugh. They had a bottle of wine in their hand. Really good stuff, actually. The kind Jilly Goulden would have sloshed around her mouth for five minutes before swallowing. Merlot was the Prosecco of the 90s, ever-so-trendy and completely middle-class. As our new neighbour swallowed her wine from the bottle, I decided to quickly test a theory:

Looking up at their top window, my suspicions were

confirmed.

She had Venetian blinds.

—I've found it, yelled Davy.

A few minutes later the front door was unlocked and we were in our new home.

Chapter 34

Reunion

A sly phone call from Donnie let me know she'd returned from London. According to her, she'd moved into a flat in Glasgow that November with her new girlfriend, Nicola. Apparently, Donnie had been trying to get in touch with me for weeks. She didn't know we'd moved out of Craigieburn Road, but saw our new number and address in the BT phonebook. The idea of my address being out in public sat oddly with me, but on this occasion I was just grateful to hear from my sister again.

—Let's meet, she suggested on the other end of the line.

I knew just the place where we could meet in private and catch-up on her adventures:

—Let's go to McDonald's.

When she spoke again, I caught a sliver of amusement in her voice.

—Aren't you vegetarian?

—Only at the weekend, I answered.

It was time to take another day off school.

Glasgow was a safe space for me so long as I stuck to the familiar shops and paths on the High Street. There was Forbidden Planet, which I visited religiously whenever I popped into the city. There was Flip, a shop that used to be the coolest place to buy clothes until people suddenly stopped being cool. Or maybe I was uncool because I still shopped there? Alien War at the Arches was always good for a day out with friends. Basically, you paid to run around some tunnels being chased by a jobbing actor dressed as The Xenomorph. Becca didn't really care for it though.

—If I wanted to be chased around dark tunnels by some ugly weirdo, I could just hang around Asda car park on a Saturday night.

She had a point.

Missing was another favourite haunt of mine. It was the hipster record store of choice. I bought *The Way Of The Vaselines* there because Kurt Cobain was a fan of their music. The selection was amazing, but the shop reeked of a busted bog and the CD cases on the grubby shelves were mostly cracked. None of that mattered. It was infinitely preferable to the shiny, sleek Tower Records and their overpriced albums.

(Why the hell did we all pay £16.99 for a CD back in the 90s?)

Donnie was waiting outside McDonald's by the time I arrived. She wore a leather jacket and tight jeans with big white Adidas trainers. She looked good, if a bit skinny. Her hair, however, was as big and crimped as I remembered. Blonde corkscrews with black roots.

—Hey, hooker, I shouted.

Her smile, a bright toothy grin, lit up her face and my life.

Suddenly I felt rather self-conscious giving her a glimpse of my wonky tea-stained grin. My teeth weren't bad, as such. They were Scottish. A testament to a childhood of sweets and poverty! But post-London Donnie put me in mind of a slightly butch Kate Moss. Working for a company like Bradford & Bingley suited both her and her bank account.

—Come here, she said. She swept me up in a big embrace, which I didn't return because I didn't know how to hug people. However, one thing I did know how to do was queue in line for a McChicken Sandwich. We engaged in polite chit chat, generalised friendly talk. But we both knew it was the prelude to a more important conversation.

158

Upstairs, in one of the booths, we got to work eating and talking.

(Not at the same time though.)

—How are you?

—I think I'm fine.

—You…think…you're fine?

—I never say, 'yes, I'm fine.' It's jinxing yourself. What if you feel fine but you aren't actually fine? Why take the chance?

Donnie looked at me, then sighed.

—You've been in Cumbernauld for too long.

—Maybe one day I'll move to London like you.

—What's the point? I'm back! And just in the nick of time.

—Hurrah!

—How's Mum doing?

—She got new Venetian blinds last month.

Donnie chuckled, sipped on her Diet Coke, then asked a question.

—Does she ever talk about me?

The fateful phone call Donnie made on Christmas Day last year hadn't been mentioned by anyone. Not even Lorna had dared broach the subject of her sister in front of Mum. This tended to happen in my family more often than not. Granny Fanny, for instance, simply disappeared after Fishtank turfed her out onto the street. Any attempt at getting information from Mum resulted in her wrath, which we were all keen to avoid.

But how did I reply to my sister?

Did I tell her the truth?

For the sake of my sister's feelings, I told her a lie.

—She asked about you the other day, I said.

—No she didn't, but thanks for being nice about it.

I looked down at my McChicken Sandwich.

It lacked flavour, but I wasn't about to complain about that in McDonald's.

Donnie asked me another question.

The answer to this one would potentially change everything between the two of us.

—Does it matter to you that I'm gay?

—No, I said immediately.

Such things meant nothing to me. I'd evolved myself past such concerns.

—Good, she said. And with that, I watched as every tight bit of tension left my sister's body through her shoulders. She leaned back, eating quietly. I did likewise. It felt good to do something normal again, or as close to normal as I could realistically expect. I chewed on a fry or two, while Donnie slurped her strawberry milkshake through a plastic straw. The sound of thick gooey ice-cream clogging up her straw was almost as loud as the background noise, the incessant sounds of eating and chatting.

—Did you enjoy your stint in London?

—No.

—Oh.

There were no fries left in my box to eat.

—I can't go back, said my sister out of the blue.

—To London?

Donnie nodded. She dumped her empty milkshake cup onto the pile of rubbish we'd accumulated. My urge to clean it all up and wash my hands afterwards was overwhelming, but I pushed back against the feeling. I didn't want my sister seeing me go back and forth to the bathroom just so I could wash dirt off my hands.

I felt it though.

In my skin.

Dirt. Filth. Grime.

Rotted dead baby.

—Glasgow's closer than London, I suppose.

—Look, sighed Donnie. —I don't want to talk about London,

okay? Not right now.

Perversely, my sister not wanting to talk about London made me want to discuss it even more. What happened? Why did she really come back? Donnie, however, wasn't done yet.

—Truth is, I need your opinion on something.

—My opinion?

—Or your approval.

—Oh God, I groaned. —What are you planning?

—I've been thinking about going to see Fishtank.

—What? Why?

—I just want him to know I'm happy being me.

—You want to tell him you're gay?

—Yes.

—Are you trying to annoy him?

Donnie rolled her eyes dismissively. She didn't like that question.

—No. I just need to do it.

—Okay.

—And I want you to come with me.

Chapter 35

On The Buses

Donnie's relationship with Mum had always been slightly stressful. For a long time I didn't understand it. Couldn't get to grips with the mother/daughter dynamic. Every now and again I accepted a vague impression that my parents favoured Lorna over Donnie. It was especially evident in the way they approached them whenever they did something wrong. When Donnie was caught smoking at school, she was grounded. But Lorna? She was sternly told not to do that ever again. She did it anyway.

Things like that can build up until there's a great big wall in the way.

I didn't understand why Lorna was Mum's princess and Donnie difficult by design

Until…

Years later, long after Donnie asked me to visit Fishtank with her, the answer suddenly came to me in a dreamless sleep. That knowledge – this *clear* understanding – literally shook me awake. It was confirmed to me when I looked at my mirrored wardrobe, the one bought for me even though I didn't want it. The reason Mum treated my sisters differently to each other was because Lorna looked more like *her* side of the family, while Donnie's features favoured Fishtank's side. Where Lorna had golden hair, Donnie had thick curly dark hair. Lorna had been born with Mum's pleasingly delicate facial features, while Donnie ended up sharing Fishtank's darker appearance.

With that knowledge came another shocking realisation.

Out of my family, I looked most like Donnie.

Which meant I looked like *him*.

Maybe that's why Donnie asked me to accompany her that day?

Either that or she just wanted a witness.

The 147A bus reeked of sweaty bums and unsprayed armpits. Donnie told me that public transport in London was just as bad, worse in fact. That seemed unlikely. Regardless, I was grateful to have someone to take me out of Cumbernauld and I was determined to be happy, even if our journey took us to the wretched Fishtank. I'd dressed for our day out, hoping to impress my sister with my refined sense of style. I had a pair of green sunglasses plonked on my nose, a black boiler suit that I got out a charity shop in Cumbernauld Town Centre, a green plastic belt pulled tightly around my waist and a pair of heavy-duty Dr Martens on my feet. Truly, I resembled a glamorous brickie.

Donnie glanced over and grinned brightly. She too had on a pair of sunglasses. They were red and white Moschino. They might have been fake, but with the money she'd made from her job in London, they were probably the real deal.

We sat on the grimy bus, looking ridiculous, bonded by thoughts of our own brilliance.

Together we were invincible.

Donnie knew where we were meant to be, so I simply followed her lead. The bus to Airdrie from Cumbernauld was a camel ride that lasted almost an hour. It gave me a chance to get all the gossip from London. Actually, I would have listened to anything my sister said. She could have rattled off recipes from a Delia Smith book and I would have gasped at the appropriate moments. For someone not used to anywhere but Cumbernauld and its surrounding hinterlands, my second-oldest sister seemed incredibly worldly-wise.

—Kate Bush's postman drank at my local bar.

—No way, I gasped.

—He said she was a nutter.

—Wow. Unbelievable.

—Pauline from *EastEnders* came in one night too.

—Was Sharon with her?

—Nah, but she looked smaller in real life.

The bus finally came to a shuddering halt outside a familiar location. A large bland building with decorative columns and lots of pigeons pecking at stray rubbish. Suddenly, I realised the bus had dropped Donnie and I off at Airdrie Sheriff Court.

—We were here for Jake's trial, I said wearily.

—Did he really do what the papers said he did?

I raised a dark eyebrow so high it nearly touched the clouds.

Donnie sighed, suddenly realising the pointlessness of asking such a question.

As we waited at the stop for another bus to arrive, I quizzed my sister on her life in London. She'd talked about Kate Bush's postman and her from *EastEnders*. But she hadn't gone into detail about her girlfriend or her old job. Also, why had she come back to Scotland? Did she miss me and her family so much she couldn't stay away?

Not exactly.

—The job itself was fine, but I got bored.

—That's a shame.

—The money was good though.

—So have you got your money or did you spend it all?

—Oh, money's not a problem.

Donnie smirked slightly. It was the smirk of a woman with a secret.

—Why not?

—Because I embezzled hundreds of thousands from the company.

I laughed out loud at her joke.

But Donnie didn't laugh.
Because she wasn't joking.

Chapter 36

The Replacement

We spent the rest of the journey to Fishtank's front door in awkward silence. Honestly, I was stunned. It wasn't that she'd stolen the money that shocked me, it was the fact she hadn't been caught yet. Surely a paper trail had been left behind? Apparently not.

—The company don't want to make a fuss about it.

—What about the people whose money you stole?

—Tax dodgers, Tories and toffs. Fuck 'em!

—You can't do that to people, I snapped.

—My new porcelain veneers say otherwise. My genuine Comme des Garçons suit says otherwise. My Patrick Cox shoes? My knee-socks? All paid for with the cash I took from those rich bastards. By the way, I paid for your McDonald's with stolen money.

—And I'm happy you did that, but…

All of a sudden I understood the truth. It was so obvious.

—That's why you want to go and visit Fishtank. You want him to see you with all this money. This is your way of showing off how far you've come. Am I right?

Donnie didn't reply, which was the response I needed to confirm my suspicions.

But she didn't understand her gesture would ultimately prove futile.

—You won't get what you want from him.

She frowned, but kept quiet.

—He doesn't care about you or me. He never did.

A few seconds later, I added:

—You look fantastic, by the way.

—Thanks.

The bus started to slow down, which coincided with Donnie getting up off the seat and onto her feet. Reluctantly, I followed. This journey was going to take me to someone I never ever wanted to see again. My chest felt tight. My stomach gurgled violently.

We got off and walked down a street, just another street that looked like any of the streets I'd walked through (or avoided) in Cumbernauld. It turned out that other places looked just as tired as my town. Whether or not that was a relief, I didn't know.

—Here we are, said Donnie.

The door was brown with glass in it. A curtain kept the inside of the house hidden. Thick drapes covered all the windows too, making it impossible to see who (if anyone) was inside. This didn't surprise me. I knew for a fact Fishtank hadn't paid a single penny in child maintenance. I'd overheard Mum complaining on the phone that he would hide every time someone chapped on the front door, terrified of being caught and made to support his own children. He took sickies from work whenever the government threatened to arrest his wages and take the money by force.

The more I thought about it, the less I wanted to be in this place. But Donnie needed me. I would never ever let her down. Besides, she owned a Comme des Garçons suit.

—Here goes nothing, said my sister.

She lifted the letterbox and slammed it down.

It brought back memories of the day we threw Fishtank out of the house.

—We don't need to do this. Let's just get...

The door opened and my mouth closed.

A woman with coarse red hair on her lip and a baseball bat in her hand stood before us.

167

Evidently, we weren't welcome.

—Who the fuck are you?

Her voice was a snarl, rough and raspy. I couldn't imagine her serving roast potatoes to Satan let alone a bunch of hungry factory workers. She was rougher than a cave bear's arse.

—Oh my God, I gasped. Though I'd never actually seen her before in my life, it seemed obvious that this was the woman Fishtank had ended up with after my mother turfed him out. She looked fearsome, a troll without a bridge in a town without underpasses. Her hair was thick and red. It clearly hadn't ever been bothered by a bottle of Timotei Extra Shine, for sure. Her eyebrows were thick and bushy. None of which was really a bad thing, as such. She was just entirely different to my mother.

—We're here to see Fishtank.

—I'm not, I mumbled.

No-one cared though. This wasn't about me.

—I know who you are, said the dinner lady suspiciously.

Donnie attempted politeness and courtesy.

—We're not here to cause any problems. We just want to see him.

—She's not getting him back! He's my man now.

I laughed, of course.

Another voice interrupted the exchange:

—Whoever it is, I'm not in!

My hands suddenly felt really itchy and dirty.

—It's two of your kids!

Fishtank came to the door, apparently unsure what to do. He looked...

Well, exactly the same.

He had on a Deep Purple t-shirt with holes all over it. His denim jeans were unironed, entirely washed-out. Fishtank had never been a keen dresser, but he hadn't ever looked so dirty and dishevelled. I'd already come to the conclusion that his new girlfriend was a boozer and together they'd found salvation at the bottom of a pint tumbler.

—Danielle. Walter.

After giving me a cursory glance, he returned his attention to Donnie.

—You look well.

—Can we come in?

The dinner lady opened her mouth to bark, but she closed it after reconsidering. Whatever she had to say, it wasn't going to be nice. She didn't want us in her house, which was understandable. We were connected to the mystery wife Fishtank had left to be with her. It was almost a certainty that she didn't know he'd tried to come back.

Maybe I'd tell her? But I knew that wouldn't happen.

—That's fine, said Fishtank. —Come in!

Donnie walked past me and I followed with my head down, which gave me an opportunity to study Fishtank's carpet. It was the colour of red wine, which was apt. It meant Fishtank and the dinner lady wouldn't need to clean the carpet if they dropped a glass or two: the colour would blend right into the fibre.

The living room wasn't much better. It was a gloomy room with some old couches, an odd tartan pattern on them. Probably flammable. What it needed instead of curtains was a nice set of Venetian blinds; of course I didn't actually come out and say that to Fishtank. He wouldn't appreciate my opinion. Neither would his girlfriend.

—Your dad wants to marry me, said the dinner lady, as though reading my thoughts.

—I'm waiting for my invite to the wedding, said Donnie sarcastically.

—You'll be waiting a long time, came the response, with added witchy cackle. Then, as if to demonstrate her claim over Fishtank, she sauntered over and grabbed his crotch.

—You tell your mother this belongs to me. Right?

—Mum doesn't care. She's got a boyfriend.

I chipped in, —And she's filed for divorce. Infidelity, apparently.

Fishtank and the dinner lady looked in my direction. I suddenly felt very itchy. The dust in the room crawled with vermin. It was all over me, eating my skin, burrowing deeper into my pores. I *had* to get away and soak my hands in boiling water.

The dinner lady spoke first, though it sounded more like a bark rather than actual speech.

—She's not divorcing him. He's divorcing her!

—Is that why you're here? Fishtank asked quietly. —Have you come to tell me your mum wants a divorce?

—No, said Donnie. —I came to tell you I'm gay.

—Fuck, I muttered.

Fishtank didn't react. Not initially. The dinner lady, however, couldn't hide her disgust.

—She's a fuckin' dyke. You're a fucking dyke.

—And you look like you've licked dog piss off a wall, I thought viciously.

—What was that?

Ah. I'd just said aloud what I'd been thinking. Donnie grabbed me and yanked on my shoulder until I fell backwards. She kept her hand on me, pulling me towards the front door. She didn't stop until we were outside. As we rushed out into the street, I caught sight of a little girl standing by herself at the top of a staircase. Dressed in pink pyjamas, she remained still, watching curiously as we left.

She was Fishtank's life now.

—What does that mean? Are you saying I'm ugly? Your dad thinks I'm sexy. He prefers me to your mum. He chose me. Right? *He chose me!*

That was Fishtank's life too.

Quite frankly, he was welcome to both.

—You're a dyke! A voice in the distance barked. —Dyke! Dyke! Dyke!

—You're a dick! Donnie yelled back at our dad. —Dick! Dick! Dick!

Their voices collided, both of them trying to drown the other out, a contest and a clash of wills. My skull felt like it might burst. Linking arms with my sister, hastily pulling her in the right direction (away from Fishtank) we pounded the pavement until my legs and lungs couldn't take it anymore. Coming to a halt, I panted and puffed. Donnie seemed exhilarated by the encounter. She kept showing off her brand-new smile paid for with stolen cash.

Once I'd regained my composure, I asked:

—Was it worth it?

—GOD YES! she cried.

—You hoped that would happen, didn't you?

—Maybe, she said.

Each of us silently waited for the other to do something. Finally, I asked a question.

—Do you know how to get back to the bus stop from here?

—No!

—I think we might be lost.

—Then let's get found, said my sister.

Chapter 37

The End Of An Era

My friendship with Becca came to a screeching halt on a wintry November afternoon while we walked home from school. It was the sort of raw cold that made cheeks red and noses run. The hood of my Kickers coat was pulled over my head, which would have been fine except the fur around the rim was too thick, making it difficult to see the path in front of me. At least my ears weren't cold. God, I hated having cold ears.

Intent on not tripping or falling on my arse, I kept my eyes focused on the path that would eventually lead me back home. Nothing else seemed so important. Not even Becca. And that was a problem, because Becca had spent the last ten minutes trying to tell me something important. Her voice was background noise. Waffle in the wind.

—Hello! She said over and over again. —HELLO!

I tilted my head, catching a glimpse of Becca's face. It took a supreme effort to listen.

—Didn't you hear what I just said?

—No, I replied blandly.

It was really cold. My hands were in my pockets, because I had no gloves.

But at least my ears were warm.

—I just told you I had a new boyfriend.

That wasn't a surprise. Becca had all but told me she had a juicy secret. The hints hadn't been subtle enough. Nothing was when it came to Becca. She'd been *gasping* for me to ask about her new boyfriend. Unfortunately, her Laura Palmer impersonation was lost on me. I had my own secrets to keep, all of which were tucked away at the back of my brain, in the dark spaces between dark places. Besides, the very idea of Becca with a secret was laughable. She was literally incapable of keeping secrets. You only told her something if you didn't mind everybody at school hearing about it minutes later.

—Yes, continued Becca as though I cared. —I've got a new boyfriend!

—Who is it? I asked, trying to fake enthusiasm the same way Anna Nicole Smith probably faked orgasms with J. Howard Marshall.

—I can't say.

—You don't want to tell me who it is?

—Oh I'd love to tell you, Walter. But…

She tried her best to look suitably dramatic, but she didn't have the range.

—It's a secret.

—Then why did you mention it in the first place if you can't tell me?

She wanted me to know she had an entire life away from our friendship, I supposed.

—Because you're my best friend, she answered.

—Do I know your secret boyfriend?

—Yes.

The wind whipped up and we squealed as a staggering burst of cold hit us. Finally, I was able to speak again, but my chittering teeth made the words slow and precise.

—Is it a teacher? I asked, trying to bring the conversation to a merciful end.

—No. Try again.

It was like playing a game of Pictionary with a blind girl.

—Could you just tell me who it is?

Becca blinked twice, her eyes watery and red from the stinging wintry wind.

173

—I can't. I'm not allowed to tell anyone. I promised. But if you guess his name…that means I didn't tell you and I didn't break my promise. Does that make sense?

We stopped at The Totem in Glenhove Road, a slum area in Cumbernauld.

Erected in 1966, The Totem is a tall concrete column resembling some great lost Native American shrine. God bless Brian Miller, the official artist-in-residence. His imagination and talent allowed him to fill Cumbernauld with wonderful weirdness. Armed with paint brushes and a hefty budget, he transformed the entire town. He painted underpasses the colours of a wild LSD trip. He designed murals that made no sense whatsoever. Best of all, he created metal sculptures purely for their aesthetic value, rather than whether or not they could kill or maim passers-by. I'd always found the idea completely thrilling. His work remained in vogue until the 90s, by which time most of it had been taken down, erased, or abandoned. The town became a far less exciting place as a result. But The Totem remained – a reminder of wilder, ambitious days, where anything was possible, even a Native American-style concrete pole in the middle of a wet town full of flat-roofed homes.

Becca waited expectantly, prepared to answer questions about her mysterious new boyfriend. But I wouldn't ask those questions. I refused to play my role.

—No, I said bluntly.

—What?

—Because I don't really care, Becca.

—What?

—I don't care about your secret boyfriend. Honestly, I don't give a shit about him.

Becca frowned, not quite comprehending the evidence of her ears. If I were her, I'd be shocked too. For the last few years I'd followed her around, laughing at her jokes, going

174

through with her stupid stunts. But she bored me now. I just couldn't stand the thought of following Becca about anymore, wearing dumb t-shirts, deliberately trying to shock people for no reason. If we were in a band like Davy Death, this would probably be the moment I declared my intention to go solo due to artistic differences.

When I spoke again, my voice sounded...weary, almost bored. I couldn't even be bothered trying to fake enthusiasm. What was wrong with me? I'd never been this candid.

Suddenly empowered, I continued.

—I'm tired of being your sidekick, Becca.

My words drained Becca's power. Mutely, she stood rooted to the concrete, mouth opening slightly, eyes narrow with astonishment. Her expression registered the slightest trace of hurt, which had been my intention, in all honesty. I don't know why, but something horrible in me wanted to lash out and to hell with the consequences. I knew it couldn't last, but it didn't need to.

Gathering herself, Becca struck back.

—What's wrong, Walter? Jealous I've got a boyfriend?

The words were weak and useless. They had no effect on me whatsoever.

—A *secret* boyfriend, I corrected mockingly.

—So what? Just because you don't have anyone!

—I have me. That's all I need.

Becca laughed. It wasn't real laughter, of course. I knew the difference.

—What's so special about you, Walter Wedgeworth? (She said my full name contemptuously). —All you do is wash your hands and moan about everything. No-one at school likes you. They're only nice to you because they're scared of your brother.

It was my turn again. I had to make sure she couldn't come back from this one.

—You're nothing. You talk too much and say nothing. Oh, and every time you open your legs, a hurricane smashes a small town in Texas.

—What the fuck?

Okay, so it made little sense. But I had an understanding that when it came to arguments, surreal or weird witticisms always worked best. One-liners, quips, or puns. They disarmed people and made them struggle to return with something appropriate. As smart as Becca was, she couldn't hope to defeat me. I'd consumed every book on each shelf in Cumbernauld Central Library and words had never ever let me down.

The battle was nearly over, our titanic fight drawing to a firm end. Becca hadn't been prepared, so didn't know how to react now that I'd turned on her. The aftershock of our argument was felt in real time. My soon-to-be ex-friend backed away. Literally, she stepped back, my words hitting hard enough to physically hurt.

That was my cue to deliver the final, killing blow.

—This is done, I said coldly.

—I don't care, she snarled.

But she *did* care. She cared what people thought of her. She cared how she looked. She cared about impressing everyone. Becca's main problem in life was that she cared too much. I cared too. But I didn't care enough to save this friendship.

When I finally turned my back on Becca, she looked almost grateful.

I walked away and never looked back.

Chapter 38

Sweet And Sour Sixteenth

My family actually remembered my sixteenth birthday, which was nice of them. Not so nice though was the fact I didn't want them to remember it. Sixteen meant I was closer to death, it meant time would speed up, flowing through me faster, rotting my cells until everything went to dust. For a long time I'd harboured a secret fear of being tossed into the wind, flying free in the breeze. Was it worse than being buried in a cardboard box out in a field? Probably not. But my fears were mostly irrational. Shortly before my sixteenth birthday, I suddenly noticed the frequency of cracks on the pavement slabs. They were enormous gaping wounds on the ground. Anyone, I thought fearfully, could trip on those cracks. I could die. I could literally die.

Mum, however, was delighted to see her second youngest son turn sixteen.

But not for the many reasons I'd initially assumed.

—You can buy ciggies legally now, she told me wisely.

—But Mum…I don't smoke.

—I'm not thinking of you.

My childhood summed up in one line.

It was 1997, the year of Girl Power. My favourite Spice Girl was Posh, because she wore black and refused to smile. It was also the year of Leonardo and Kate. I saw *Titanic* in Glasgow's Odeon, but I didn't think much of it. The film seemed to last forever, so much so that I left my mother, Leo, and Kate halfway through to go out and get some ice-cream.

When I returned with a chocolate chip Cornetto in my hand, the Titanic had already hit the iceberg. I'd missed the best part of the movie! The one scene I'd really wanted to see and it had been ruined.

The rest of the movie sank without trace for me.

Sensing my disappointment with my birthday treat, Mum made a promise.

—I'll take you out to a fancy restaurant, she said.

The Wedgeworth family went to New City Palace in Glasgow as a birthday treat and an apology for making me watch *Titanic*. Mum told me to invite my friends, but I didn't have any friends. This led Mum to enquire about the status of my friendship with Becca.

—We aren't speaking anymore.

—Why not?

—Because I don't like her anymore.

As explanations went, it was venomous in its blunt simplicity. But how else could I explain what happened between me and Becca? There weren't any really shocking revelations, no plot twists or turns. We'd simply drifted apart. I think the main problem, apart from her constant need for attention, was that she always talked about herself, never asking me how I felt about anything. Really, she didn't care. I stopped caring too.

—I never liked her, Mum told me.

—What a shocker.

The sarcasm oozed like discharge from a freshly-squeezed pimple.

—The problem with that girl was that she was all about herself.

—Yes.

—A bit like that moany cow in those books.

—Erm…what?

—You know. The fat one with the diary.

Mum struggled to remember her name. Later, during our journey to the restaurant in Glasgow, Mum suddenly remembered the name as it dropped back into her memory. She cried out in excitement at finally solving the mystery. Startled by the noise, Laddie nearly leapt out of his seat, accidentally revealing to everyone in the car that he hadn't buckled his seatbelt. Davy was a nervous driver, forever terrified of crashing into other cars or accidentally killing people. He had a real terror of causing vehicular manslaughter.

—Bridget Jones, exclaimed my mother.

—Who?

—Her with the diary. She's always going on about herself, isn't she? That's who Becca reminded me of. Bridget Jones. Self-obsessed and plain.

My mother hadn't read a book in her life. The closest she came to reading a book was any time she got the latest issue of the Littlewoods or the Argos catalogue.

How the hell did she know about Bridget Jones and her bloody diary?

We met Lorna and Declan on Sauchiehall Street, at the entrance to New City Palace, which wasn't ideal because I didn't want my sister's boyfriend at my birthday dinner. Everything about him made my teeth tingle; his black suits, all cheap nasty polyester, made me shudder. His slick quiffed hair, gravity-defying in its stature, thanks to the Brylcream he slathered into every follicle. Even his dimples irritated me. But I couldn't do anything about him. My sister was in love with a man who kissed her after kicking her.

—Hey, pretty lady, said Declan as Mum approached.

—Hey, sonny-boy, said Mum in return.

I nearly vomited all over my nice new Dr. Martens, a birthday present from Davy Death.

—Happy Birthday, said Lorna.

She embraced me.

I didn't know what to do.

Declan came to me and tried to be civil. He knew though. He sensed my searing hate.

—You're a man now!

—What was I yesterday?

We all laughed.

Then Jake arrived, announcing his presence with a whooping loud shout that turned heads all around us. He staggered up the street, off his head on something. Physically, his body was on Sauchiehall Street with the rest of us. Mentally, it was in another dimension.

Davy Death looked mightily uncomfortable.

They were oil, water. Sugar, salt. Whatever.

—Happy Birthday, shouted Jake.

It would have been a lovely sentiment if not for the fact he said it to Laddie.

With my head lowered, we headed upstairs to the restaurant and good food.

My birthday present to myself was the gift of not being a vegetarian for this meal. I went for my default dinner of Chicken Chow Mein with chips. I loved chips cooked in a Chinese restaurant. They were always really crispy and tasty, the sort of chips I'd ask for as a last meal if for some reason I ended up on Death Row.

Jake started up his usual fuckery a few moments into the meal.

—What would you like to order? The waitress asked.

In his best Charlie Chan parody, Jake asked for 'Plawn Clackers' instead of prawn crackers. He spoke in a ludicrous caricature of what he considered to be a Chinese voice.

—Ooooh ah wanta some Chicken Noodle Soup.

—Shut him up, I hissed between gritted teeth.

Honestly, I couldn't go anywhere with my family. It had always been this way.

Mum kicked Jake beneath the table.

Unbeknownst to her, Lorna had also decided to kick him.

Me too. I put my brand-new Docs to the test.

—FUCK OFF! Jake exploded.

We fell into a collective silence and let Jake eat his Prawn Crackers. When his soup arrived, he polished it off loudly, slurping each bit of noodle like an animal. His teeth, rotted through years of drug abuse, reacted to each spice in his Kung Pow Chicken. Punching the table in pain, he wept and wailed. Everyone in the restaurant couldn't take their eyes off my family. It was more entertaining than their conversation.

Then *she* arrived.

No-one noticed her at first, but my grateful smile was a beacon to guide her to our table.

Donnie strode over to the table and waited for acknowledgement.

Wordlessly, Mum got up and hugged her.

Lorna burst into tears.

Laddie looked at me and grinned.

Davy Death struggled to work out whether or not he wanted a dessert.

And Jake? He fell asleep on his plate in a druggy daze.

We left him there and I finally got to enjoy my sweet sixteenth.

Chapter 39

A Favour For Lorna

Lorna called me up when I was supposed to be at school.

—How did you know I took the day off?

—Because you always take the day off, Walter.

—Actually, I don't do that now. You see, sis, instead of staying off every day, I only stay off every *other* day.

—You'll still do better in your exams than Jake ever did.

Then half a heartbeat later she added:

—I need your help. Can you come to mine as soon as possible?

She didn't need to ask twice.

Then again, with Donnie back on the scene…she wouldn't have needed to ask twice.

Lorna's apartment wasn't too far away. She lived with Declan in Douglas House, a hefty tower block in the Seafar district of Cumbernauld. It could only be accessed via an intercom buzzer. The sound of the buzzer as I jabbed the button made me wince slightly. The electronic shriek scratched all the way to the back of my brain. It set my teeth on fire.

The noise suddenly stopped, only to be replaced by my eldest sister's calm tone.

—Walter?

—Yes, it's me.

—Okay. Come in!

The locking mechanism clicked, releasing the door, which I took by its handle and heaved until I could get inside. My arms weren't used to lifting anything heavier than a hardback novel, so large metal doors were somewhat problematic. Eventually,

I entered the foyer of Douglas House. There was a large mural on the wall opposite the lifts.

That's when I realised this was the first time I'd been to Lorna's flat.

Oh, I knew where it was. We all did. It was just…well, she hadn't ever asked me over. Excited to see whether or not my sister kept her skirting boards clean, I pressed the button on the panel for Floor 8 and waited. While waiting, I studied the weird psychedelic mural in detail. It was mesmerising. Another Brian Miller design. Some of it reminded me of The Totem, with little holes and shapes moulded out of coloured concrete. Gently, I reached out and touched the shapes with my bare fingers, but pulled away when I suddenly realised there might be microbes all over the wall. Vile disgusting germs waiting to burrow into my flesh, eat me from the inside out with filthy efficiency.

The doors to the lift pinged open, revealing a brown wood-panelled interior.

As I got in, a little pensioner hobbled into the lift with me.

—I didn't think I'd reach it in time, she said wearily.

Dressed in a peach rain jacket, sporting a blue rinse through her hair, she looked like a typical Cumbernauld pensioner, very Dame Edna Average.

—Which floor, I asked politely.

It was muscle memory the way I immediately parroted the words 'which floor' if I ever had the misfortune to enter a lift before anyone else, but I'd been raised to be polite to everyone – even people I despised. The pensioner in the lift seemed lovely though, so I was more than happy to be helpful.

—Floor 13, she replied.

I went to press the button for Floor 13 only to discover there weren't actually thirteen floors in the block. It went up to twelve floors only. Politely (and thoroughly puzzled) I looked around at the old dear and said as much. If she heard me, she didn't show it. Really, I should have laughed in her face. But I couldn't. I actually understood the little old lady standing in front of me. After all, wasn't I also trying to get somewhere in the world that I couldn't quite reach?

—Lawyers and judges used to live here, she said proudly.

—Was it quite a place back in its day?

—Oh yes, she said, warming up to her subject.

—Where did they all go?

After thinking it over, she finally answered:

—Byres Road in Glasgow.

Byres Road had always been where the middle-class contingent of Scotland lived. I'd once been to Byres Road, years ago with Fishtank, when I was about seven years old. It happened because he needed a spare part for his crappy CB radio contraption. Eventually, Fishtank tracked down someone with the necessary electronic element and arranged to buy it from him. Bringing me along with him as protection in case his appointment turned out to be a gay serial killer (but clearly not giving a shit if he killed children), Fishtank made me sit quietly on the bus into Glasgow. At Buchanan Street Station, Fishtank flagged down a taxi to Byres Road. Then we had to walk up alleys, through backstreets, navigating past rubbish bags propped up against red-brick walls outside large gardens.

—This looks like the door, said Fishtank.

Leaning in, Fishtank knocked twice. The door opened to reveal a skinny little man with pale skin and a slightly accented German voice. Not that I recognised that at the time, I just assumed he spoke funny. Anyway, we waited until Fishtank got what he wanted and eventually (after a quick trip to Wimpy) we headed back to Craigieburn Road.

—One day we'll live in Byres Road, vowed Fishtank on the return bus trip.

—With all the other rich people?

—Yes, he said with the intensity that only delusion provided. Then:

—How do you know they're rich, son?

—All those bins. Rich people have lots of rubbish, don't they? Fishtank looked at me with what I could only assume was grudging respect. It was as though I'd guided him towards enlightenment. I soon guided him back to cold harsh reality.

—We don't have much rubbish to throw out, I said candidly.

The pensioner in the lift at Douglas House would probably remain there, fated never to reach the non-existent thirteenth floor. I got out and made my way towards No. 91, which was my sister's flat. Or that's what she'd told me. I hadn't even raised my hand to knock on the door when it swung wide open, a hand from within snatching at me.

—Bloody hell!

—We need to be quick, said Lorna.

—What's happening? Are you okay? Why did you phone me?

—I'm leaving Declan.

I paused, waiting for the punchline.

It never came.

—About bloody time!

—He doesn't know you're here helping me pack my stuff. If he found out, he'd kill me.

—Right.

—He'd kill you too.

Immediately, I started helping my sister pack her stuff into suitcases and Asda bags. Putting her worldly possessions into Asda bags was insulting, or so she thought. Lorna had a real hatred of people who used shopping bags for anything other than shopping. I didn't have the heart to tell her about Davy Death's strange habit of wrapping a poly bag around his head whenever it started raining, simply because he didn't have a hood on his jacket.

Together, we managed to get my sister's stuff packed away. It wasn't as tidy as I'd have hoped for, but it was enough to make a sharp exit.

—Why?

Lorna didn't quite understand my question.

I tried again.

—Why *now?*

Lorna slumped down on her couch (a nice leather settee that Mum would have pawned her secret stash of Patsy Cline tapes to buy for herself) and let out the longest sigh in the world. From the outside, she looked like she had everything. The nicest flat, fabulous clothes, expensive jewellery, the trendiest hairstyle...

But she wanted more.

I knew that. I sensed it.

Not only did she want more, she *deserved* more.

—I'm living a life that I didn't want to live.

I said nothing. It wasn't necessary. She'd speak and I'd listen. That was the transaction.

—I'm sick of hiding my bruises. I'm sick of lying to everyone. I'm sick of telling people I tripped up again. I'm sick of feeling sick. Honestly, I feel like shit all the time. The tension...it's fucking horrible. I'm tired. He's never happy and I'm never happy.

With quivering hands, Lorna lit up a cigarette that seemingly came out of nowhere.

—I'm not even allowed to smoke in my own flat. And it's my flat...or...my name's on the lease. All the money I earn goes into Declan's account. I've got nothing when I should have it all. I wanted to go places, Walter. I thought I'd go places.

Just like Mum before she met Fishtank.

Aloud, I joked:

—Papa Docs?

Lorna laughed slightly, but it wasn't enough to push the tears back up into her eyes. They flowed freely, dripping wet glistening droplets. She didn't give a fuck any more. We all knew about Declan, of course. But no-one wanted to say anything. Lorna had always been a firm influence on our mother, a wise and sensible presence that helped us all through the nightmare of having Fishtank for a father. Yet her problem was obvious:

—You've made the same mistakes Mum made.

She looked up at me, took a long drag of her cigarette and then...

Laughed. My sister laughed as though I'd told the funniest joke in the world.

—You're right.

My words seemed to spur her into action. I watched as Lorna got up off the couch and started the process of shifting her bags into the hall. Silently, I helped. Together we must have emptied the flat of nearly everything that belonged to my sister.

Truth be told, it was a bit bare afterwards.

—It's alright for you, she said out of nowhere. —You don't have any worries or cares.

Lorna had no idea. She didn't know. How could she? I'd never said anything about the dead baby. I wanted to tell her, but something stopped me. Something always stopped me.

—I don't have a lot of rubbish either, I said. —God, I wish I had a lot of rubbish.

The reference was lost on my sister, of course. Only Fishtank would have understood.

—Where will you go? I asked.

—Where else? Cumbernauld's Battered Wives Home.

—Aunt Edith's house?

—Yep.

—Say hi to her for me.

—I won't be there for long, she vowed.

Together we got into the lift with the first bundle of luggage. Once inside, we were greeted by a little pensioner with a blue tint in her hair.

—I'm trying to get to Floor 13.

—I hope you find it, I said.

Chapter 40

Escape From Cumbernauld

My first bid for freedom came shortly after sitting my Highers. My exams had kept me busy for months, but in the end I scored some good strong results in English, History, and Computing. Learning from textbooks worked better for me than suffering in a classroom. But it wasn't all good, or easy, during exam time. My Maths result flopped worse than an OAP without Viagra on his honeymoon. I knew it would happen and I wasn't surprised. My brain wasn't equipped to deal with complicated sums. I tried my hardest, but numbers were mysterious unknowable things that refused to work without the help of a calculator.

Everyone seemed happy with my results, and I should have been happy too.

But…

I just couldn't bring myself to feel anything other than deep unhappiness.

I wanted out of Cumbernauld.

No. I *needed* out of Cumbernauld.

There had to be somewhere for me to go, a place to be fabulous and wonderful, where people didn't throw dead babies into a soggy box. The instinct to flee overpowered every thought and idle daydream. Donnie had felt it too at one point, choosing to abandon everything in a hasty move to London. I wasn't brave enough to drop everything and move to a completely different part of the country. Not yet. I had to be pragmatic.

My lifeboat appeared in the form of someone I never expected to see again.

*

It was during a stuffy summer evening in 1997 when my life suddenly changed for the better. Mum came into the living room after an hour of chatting on the phone to someone. Honestly, I hadn't paid any attention. Mum was always on the phone, nattering away with a friend, bitching and moaning about someone at work. In the various jobs she'd worked at over the years, there was always one nasty manipulative person that my mother took an instant dislike to. They became her ultimate enemy, until another one came along. Eventually, I came to understand that my mother needed to fight, she had to have an antagonist to battle against. Goodness knows why she needed that kind of drama in her life, but it *always* happened.

This phone call, however, wasn't about someone at her work. It was about…me.

I'd been in the middle of watching a particularly good episode of *Buffy The Vampire Slayer* on BBC2 when Mum popped her head around the door to ask a question.

—Walter, she said. Could we speak for a few seconds?

—I'm watching Buffy!

—It's important.

—If it's Mr. Boyd, tell him to sod off. I'm leaving soon.

—Mr. Boyd?

—Herr Shitler, my headmaster!

—That tosspot? No, it's not him. Let's talk.

Sighing, I climbed off the couch and followed Mum downstairs to the kitchen. Hopefully, what she wanted to discuss wouldn't take long and I could get back to watching Sarah Michelle Gellar poking vampires with sharp sticks.

A few minutes later, I found myself seated by the kitchen table.

Davy Death was upstairs having a bath and listening to The Cure. Laddie was in his bedroom with some pals, playing a shooting game. No-one could interrupt this talk.

190

—I'm just off the phone to your Granny Frances.

—Granny Fanny! I blurted.

—We don't call her that, okay?

—Is she okay? What's she been up to?

My last memory of my grandmother was watching her be tossed out into the street like garbage by her own son/grandson. It wasn't a nice mental image, but in terms of horrible visions to see whenever I closed my eyes…well, I had far worse to choose from.

—She's been living in a nice little house in Bonnybridge, actually.

—How did she end up in Bonnybridge of all places?

—She used up the rest of her life-savings and bought it.

—I thought she had no money. Wasn't that the reason Fishtank threw her out?

—She's always got money stashed somewhere.

—Why didn't she get in touch with us?

—A few reasons. She didn't know we got shot of Fishtank. She didn't know we'd moved out of Craigieburn Road, and she didn't have our phone number. She's not daft though. I knew she'd find us if she wanted something.

—Fair enough. What did she say?

—She needs help.

The circumstances behind the phone call soon became clear. Someone needed to help Granny Frances, and there was only one person with enough free time to dedicate to her care. I was on the verge of leaving school without a job. I didn't start my journalism degree at The Glasgow College of Building and Printing for another few months. It made sense that I'd be asked to go and help Fishtank's mother/grandmother.

—What sort of help? She can't stay here. Not after last time.

Mum shuddered at a vivid post-traumatic flashback of her hall carpet being shat on while she and Lorna tried to shift a big bag of bones up the stairs. It was all in the eyes. I recognised the indefinably dull expression of horror, because I saw it in the mirror.

—She needs help with little things. Meals. Cleaning. That sort of thing. She's fine using her toilet. She has a snazzy new Stannah Stairlift.

—How modern!

—It would mean going to live with your granny in Bonnybridge for a while.

I stopped. Whatever I had to say didn't matter anymore.

Had I received and understood that correctly?

Did my mother just say I'd need to leave town in order to help granny?

—You'll be there rent free, of course. But you're already used to that, aren't you?

—I'll pay rent when I get a job!

—Helping out your grandmother can be your job.

I would need to be a carer for my grandmother, which sounded good in theory, but I realised I'd be a terrible carer, simply because I struggled to care about anything. Could I actually do it? Mum was determined to make it happen. She probably didn't want the hassle of dealing with her mother-in-law. Who did?

—Come on, son. This is your grandmother.

—Technically, she's my great-grandmother.

Mum struggled to smile. Bless her, she tried but ended up dislodging her false teeth.

—Look, she said snappily after fixing her smile. —Do you want to do it or not?

To escape Cumbernauld was an opportunity too good to pass up. Actually, I'd already decided to do it, if only because I wanted to get out of this little town, the only place I'd ever known. I was only sixteen, yet I felt close to death. Something had to change.

—I'll do it, I said.

—Thank fuck for that! Mum exclaimed. —You'll need to get your stuff into boxes.

That wouldn't be necessary.

I'd never bothered to unpack my boxes from the last time I moved.

Somehow, I knew this day would finally come.

Freedom, at last!

Granny Frances died two days after I arrived in Bonnybridge.

Three days after that, I was forced out of 'her' house by her landlord.

I had no choice but to return home.

Turned out, I wasn't the only one.

Chapter 41

Various Uses For Tin Foil

My bedroom was no longer *my* bedroom.

—Okay, said Mum remorsefully (whilst grilling some cheese on toast for her new lodger). —While you were away, Jake came by and asked if he could stay for a while.

—I was away for a week.

—No-one thought your Granny Frances would die that quickly.

—Less than a week!

—I know. I know. I'm sorry, but what else could I do? He's my son.

—I'm your son!

—Look, Jake's been through a lot. He's out from rehab…

—Did he jump the fence?

—Yes, he did. But that's not the point. He went, he got clean, now he needs my help.

—No-one can help him!

Mum recoiled at the sound of my voice. This was far more emotion than she was used to getting from me. Was it so surprising, though? I couldn't help but feel cheated, like the universe had conspired to fuck me over and give me everything I'd ever wanted, only to snatch it away again. It was like being at a really shit birthday party, playing Pin The Tail On The Donkey, then discovering there was never any donkey and you'd been left holding the ratty tail you didn't want in the first place.

The donkey was freedom. The tail was Cumbernauld.

—He won't be here for long, okay?

—He'd better not be!

—A few more days at the most. Then he'll be away in a flat of his own.

I sniffed the air. It smelled crispy.

—You're burning the toast, I said.

—I'll just scrape it off, said Mum glumly.

Honestly, I could have wept.

The first thing I noticed about my bedroom was the smell. It wasn't there last week, which meant Jake had introduced it while I'd been gone. Fruity, almost *too* sweet, the stink brought about an involuntary gag reflex in me. What made it worse was that Jake had tried to disguise the smell with an entire can of Glade air freshener. Rushing over to my window, I battled against the venetian blinds before finally turning the handle, letting in some clean air. It would probably take a few hours for the stench to shift, or so I thought.

—What has he been doing in my bedroom, I asked myself aloud.

There was also a rather bulky box balanced precariously on piles of MY books.

A box with a screen.

Yes, he'd put a television on top of my books.

A television.

My immediate instinct was to topple the telly onto the carpet, but I reconsidered my course of action (as I always did) and settled for removing my books. Who used books as a substitute for a shelf anyway? My brother, apparently.

But the final change in my bedroom was something downright bizarre, stranger than the smell or the television on top of my books.

There were empty Polo Mint wrappers strewn across my carpet.

A glance into my waste basket immediately revealed piles of

uneaten Polo Mints inside, not just a few little portions, but the entire bin was almost full of them. A few Kit-Kat wrappers too, though not the chocolate. Just the outside paper.

Who the hell buys Polo Mints and doesn't eat them?

The front door to the house opened and Jake announced himself with a bellowing —MUM, I GOT YOU A PACKET OF TWENTY CLUB KING SIZE.

My bedroom was literally adjacent to the front door of the house.

Which meant…

Before I could complete my thought, Jake walked into my room.

His room?

—Hi, I said brightly with a fey wave of my hand.

He looked tired, big dark circles beneath his eyes, skin like a wrecked old handbag. His hair looked greasy and gross. But his teeth were the worst. They were dark and dank, full of uneven gaps, his tongue (an undercooked raw pink) visible in the spaces.

My big brother looked like shit and though I was happy to see this, I also wanted to see it somewhere other than my own bedroom.

—Hey Walter. I'll not be here for long. I'll even sleep on your floor.

—Sleep on the couch, I told him.

—Nah, I'll be here next to you every night.

It didn't escape my attention that the words sounded vaguely threatening.

—You better not interrupt my reading, I said.

—You better not interrupt my wanking, he said.

I screamed so loud that the sound filled the entire house.

Eventually, Mum got involved. She had to, for obvious reasons.

—Who wants some cheese on toast?

Crisis averted. For now.

196

*

Over the next few days there came to be an uneasy truce between my brother and I. What choice did we have? Both of us wanted that room, but we didn't want to piss off the one person who could kick us out into the cold. Mum was determined we get along. It wasn't just Mum, of course. Laddie was delighted to have Jake back in the house, though that was due to a bit of hero worship and the fact Jake could play International Superstar Soccer Pro on the PlayStation. I couldn't even play football in real life, never mind a video game version of it. But Jake enjoyed spending time with Laddie. Playing games kept his mind off whatever was bothering him. And something really had been bothering him. His mood swings gave it away, initially. The long visits to the toilet were another sign something wasn't right. Worse, Jake actually fell asleep playing Mario Kart. Laddie, an avid fan, was horrified to see my brother zoom off the Rainbow Road over and over again. But what could we do? Whenever I complained, people shut down.

I'd become a tedious moany git. I hated myself for it.

Things weren't so bad if I ignored Jake's spontaneous farts, his snoring, the weird sounds he made when he had nightmares (every night), or the gamma ray blue glow of the television set that seemed to last all night long.

Revenge, of sorts, came when I accidentally stood on Jake's face one night. Needing to pee, I swung my legs around, hopped off my bed – and landed on something breathing. Instinctively, Jake's fist shot up, but I leapt away with effortless grace.

A few nights later, Jake got his own back.

We still haven't spoken since that night.

Here's what happened, in the only way I can explain it: I'd trapped myself in my room so Jake couldn't take over. He spent an inordinate amount of time in the bathroom upstairs, apparently eating Polo Mints. It was just weird. The smell from the bathroom was sticky sweet, like rotten fruit. I had no idea what he was up to, which in hindsight was really stupid of me. None of us knew. We simply didn't know enough about addiction. We thought addiction was something that only happened to junkies, not people like us.

Anyway, while Jake was upstairs in the bathroom, I stubbornly remained in my room (and it was MY room), reading until my eyes felt heavy. As a result, I fell asleep early on. But it didn't last. Sleep was a guest in my life and a few hours later (if that), I awoke to find my brother on the floor.

With a girl.

I froze. What could I do? Should I pretend to be asleep?

Lying on my bed (and lying about being asleep) I fake-snored from time to time, just to keep the illusion up that I was in a deep sleep, the sort that never happened to me. Both Jake and the girl made soft animalistic sounds as they had sex on the floor of my bedroom. It got louder, rhythmic, both of them caught up in their not-so-private passion.

While I lay in bed, I remember thinking:

—They'll be at it for hours.

Three minutes later they finished.

—That was great, said the girl.

Her voice. I *knew* it. Suddenly I felt an awful sickness moving through my belly, a sort of physical manifestation of the absolute betrayal I felt in that moment. Fighting off the waves of sickness, I finally calmed down. I lay in the gloom of my bedroom, pretending to be asleep, whilst plotting violent revenge on my enemies, one of whom was my brother.

And the voice giggling on the carpet beside him?

It belonged to Becca.

Chapter 42

Grassbag!

Mum's daily routine made it easy to get her alone. Every morning she did the same thing with the dogged obsessiveness of someone stuck in their ways. She switched on the kettle, opened the patio doors, had a cigarette, drank coffee, ironed her clothes, had a cigarette, ran a bath, did her hair, had a cigarette, then headed for the bus.

She was at the kettle-boiling stage of her morning schedule when I approached her. The scenario I'd planned in my head might not happen in reality, if only because my mother didn't always react the way I expected. She was at the patio doors with a cigarette in her mouth and a key in her hand.

—Good morning, I said quietly.

—What's so good about it? she asked.

—Not much. I've got some bad news for you.

Mum blinked twice, then unlocked the patio door. With all the strength available in her wiry arms (not much but strong enough to hold a catalogue for hours), she managed to heave the large metal frame to the side, sliding the glass door along until it met the edge of the wall. It should have been easier to shift, but we had no WD-40 left. Jake had probably sniffed it all. With the patio door wide open, Mum managed to light up a cigarette despite the cold. As she poked her head outside, a gust of cold, early morning air blew past her.

The frigid air crawled all over me, sharp and sore, turning my breath into a fine mist.

If I'd still been half-asleep, I was fully awake now.

—Right, what's going on?

—I think Jake's on drugs.

When I said it aloud, it made my secret, silent suspicions real.

My brother was on drugs. He'd probably never been off them, of course.

For a second, just a little sliver of time, I actually felt bad for selling Jake out to Mum, telling her that he was still a rampant druggie. But like gas, it passed. I couldn't forget what he'd done to me. It wasn't possible to just erase the previous night, where I'd pretended to be asleep while he had sex with my ex-best friend. I had had to fake snores while Becca faked an orgasm. Never ever had I expected to be in that situation.

The memory made me shudder.

Mum simply assumed it was the cold from the garden

She took a drag on her cigarette, savouring that first-thing-in-the-morning taste.

—You really want him out of your room, don't you?

—It isn't about that, I protested.

—Davy doesn't want him here either.

—I didn't think so.

—Look, I'm not stupid. I know Jake's a bit of a handful…

—A handful? He's a psycho.

—He's your brother.

—And he's on drugs!

—What drugs? He only does speed, Ecstasy and weed.

—He's smoking crack.

—He can't be, said Mum calmly. —I'm not stupid, son. I thought he might be on that shit, but I checked the cupboard. There's plenty of tinfoil. He's not smoking crack.

—Yes, he is. He's filled my bin with Polo mints. Where are the wrappers? Why mints? And Kit-Kats? They're wrapped in foil, that's why. It makes sense, Mum.

She looked unconvinced. I had to admit it seemed a bit stupid.

A packet of Polo mints seemed like an unlikely addition to the drug abuser's kit. But I knew I was right.

Mum eventually headed out of the kitchen through our hallway towards my bedroom. I pulled the patio door over, closing it tight, blocking out the early morning frost. My heart pounded heavy and steady, my stomach responding with the same nervy sickness that I'd felt only a few hours earlier. If this didn't work, I had no doubt Jake would fuck me up.

A few minutes later I heard something being smashed in my bedroom.

—Not my stuff, I wailed.

Really, I should have been more worried about what I'd unleashed on my mother's safety. Maybe, just maybe, I could have worried about my brother too. No, my first thought was my books and my bed. The fear they could be compromised terrified me. I'd worked hard on creating a safe bubble, which had been invaded by my brother and my ex-friend.

Selfish people don't realise they're being selfish. That's why we're selfish.

—Bastard, screamed Mum's voice from inside my bedroom.

—Whaaaaat?

Jake wasn't quite awake yet. His voice sounded sleepy.

Becca screamed. I flinched at the sound.

Something else crashed down on the floor.

I rushed in and found Mum skull-dragging Becca across the carpet. Her hair was a tangled mass within my mother's fingers, twisting and yanking, each time soliciting a scream from my ex-friend. Jake was fully awake. He knew exactly who was to blame for this:

—This is all your fault, he shouted.

Upstairs, I heard Davy Death moving around.

—Get the fuck out of here, screamed Mum.

She released Becca and hurled her in my direction, which was unfortunate because I didn't want to catch her. She fell forward, crying. And I felt for her, I really did. But she was collateral damage in the secret battle between me and my brother over my bedroom.

Becca opened her mouth to say something cutting and oh-so-witty.

She didn't get the chance.

—Go, I snarled.

Becca picked her things up and left.

The front door slammed shut a few seconds later.

At least I'd discovered the identity of her secret boyfriend.

Mum's voice brought me back to the situation in my bedroom, the one I'd caused to happen. She was screaming at Jake, loud enough for our neighbours to hear. Not that she cared. Her anger needed a place to go and her oldest son was its destination.

—What's this? FUCKING POLO MINTS!

Mum kicked my wastebasket over and hundreds of little hard mints rolled out, covering my carpet in even more mess. I winced. My revenge had spiralled into a proper brawl. Jake looked at me with unrestrained fury, probably thinking how good it would feel to kick my arse with his Adidas. Mum, meanwhile, was busy kicking his arse with her slippers.

—Have you been smoking crack?

—Aye. So fuck?

Mum responded by bouncing the basket off my brother's head.

—I want you out of my house. I mean it. Get the fuck out.

—I've got nowhere to go!

—Go and stay with that little tart you snuck in here last night.

Mum stormed by me, but had a final parting shot before the matter was ended:

—You've got your room back. Are you happy?

I couldn't answer that question because I honestly didn't know.

Chapter 43

Flatmates In My Fantasy Flat

In a bid to stop Declan finding her, Lorna kept the location of her new flat secret. In fact, it was so secret I didn't actually know where she lived for a good few months. She popped over for the Wedgeworth New Year Party which I always tried my hardest to avoid. The festivities were too noisy and everyone got smashed on Davy Death's homebrew, which smelled like burned socks. For a while I thought Lorna was ignoring me after what happened to Jake, that she held me responsible for getting him evicted. But my worries disappeared one night when Donnie phoned me. I was in my bedroom watching repeats of *This Life*, the best thing on television, when the house phone started ringing. Wearing an ugly tracksuit, I answered the phone, grateful that no-one could see me. Cool Britannia what? The tracksuit had been another birthday present from my mother, but I hadn't worn it outside the house despite vague promises. It wasn't just a tracksuit to me, it was tangible evidence that my own mother didn't know me. When had I ever gone out dressed in a tracksuit? Really, she might as well have bought me a football and a line of coke too.

Donnie, however, understood me. She would never have bought me a tracksuit.

—Hey Walter. Listen, I'm back in Cumbernauld staying at Lorna's new flat...

As she spoke, I came to realise that this call was special for two reasons:

Firstly, she told me she was living with Lorna in her secret flat.

Secondly, she wanted me to know she had a fancy new gadget.

—I'm talking to you on my new mobile phone.

—A mobile phone?

—It's great, isn't it? A state of the art, top of the range, business bitch phone.

—So, you and your new mobile phone have moved in with Lorna?

—Yeah. I've split up with my girlfriend.

—That's a shame, I said sympathetically.

—Also, I think men from London are after me.

—Men from London?

—Yeah, I stole their money. Remember?

—I thought you embezzled it from that company you were working for?

—Walter. You're the smartest person I know, but you're thick as shit about some stuff too. The company was a front. I snuck in through the back. Then I treated myself to their cash.

—Is the cash untraceable?

—I wouldn't have taken it otherwise.

—GOOD.

—Anyway, I thought they were up in Glasgow looking for me, so I ditched my flat and came back to Cumbernauld. I'm hiding out with my sis. I mean, we've both broken up with our not-so-better halves. It makes sense, don't it?

—You could go anywhere and you've chosen this dump. You're mad.

The bitterness in my voice was difficult to mask, but if Donnie picked up on it, she didn't say anything. In hindsight, I was glad. I hated explaining my feelings to people. Before I gave Donnie an opportunity to say anything else, I gently changed the subject.

—You're in Lorna's new flat? What's it like?

—It's fantastic. Honestly, it's really nice.

—Where is it anyway?

—It's in Hillcrest.

—Not the pensioner flats, I gasped jealously.

—Yes! The very ones.

I'd always wanted to live in one of those wonderful pensioner flats in Hillcrest. Pensioners always had nice gardens, the sort with quaint little wooden benches, fences painted with preservative and colourful little gnomes dotted around the locale. I knew I'd make a great resident in Hillcrest. Oh, I'd water my plants and listen to *The Archers*. I'd mow the lawn and boil pasta in nice little ceramic pots. I'd drink Earl Grey tea and have Wimbledon playing in the background, even if I didn't understand the rules AT ALL.

—Can I come and see you?

Donnie laughed down the phone. It sounded nice.

—Why else do you think I've phoned you?

I found myself grinning madly, a grin soon wiped off my face when Donnie added:

—But make sure no-one follows you.

It was the worst possible thing anyone could say to a neurotic like me. My sister probably wanted to freak me out for a laugh. As a parting gift, she gave me the house number and disconnected the call or whatever mobile phones did when the conversation was over.

It was 1998.

I was still trapped in Cumbernauld.

It was a rare sunny day when I headed over to Hillcrest Road to view Lorna's new flat. Actually, I was excited to see it. As I pounded the cracked pavement in my Docs, I contemplated all the lovely colours Lorna could paint the walls of her new flat. I fell into a sort of trance, deeply lost in a vision of fuchsia paint being applied to fresh white walls.

Daydreams were always better than real life.

My legs, however, were independent of my brain and they took me in the opposite direction from Hillcrest, moving me somewhere else.

Somewhere I hadn't been in years.

In the end, the power of the past was too strong to resist. Before I knew it, I found myself standing in the shadow of a cluster of apartment blocks in Sandyknowes Road, beyond which I'd found Baby C's corpse over six years ago. Six years had passed. Six whole years where everything had changed, yet I was still being smothered, locked in limbo.

This town was slowly grinding me down.

Why had I come back?

What was the universe trying to tell me?

Sometimes, I wondered if I'd done the right thing in keeping it all to myself.

It wasn't as though I did the wrong thing. I told the police, didn't I?

Cautiously, I moved down a path that connected to the spread of trees I'd fled to after Gary Dowds and his friends came after me. I snorted disdainfully at the thought of ever being afraid of that loser. He should have been afraid of me, really. Thinking of Gary made me recall more details about Langland's Primary School. People and places I hadn't thought about in years: Mrs. Robertson, the common room, Poppy, Moo and Billy The Squid.

I even thought about Fishtank again.

The forest behind the flats was just a few more steps ahead of me.

But I couldn't go through with it.

I'd seen what that place had to offer and it wasn't for me.

Once again, I turned and walked away from my past.

Fifteen minutes later I reached Lorna's secret flat in Hillcrest Road.

Lorna was sitting outside in her little garden with a cigarette in her mouth.

She reminded me of someone.

Who, though?

The answer came in a flash of recognition.

—Hello Mum, I said.

—Piss off, snapped Lorna in return.

Suddenly I felt sorry for the poor pensioners in the nearby houses.

—How did you get this place?

—I secretly stuck my name on the council house register a while back. This place came up at the right time. Declan isn't going to look for me in a street full of mouldy oldies.

—Where's Donnie?

—She's in the living room on her daft phone.

—I've got to use it. Just once.

—But Walter, who would you phone?

Ah. There was no-one.

—Bugger, I said.

Lorna looked so sorry for me that she got up and went into the kitchen to do the one thing she knew would cheer me up. She wasn't gone long when I heard the best sound in the whole world: the bubbling of boiling water in a kettle.

Despite not yet being invited, I headed into the flat and looked around.

Donnie was in the living room dressed in denim dungarees, the worst outfit ever, nearly as bad as my ghastly birthday tracksuit. I would have told her to never wear dungarees ever again, but she was too busy shouting at someone on her little phone. I managed to get a look at it up close: it was small, of course. Metallic blue with transparent plastic wrapped around it and Motorola's ubiquitous logo at the top.

Suddenly aware of me, Donnie paused and covered the phone with her spare hand.

—Walter, you've got a bank account. Haven't you?

—Yes?

—Good.

Then she went back to her conversation. Apparently, it was her ex-girlfriend.

—Why do you need to know if I've got a bank account? I asked.

—I'll get back to you on that one.

—Donnie, I started. —I'm not letting you use my bank account.

She looked offended, which really was rather galling.

—Do you think I'm going to rob you or something?

—The eighty quid a week you'll get from the Job Centre when you leave school will really go far, cackled Lorna.

Finally, Donnie returned to shouting into her hand about whatever it was lesbians shouted about during breakups. There was nothing else I could say or do until the fight was finished, so I headed into the kitchen and drank tea with Lorna on her fancy backless wooden stools. We talked about everything from Tony Blair's creepy smile to whether or not Princess Diana had faked her death, before our conversation finally settled on something we both had in common. Weirdly, it was our shared hatred of Cilla Black. Actually, I didn't mind Cilla…but Lorna despised her intensely for the silliest of reasons. In fact, she couldn't make her mind up *why* she hated her. It changed on a weekly basis. Sometimes it was Cilla's voice that enraged Lorna (—Bitch sounds like a cat being castrated), other times it was the way she dressed (—Spam dressed as glam), but I always suspected the real reason my eldest sister loathed Cilla Black was because of her hair colour. As a child, Lorna had bright ginger hair. Now I'm no psychologist, but I suspect Lorna hated in Cilla the qualities she hated in herself, namely her bright orange hair. I nearly put this to her, but decided it wasn't worth being hurled out of her lovely new pensioner flat.

—She wouldn't rob you, said Lorna abruptly.

She'd overheard my conversation with Donnie, but didn't quite understand it.

—I know she wouldn't.

—Donnie's many things, but she isn't a thief.

Lorna had no idea what her little sister had been up to down in London.

Luckily, I was good at keeping secrets.

I was also very good at making unwanted suggestions.

—Have you ever considered painting your flat fuchsia?

Chapter 44

New Labour, New Deal

My final day at school felt like every other day at school. Long and uneventful. I felt nothing as I walked away for the last time. I knew exactly where I was going. I'd already sent off an application to study journalism at The Glasgow College of Building and Printing. Journalism seemed like a good fit for me. Okay, it wasn't a degree, just an HND, but if I demonstrated an aptitude for the work, I could finish off the degree at Napier University. It didn't take long for my application to be accepted, which was brilliant for my ego. I was still at the point where I could be anything I wanted. Dreams have a way of disappearing after school, when you realise you can't be a popstar or a lawyer, but being accepted into college meant I could still be a journalist.

I had a few months to muddle through before I enrolled.

Until then, I had no job and no money.

Mum insisted I get out and sign on.

My first visit to the Job Centre was depressing and impersonal. The smiles on the faces of the staff never reached their eyes, something I noticed very quickly. I'd always despised phoniness and the Job Centre was full of phony people on phones. Stands dotted around the room had cards on them, little squares with information about new jobs. I didn't really need a job yet. My plan was to wait it out for a few months until college started. As far as I was concerned, this was a realistic option. Every Wednesday I put myself through the humiliation of signing on. Every Wednesday I lied about my job search. I sabotaged every attempt at getting employment. My interview for a part-time checkout assistant in Tesco was a disaster after I told them I shopped in Asda.

For months I signed on every second Wednesday.

I learned to hate Wednesdays.

I nearly managed to get away with it.

Months passed by. I signed on. I got my money. I didn't get a job.

Then one Wednesday I was summoned to speak to someone about my lack of progress.

In their infinite wisdom, the Job Centre had assigned a career advisor to help me out.

—So what would you like to do?

My career advisor didn't look at all interested in the answer to her question, but I decided to humour her. After all, she was only doing her job. Apparently, she was new to it as well. At least, I hadn't seen her before that day, the last day I signed on at the Job Centre.

—I'm going to start college soon. I'm training to be a journalist.

—Oh, you like writing?

—I'd like to be a famous writer, I said.

—A famous writer?

—Well, I'd rather sign autographs than sign on.

She didn't laugh. Sheepishly, I retreated into silence. What a bitch!

—I can't see writing jobs, she said whilst looking at her very large computer screen.

Her name badge identified her as SUSAN. The badge was green, like her makeup. She also had the start of a monobrow, but I did my best to keep quiet about it.

—What other jobs can you find for me?

Susan looked again, but I could tell from her facial expression that she didn't have anything for me. The more she looked at the screen, the more I looked at her forehead. That monobrow had started to affect me on a really deep level that couldn't be consciously explained. Why did I dislike it so much? It was just a thick eyebrow, wasn't it?

—Can you drive?

—No.

—Okay. Do you have experience in washing windows?

—No, but I like to dust skirting boards. I have really clean skirting boards.

—Okay. How about a job washing dishes at Dullatur Golf Course?

—That sounds easy!

—It should be within your qualifications.

The way she said those words made me want to shave off her monobrow with the rustiest razor I could find.

—I'll arrange an interview for the job. You should hear something soon.

—What? A job interview? For washing dishes?

—Lots of people are after that job.

—Oh.

Susan tip-tap-tippity-tapped the keys on her keyboard. The way she typed wasn't right; her forefinger was on the wrong button, for a start. Also, her thumbs should have remained rested on the space bar. I'd always been good at typing, having enjoyed using the keyboards at school during lessons. That was about the only thing about school that I'd enjoyed.

—I'm a good typist, I told Susan.

She didn't care.

—Do you play any instruments?

I thought about it, wondering why she'd asked such a strange question. Was it a trick to catch me out? Would my answer determine how much money I received from the state? It didn't take long for me to realise what might be happening.

There had been a news story on *BBC News At Six* about a brand-new initiative from Tony Blair called New Deal. It was a special grant that paid for musicians to buy instruments and book studio time. New Labour, New Ways To Waste Money.

Why else would a career advisor ask such a specific question?

—Yes, I said boldly. —I'm gifted with substantial musical talent.

—What instrument do you play?

—I'm a multi-instrumentalist.

That sounded terribly impressive, or it would have to anyone else other than Susan.

—Okay. I play guitar, bass, glockenspiel, and the spoons.

It was all lies, of course. I couldn't play an instrument if the ghost of John Lennon himself took control of my body for a Beatles reunion at T In The Park.

—Honestly, I play all those instruments in my band.

—Oh, said Susan with a crafty grin. —And what's the name of your band?

I froze. Nothing came to mind. My brain was blank. Shit.

Thankfully, I improvised a story out of nowhere.

—I'm in a punk band called Savage Wank. We've got lots of albums and I tour quite a lot. Really, we're better than the name suggests. Except for the third album. That sucks.

This was all meant to impress Susan into signing off a fat New Deal grant for me.

Tony Blair was about to empty his pockets right into my hands.

But instead of impressing Susan, she looked…confused.

It didn't take long for me to realise something wasn't right.

—You aren't the lead singer of Savage Wank, she said with a furrowed forehead.

—Yes, I am.

—No, you are not. I saw them live back in '82 at Paisley Town Hall.

And just like that, any chance I had of scoring some extra money, courtesy of Tony Blair's New Deal fund, went the same way as Babylon Zoo, Menswe@r, and Gay Dad. As for the dishwashing job, I actually applied for it. I spent hours working on my personal statement, carefully crafting each word on the form, explaining in detail why I was the best person to soap their plates and clean their cutlery.

They said I lacked the proper qualifications.

I didn't get the job.

Chapter 45

Death At A Party

Jake committed his first murder on a night out with some friends. This might have been surprising for some people, the sort who only knew his appealing face and slick patter, but for me this murder was the logical conclusion to my brother's erratic behaviour. He'd started off with armed robbery, graduated onto poisoning little kids, until finally...murder.

The only thing that surprised me was that it hadn't happened sooner.

Mum and Davy got everyone together in one room, something that usually only happened at Christmas. Lorna. Donnie. Laddie. Me. We sat in the living room, waiting anxiously for someone to tell us what was going on. I knew it was about Jake, simply because he wasn't with us. My hands felt dirty, but I couldn't go and wash them.

Family gatherings always made me nervous. There was too much that could go wrong, too many accusations, fights, and flashbacks to all the horrible events of our lives.

Davy seemed pensive. That's how I knew something was wrong. Not just wrong. Terminally serious. Mum, meanwhile, looked as worried as I felt. She was seated on the main chair over by the TV. I sometimes curled up on that chair to read books, because that spot in our living room always caught the sunlight until the very last ray went away. She had a cigarette drooping between her lips. It looked like she'd forgotten to light it.

—What's happening, Mum?

Lorna had fallen neatly into her traditional role as the sensible

215

eldest sister, the one who asked the sensible questions. She'd already come to the same conclusion I'd reached when Mum started talking: whatever was happening had something to do with Jake. He wasn't with us. That meant he was the topic of this spur-of-the-moment meeting. But what had he done this time? Did I even want to know?

Noticing the cigarette in her mouth hadn't been lit, Mum removed it and said:

—He's up at the police station. He's been there since last night.

—Okay. Is it bad?

—Very.

Donnie interjected with the question I wanted answered:

—What did he do this time?

We weren't even pretending Jake was innocent of whatever crime he'd been arrested for. Why bother? Thinking back on that day, that is what I remember most clearly: all of us knew before we actually knew. Mum, however, seemed to take exception to Donnie's tone, the way she often did. Had Lorna asked the same question, it probably would have been met with the opposite reaction.

—Yesterday it was Grievous Bodily Harm.

—Yesterday?

—My favourite Beatles song, I added with a smirk.

Actually, my favourite Beatles song was (and still is) *Paperback Writer*.

My family didn't reply to my ill-timed joke because they didn't care.

—Yesterday. It happened at a party. He got into a fight over football. The boy he battered died in hospital this morning. Jake's being charged with murder now. He called me from the station. I went to see him and he told me he didn't do it.

She paused, took a breath, and then said:

—He's pleading his innocence.

216

Donnie's eyes caught mine.

They carried a message.

I understood it perfectly.

—You…think he's innocent? I asked sceptically.

—Oh, I *know* he's guilty, snapped Mum.

—What actually happened?

Donnie still wanted to know the finer details.

—I've *told* you! He was at a party…

—Mum, there's no point in shouting at me. Just take a deep breath and tell us the full story. What happened after the fight?

She wasn't happy about it, but Mum eventually explained what occurred after the fight.

—Most of the witnesses are already denying being at the party, but the guy Jake battered was there with his brother. And he was there with his girlfriend. They aren't backing down this time. Jake's terrified he'll go to jail. All this over a football strip!

I had to know what happened. I *always* had to know what happened.

—What did he do to the poor lad?

—He hit him from behind, fractured his skull. Then ran off with the weapon.

Mum puffed on her cigarette again, sucking it dry until there was a little stub in her fingers. She looked tired.

—Where did Jake stash the weapon? Donnie asked.

—He left it in our bin, Davy said bitterly.

That was the only time he spoke up during the entire meeting. My heart sank for the poor man.

—It's a metal walking stick, continued Mum.

—Jake had a walking stick?

—Yes, explained Lorna. —It's a crutch, you know, one of those NHS ones they give to people who break an ankle. He took it with him to the Job Centre whenever he wanted to claim disability allowance. Lots of people have benefit sticks.

My jaw dropped in disbelief. I couldn't even fake my way into getting extra money from the New Deal fund, yet my brother literally faked disability to snatch more cash. Life was terribly unfair. For that reason, I felt (and battled against) a surge of unreasonable jealousy.

—Yes, he left his bent crutch in our bin.

—Bent?

—He hit that lad so hard it bent the stick in half.

I gasped. It was too horrible to contemplate. Did that boy look up and see Jake holding the crutch over his head? Was that the last sight his eyes caught before everything went dark? Who was he? Why did he need to die? He had family. He was someone's son. But unlike Baby C, he'd been given a chance to live and grow. Until he met my brother.

—Where did you hide the stick? Donnie asked.

Mum laughed in her daughter's face.

—Hide it? Don't be daft. I didn't hide it.

She lit up another cigarette and savoured the flavour.

—I took it to the police right away, she said.

Chapter 46

Walter Wedgeworth Gets A Job

Everything seemed to improve after Jake went to prison. Not that he was responsible for all the problems in my life. In fact, I barely saw him after Mum threw him out again. I didn't even attend his trial, not after what happened last time. But the fact remains that things got better in his absence. College plodded along nicely, the coursework well within my capabilities. I met some new friends there too. Not real friends, just college friends. There was never any desire on my part to get close to anyone.

People always disappoint me in the end.

Thankfully, I also got a job at Cumbernauld Central Library and the chance to get some cash. I'd seen a poster advertising a Saturday job there and my heart soared at the prospect of working in the place I considered my real home. So I contacted them via the phone number on the poster, gave out my details (despite Mum telling me to make sure no-one knew where we lived in case the catalogue man found us) and waited.

And waited.

And waited a little more.

Eventually, one Tuesday night, I received a phone call from North Lanarkshire Council. At first Mum thought they were trying to get her to pay some Council Tax, but I assured her the call was for me. She handed the receiver over to me.

—Walter? A voice said from the other end.

—Hello, I gasped.

—I'm Morag, the librarian at Cumbernauld Library.

—I'm Walter Wedgeworth, I've read a lot of books in your library.

—Oh I know. I've seen you. We've all seen you.

—Is...that a good thing?

—Absolutely. You're a loyal borrower. Anyway, I'd like to offer you a Saturday job.

—Really?

—Yes. Can you start this Saturday?

—You bet! I would probably be there anyway.

—Okay, I'll see you on Saturday. Have a nice week, Walter.

—You too, Morag!

Once I was sure she'd put the telephone down at her end, I allowed myself a little squeal of joy. In fact, I did a little dance in the hallway of my house where the phone sat on a ledge connected to the wall. I wasn't just a college student. I worked in a library. Not just any library, but *my* library, the one that had offered me a place to go when I needed to escape from the world.

Life was finally working on my behalf.

Sadly, my good fortune didn't last long.

As I said: people always disappoint me in the end.

Sometimes, I disappoint myself.

My first day working in the library ended in a disciplinary when staff complained about the number of times I left my workstation to wash my hands. In my defence, I had no idea customers could be so dirty. They returned hardbacks with torn pages (—That's how I mark my place), paperbacks stinking of cigarette smoke (—Everybody does it), and video tapes with blood on them (—I cut myself making my husband's lunch). My skin wouldn't let me stick around. But soap didn't seem to shift the filth I felt all over me.

Eventually, I was called in to the librarian's office.

Morag wasn't what I expected from a librarian. She was young, for a start. Cool, even. She dressed in a leather skirt and knee-high leather boots. Her hair was done in the elegantly choppy style that Jennifer Aniston had made famous. Morag also wore an array of stylish spectacles that seemed to change daily. As I entered her office, I observed her wearing a pair of large NHS spectacles, the sort Morrissey might have worn in the 80s.

—Sit down, Walter.

—Thanks, I mumbled.

This couldn't be good. I knew it. I *sensed* it.

—I've been hearing from staff that you keep leaving the counter. Normally that's fine. If you need water or a cuppa, I'm fine with that. As long as the work gets done. But you keep going away. I don't want my staff to think I've hired the wrong person for the job.

Morag smiled. It was a nice, genuine smile.

I tried imitating it, but the feelings weren't there.

Even faking happiness seemed difficult.

—Where do you keep going during your shift?

My first instinct was to lie, because the truth was too ridiculous.

However, I ended up being honest.

—I wash my hands. A lot.

—You wash your hands?

—I can't help it.

Morag actually seemed sympathetic.

—Sometimes borrowers return our items in a state. It's not nice, but it happens.

—Physical contact makes my skin feel weird. Not nice.

—Oh Walter, I'm sorry.

—I don't need sympathy, I said, surprised.

What was I supposed to say? How could I explain I hadn't been the same since I pushed my hand through the mouldy fold of a sodden cardboard box in the pouring rain, touched the slick skin of a rotting corpse, a dead baby buried half-heartedly in the muck. More than that, I had years of bullshit

221

in my brain. Fights, abuse, violence, manipulation...and that was just dinner time at my house. My childhood was fat I couldn't burn off. With everything that had happened, was it really so surprising I wasn't quite normal.

Morag, bless her, had a theory of her own.

—You might have Obsessive Compulsive Disorder.

Finally, a name for my problem.

—We have books in the Psychology section about it. I could get you a few, if you like.

What else could I do other than accept her offer?

—Good. Now try and keep it under control. I don't want this to affect your work.

—Thank you, I said.

Leaving Morag's office, I headed out into the main library.

I approached the Psychology shelf...

Then walked right past so I could go wash my hands.

The Kopper Kettle

Donnie met me in The Kopper Kettle in Cumbernauld Shopping Centre. It was a nice enough café except (if I believed my sister) one of the waitresses had a severe case of Hep C and the hamburgers looked like something that had been fished out of a toilet and pressed into a patty. Luckily, I was in the midst of another vegetarian phase and only wanted chips. Donnie offered to pay for my meal, which should have alerted me to the fact she needed a favour from me.

I immediately told her I wasn't going to visit Fishtank again. She understood. Of course she did.

—I wouldn't visit that wanker if he went to the hospice and needed grapes.

Grapes? Don't make me laugh. Fishtank was the sort of person that thought a Muller's Fruit Corner counted as part of his five-a-day.

—You look good, I said politely as my sister caught my eye and smiled. It wasn't a hollow compliment. Donnie's face was framed by a large crown of frizzy peroxide blonde hair, the roots an inky black. It created a clash of colour that my sister liked on herself. She wore an expensive denim jacket, the sort that sat easy with everything she wore. I had no doubt her jeans and fancy designer shoes were likewise expensive. Though I wasn't as expensive, I still tried to look exciting, using my body as a billboard for brightly coloured clothes and incompatible palettes. If Donnie liked my clothes, I felt bright and happy.

—Here's your chips, said the waitress as she placed a bowl on the table.

The fact my sister had ordered a cheeseburger didn't stop her fishing for chips.

—Okay. I need a favour.

Well I hadn't seen THAT twist coming my way.

—I'm shocked, startled, and astonished.

My sister sniggered.

—Oh, you're sarky today.

I popped a chip into my mouth and smiled with chubby food-filled cheeks.

Donnie finally got to the crux of our lunchtime meet-up.

—I've got to transfer money out of my bank account.

—And you want to use mine?

—It's only for a while.

—I don't want to be involved in your shenanigans and nonsense.

Donnie gave me a pained expression and I let the matter drop. Her approval meant everything to me and her disdain was catastrophic to my self-esteem. Honestly, I felt like shit whenever we fought. The last time she'd asked about my bank account, I'd lashed out and all but accused her of trying to steal from me. I knew she'd never do that, but when Donnie was up to something, I felt...apprehensive. My worry was that she might make a mistake and pull everyone into the hole she'd blown in the ground.

Sighing dramatically, Donnie cut her burger into tiny pieces. A habit she'd had from the days of eating dinner in front of Fishtank. I waited for her to say something.

—Do you know what your problem is, Walter?

—I don't have any problems.

—That's your problem.

—What *are* you going on about?

—You're always trying to avoid everything. You're outside staring in, watching everything around you, waiting from a safe distance until you're ready to do something. You always have a barrier up between yourself and everyone else. Even me, sometimes.

I said nothing. What could I say? She was right. I wasn't living the life everyone else lived. I'd already come to the conclusion that life…a real normal life…wasn't for me. But there was no map for people like me. Everyone my age would grow older, marry someone they loved, start a family, pay a mortgage, go into arrears with their council tax, go on holidays abroad, fight, fuck, love, lie, and leave their mark on the world. Me? I wasn't going to marry. I wasn't going to be with anyone. I didn't feel that fire in me, that push or pull towards love and the life it brought. I was alone, even in a room full of people. But I wasn't sure what to do with this knowledge. It was something I thought about often. If you didn't have sex, marry, start a family…did you actually matter? I had a terrible fear of being trapped in a sort of perpetual adolescence, a piece of me frozen forever in place because of my asexuality. My entire existence seemed to defy convention and sometimes I was very proud of that, but other times I didn't know how to accept it.

Despite feeling out of sync with the world around me, there were occasions when I felt like things weren't so bad, that life could be nice and normal. Spending time with Donnie, laughing at the drama in her life. Watching old TV shows with Davy Death, talking into the early hours of the morning. Reading books where I could be other people, experience their lives through letters, words, and sentences.

But it never lasted and I always found myself alone with myself.

Donnie ate a little more of her burger, then paused for what I thought would be a moment of introspection. But she went and ruined everything by saying the wrong thing.

—Things get better when you come out of the closet.

—What?

—It's okay to be gay.

When I shot back, my voice came out a little bit too loud.

—I'm not in the bloody closet. You don't understand a thing about me!

Donnie reacted by raising her voice to a similar pitch as mine. She wasn't the sort of person to let anyone shout at her, not even her brother.

—Then tell me!

People in the café tried to look like they weren't staring, but they couldn't help themselves. There was something unfolding before their eyes and they didn't want to miss a single moment of it. I would have been the same, to be fair.

In this place, I tried to explain myself.

But I couldn't.

Instead, I handed over my bank details on a piece of paper from a notepad I always carried. It was used for college. I'd been learning Teeline Shorthand for all the future front-page headlines I intended to write. It wasn't what Donnie expected to happen, but she'd set in motion something between us that had to be resolved. She'd wanted to hear me out. Listen to what I had to say. In the end, that mattered. That, and our history together.

—Ta, said my sister as she took the scrap of paper.

I decided to tell her the truth, if only so she understood *something* about me.

—It's true, I have something to tell you.

—Oh, said my sister with a big wide grin. —This sounds exciting!

—It's not what you think, but I want to tell you anyway.

—Is it about Fishtank? What he did to us?

—No, it's about Baby C.

Donnie frowned. I could see her rifling through her memory to recall why 'Baby C' sounded so familiar. Eventually, she remembered. Her expression changed quickly.

—The baby in the box? The one down in Sandyknowes Road? But didn't that happen years and years ago?

—Not that long. Not really.

Actually, it felt like another lifetime, but only six years had passed. Nearly seven.

—Okay, said Donnie. —I remember Baby C. What about it?

—*Him*, I swiftly corrected.

—Sorry. What about him?

—Do you remember anything else about Baby C?

—Not much. I was too busy getting high at raves. I think he was found behind some flats, wasn't he? Someone phoned in an anonymous tip that led the police to his body.

—Yes. That was me.

Donnie didn't quite grasp what I was trying to tell her. I tried again.

—I found the body and phoned the police.

—Are you for real?

—Yes.

—Sandyknowes Road is full of crackheads. What were you doing there by yourself?

—Crackheads? Our brother's a crackhead and he's cracked a few heads too.

Donnie made a face that said everything I needed to know on the matter of Jake's habit. Immediately, I regretted mentioning Jake. Back on topic, I continued.

—It was a baby. A dead baby. In a box. I didn't know what to do, Donnie. In the end, I called the police. Obviously, I didn't give them my name. But it was me. I found him.

—Fucking hell!

Another voice cut into the conversation.

—Did you enjoy your meal?

We both looked around as the waitress sauntered past, her arms full of plates and cutlery. Neither of us answered and the wait for a compliment became unbearable. Within seconds, the poor waitress had moved to the counter at the back of the café.

—You found a dead baby. And you didn't tell us?

—I didn't tell anyone, I said.

—Oh my God. That's why you're always washing your hands.

—Excuse me?

—You've got a thing about washing your hands. It's about control, isn't it? Or maybe you're trying to wash away…

I immediately cut her off.

—Don't you *dare* psychoanalyse me.

—I didn't meant to come across like I'm your psychiatrist or something.

—I should never have told you!

—Look, I'm glad you did. It explains a lot.

Raging, I jumped up with such force that my chair fell over. My pinstriped suit jacket was speedily flung around my shoulders. Then I spun and made for the main door. Donnie didn't try to stop me, having already got my bank details.

As I put my hand on the door to shove it open, I heard my sister's voice.

She sounded amused.

—Thank you for helping me out, Walter. I mean it. Thanks.

Tutting, I stormed off and left my sister behind in The Kopper Kettle.

Four days later, she was dead.

Chapter 48

Things Can Only Get Worse

When I first heard the news of my sister's death, I assumed the men from London had managed to track her down, make her suffer for stealing their money. It seemed like a logical sequence of events to me. When Mum first heard the news, she reacted not with a scream, that would have been too dramatic, but with a little cry of pain. Her youngest daughter was gone. We were all lost. Apparently, Jake reacted to the news with violence, punching the warden of HMS Barlinnie. He was sent to solitary, or so I was told.

I didn't know how to react.

Even with the death of my sister, I struggled to react the way others around me reacted.

I didn't cry. I couldn't. I tried, honestly, I did.

Lorna wept. Laddie wailed.

Instead, I dug out some old boxes and found something that made me happy.

A stack of old Nancy Drew mystery novels.

I hadn't read them in years, having moved onto Agatha Christie.

In the days and nights that followed my sister's death, I retreated to the town of River Heights where bad things were kept at bay by a girl detective with a rich dad.

We had to wait for the post-mortem to be carried out. Rumours had already spread across town, various iterations of the story told and retold, evolving, mutating, taking on new twists and turns. Donnie had been taken out by a hitman. She'd committed suicide because her girlfriend broke up with her. It was drugs. It was depression. It was food poisoning at The Kopper Kettle. It was whatever the story needed it to be, which was everything but what actually happened. Everything but the truth itself.

We had to wait for that.

It felt like forever.

A week after Donnie's death, we all gathered at the house for the results of the post mortem, which came via a phone call. Laddie sat by Lorna, his hand in her hand. Jake wasn't with us, being some distance away in a cell. I sat alone because there was no-one to sit with me.

Eventually, Davy leaned over from behind the chair and whispered:

—This is bad, Walter. It won't get worse than this.

—It always gets worse, I said flatly.

Davy didn't reply. What else could he say? For us, it was true.

Mum entered the living room, where we were all seated. She looked shell-shocked. Oh, she'd looked that way since we were informed about Donnie's sudden death, but now she looked completely out of it. She was so stunned that she'd forgotten to light up a cigarette.

—She died from heart failure, said Mum.

—Heart failure?

Lorna could scarcely believe it.

—At Donnie's age?

—Her name was Danielle, corrected Mum.

—Her name was Donnie! I said, correcting her correction.

It turned out that my sister had been born with an irregular heartbeat. Undiagnosed, it was only a matter of time until something went wrong. An arrythmia, said Mum. That was the medical term for Donnie's condition. Worse, it looked like it could be hereditary.

—Do you have this on your side of the family? I asked Mum.

—No. But your dad's mother died from heart failure giving birth to him.

The arrythmia had come from Fishtank's side of the family.

He'd finally got his revenge.

There's a period when someone dies in which nothing really changes when in fact *everything* has changed. That's what I felt in the days following Donnie's death. The period between her death and her cremation was filled with routine. I threw myself into monotony, embraced the little necessities of daily life. What else could I do? My only option was to do what was right for me. Crying with my family wouldn't help. Talking about it served no purpose. Fixating on the how and why of my sister's death wouldn't make the situation better. All I could do was wait and let time take it all away.

Mum organised the funeral.

I wore my best suit, a shiny metallic two-piece.

We all shared the same car, except for Jake who wasn't allowed to attend the service.

Apparently, he'd shanked someone in prison for stealing one of his cigarettes.

The service took place on 16th February 1999. Yet another date I'll never forget.

I had to help carry the coffin down to the hatch where a firestorm would turn my sister's body into ash. When I realised what was happening, I reacted in horror. It was probably the strongest emotion I'd displayed during the entire ordeal.

—You didn't ask me! I hissed when Mum explained the procedure.

—I just assumed you'd want to send your sister off.

—Please, I whispered. —Please don't make me touch that box.

Mum looked at me with vacant eyes.

—It isn't a box. It's a coffin.

Later, after we watched my sister go into the fire, I had a strange notion that perhaps Fishtank would come to see his daughter one last time. He was a horrible bastard, but he was still her father. Surely he'd want to be at her funeral.

But he wasn't.

What sort of father didn't attend his own daughter's funeral?

Scumbag.

The service was over and we all exited the crematorium to a light sunny day. I filled my lungs with heavy gulps of fresh air. It felt good. We were all heading to our cars again, so we could go to The Legion in Cumbernauld where my sister's wake was to be held.

As we walked, I looked back. The crematorium was filling up with crowds of people.

My initial assumption was that they'd come to pay tribute to my sister.

But I was wrong. They were there for someone else. A loved one.

Death was a business. It had a timetable.

I bunched my hands into fists, ready to fight off the urge to scrub them red raw.

Chapter 49

Tips For Good Journalists

The library paid me every four weeks, depositing my wages into my account on the first Tuesday of each month. After checking the bank to see if my wages had gone in (they always went in), I immediately headed into Glasgow to spend my hard-earned cash on books, CDs, food, and clothes. Mostly books, though. Mum eventually joked that I had more books in my bedroom than on the shelves at the library. She wasn't wrong. The weight of books on the shelf caused it to topple over and fall on me while I was asleep in bed. It happened quickly: the shelf was on the wall beside my *Scream 2* poster, then it was on top of me. Every book on that shelf, every *Nancy Drew*, *Doctor Who*, Stephen King, Banana Yoshimoto, Agatha Christie, Truman Capote, Kathy Acker, JT LeRoy... literally every single book I owned fell and hit me from a height. Worse, a particularly heavy edition of *Gone With The Wind* smacked me right between the eyes. The next morning, I felt the tightening of skin as a tell-tale bruise formed on my face

How could I tell people I'd been headbutted by a hardback?

I couldn't. So instead, I told them I got into a fight with a mugger.

It was far more believable than the actual truth.

Muggers were as common in Cumbernauld as buses that didn't turn up on time.

If you were really unlucky, you could be mugged on a bus that didn't turn up on time.

*

College was fast becoming a bit of a bore. I turned up with my notepad, thinking of stories to write for the student newspaper, praying for shocking scandals to expose – only to be sent out to write about jumble sales and Britpop bands whose music and haircuts were interchangeable with those of Noel and Liam. What was the point? Britpop was done. Everyone knew that. Well, everyone who'd sat through *Be Here Now*.

The real problem with trying to be a journalist was that I'd assumed it would be far more exciting than it actually turned out to be. Two specific incidents really clarified my complete unsuitability for the profession of journalism.

The first incident happened during a visit from The National Union of Journalists...

We were in our classroom on the top floor of Glasgow's College of Building And Printing, the oppressive heat from the afternoon sun slowly boiling us alive. Thank goodness I had a full can of Lynx in my rucksack. The heat was so bad I almost fell asleep on my table. But I didn't get the chance. My lecturer, a jolly ex-journalist for *The Sun* named Jock (who'd later be convicted for phone hacking), loudly informed us that someone from The Union would be visiting, ostensibly to answer questions about the profession, but really to increase membership. We weren't stupid. Well, I wasn't. I couldn't really say that about all my classmates; one or two wanted to work for *Loaded* magazine. All they talked about was scoring on the pitch and in the bedroom. I hated those people.

Eventually, after what felt like hours, The Rep from The Union arrived in our classroom.

She was a large sweaty woman who immediately put me in mind of a demonic boiled egg. Her suit was functional and ill-fitting and possibly on the verge of splitting a seam.

Soon enough, The Rep started her persuasive pitch for Union membership.

She didn't even tell us her name. She was simply The Rep from The Union.

—The newsroom is a fast-paced environment. It can be stressful. It's definitely competitive. You need your union to protect you. Without protection, you're exposed.

I shuddered at the thought of being exposed in a newsroom.

—Anyone here could get a job at a newspaper. But what happens if your editor takes a dislike to you? What protection do you have? Well? Tell me?

Of all the people The Rep could have picked to make her point, she chose me. As she motioned in my direction, everyone turned their heads to look over at my desk. I did a doubletake, just to check whether or not someone was seated behind me.

I wasn't that lucky.

—What's to stop your editor from saying LOOK AT THAT POOFY REPORTER. LOOK AT HIS POOFY HAIR. WHY IS THAT POOFY LITTLE MAN STARING AT ME? What's to stop him from saying that? I would never say that to anyone. But not everyone is as fair and impartial as I am.

Everybody in the room burst out laughing, including The Rep.

Two minutes passed and they were still laughing.

I seethed in the background, boiling quietly in my own impotent fury.

The Rep looked right at me. Her eyes met mine.

She clasped her hands over her chest and said solemnly:

—Remember. You need your union.

I knew what The Rep needed, but she'd be dead within seconds of swallowing it.

The second incident that put me off pursuing journalism as a future career happened one afternoon during a deathly slow lesson. We were trying to learn shorthand, a seemingly essential requirement to pass the course, despite the fact we'd been told to go out and buy a Dictaphone from Argos. Actually, I was rather good at shorthand. I picked it up quickly and easily. If I enjoyed something, I usually worked hard to excel at it.

A loud theatrical sigh at the front of the room made me aware that Jock really wasn't in the mood to teach. Dropping his pad and pen, he looked at the room, his eyes seeing everyone, but making us all feel like he was looking at each of us specifically.

—Okay, it's too nice to stay in here today.

Everyone in the room cheered except for me.

The pollen levels were insane and my eyes were puffy and thick.

—We're going to go somewhere that all journalists go for stories, said Jock with a shit-eating grin. He seemed terribly pleased with himself. Me? I'd suddenly perked up at the prospect of joining real journalists on the hunt for exciting stories.

—Where are we going?

I don't know who asked the question, simply because I hadn't bothered remembering the names of my classmates. There was no point. I wouldn't see them ever again.

—Somewhere special, said Jock playfully.

He took us out.

He led us down the street.

He revealed the one place where every journalist in Glasgow could be found.

It wasn't a newspaper office.

Nope.

It was a pub.

—But I don't drink, I said.

Jock's expression seemed sympathetic.

—You'll start once you get a job at a newspaper. Trust me.

The very thought of getting steaming drunk and waking

up with a hangover made me want to run in the opposite direction. Drugs, sex, and booze held no appeal for me.

Determined to prove Jock wrong, show him that I could flourish in the booze-soaked world of print journalism, I tagged along with my classmates as they surged into the pub. Immediately, I was confronted by the sight of journalists sitting around tables with pints of beer and empty glasses. They were chatting and laughing, but more significantly (and I saw this with my own eyes) they were *looking* and *listening*.

Looking for headlines.

Listening for stories.

It didn't take long for me to realise this wasn't where I belonged.

They were dressed in coats and trousers.

Me? I wore a French beret and a black turtleneck sweater with matching gloves.

They had pints of Guinness in their hands.

Guinness? Sod that. I wanted a cup of Typhoo.

The confusion threatened to burn my brain.

In the end, it didn't take me long to come to a decision.

I immediately quit college and stayed in bed for months eating Maryland Cookies.

Chapter 50

A Birthday Breakdown

Mum took a trip on what would have been Donnie's twenty-seventh birthday. Coincidentally, I was due to pay rent so I could continue to live in the style to which I'd become accustomed. As for Mum's trip, well she didn't go alone. Trips are boring without company. But she didn't invite me or Lorna. Mum didn't ask her boyfriend either.

So who did she take with her on her trip?

She took Donnie.

Actually, she took her ashes.

They were sealed inside a large ornate blue urn. The most expensive in the catalogue. Mum had insisted on opulence for her daughter's final resting place.

I was the first one to realise the ashes had disappeared from the living room mantelpiece. I'd spent the morning dusting the skirting boards, cleaning the dishes, hoovering the floor, and wiping the Venetian blinds. However, where only twenty-four hours earlier the urn had been displayed on a makeshift shrine in our hallway, now it was now gone.

—Bugger, I muttered.

All the signs had been there that something was wrong with Mum.

She was only smoking a few cigarettes when she used to smoke packets per day.

She hadn't dyed her hair for quite a while.

She hadn't ordered anything from Littlewoods or Kays.

These things on their own might not signify much, but put together with Donnie's missing urn, they told me everything I needed to know about my mother's state of mind.

First, I phoned Lorna to ask if Mum was over at her flat.

No, she was not.

Where could she be?

She couldn't visit Donnie's grave, because she didn't have one.

That left one obvious place to check.

I headed to the bingo.

The Mecca had a terribly depressing atmosphere; the forced gaudiness, the lost souls wandering about looking for something they might never find, the carpet with its weird patterns that changed every time the eye fell upon it, the moulded plastic décor that was supposed to make the hall look bourgeois but instead made it look fucking hideous.

Mum loved it. She had to love it, because she spent enough time under its roof, playing to win, never winning anything. Not that she cared. It was all about getting out and having a nice night. Different strokes, different folks. Etc. Etc. Whatever.

The hall was TARDIS big, with tables neatly arranged in rows, barriers split players off so they could play in peace. It used to be The Hollywood Bowl. I'd spent a lot of time there when I should have been at school. There was a *Doctor Who* pinball machine, which I loved because I loved anything to do with that mad old TV show. But The Hollywood Bowl didn't last. Like everything good in my town, it closed down due to lack of interest.

The bingo didn't have that problem.

After a few seconds of looking, I finally found Mum.

She was sitting alone at a table in the far corner of the hall.

The urn was next to her.

This wouldn't be easy.

I crossed the hall in a few steps and took a seat alongside my mother.

—Hey, I said gently.

—I only need three more numbers.

—We were worried about you.

Mum clicked her tongue, making a sharp noise that perfectly communicated her displeasure.

—I'm only at the bingo.

—You took Donnie's urn.

—It's her birthday, so I wanted to get her out that house.

—Mum, you can't take her urn about in public.

—Don't tell me what I can and can't do, Walter.

—Mum…

—Cup of tea. You and me.

My ears perked up at the mention of tea. I didn't understand bingo terminology. It was a language I hadn't learned.

—Three, said Mum helpfully.

She dabbed her pen onto a number in her card. There were a few cards scattered around the table, next to my sister's ashes. Actually, Mum had been doing quite well so far.

—I can take the urn back home, if you like.

—Don't touch it.

—It's probably really heavy…

—Leave. It. Right. There.

—Okay.

We sat there in silence, the only sound in the room being the inaudible group-mutter of the pensioners playing bingo, and the loud (and somewhat irritating) voice of the caller.

—Rise and shine. Twenty-Nine!

—Legs eleven! Eleven!

—The Lord is my shepherd. Twenty-Three!

—Lucky Seven. That's number seven!

—Dirty Gertie! Thirty!

—For fuck sake, I muttered.

This was beginning to send me loopy.

Thankfully, the game ended.

—I only needed two more numbers to win the Jackpot, said Mum.

She burst into tears.

—There, there. I said. —You'll win next time.

—Do you remember when she phoned at Christmas and I put the phone down on her?

Her tears weren't about losing at the bingo, obviously. Well, it would have been obvious to someone in touch with normal humanity, and not a weirdo. I sat there wishing Lorna had found Mum instead of me. She would know what to say. She could tell Mum what she wanted to hear, not what she needed to hear.

I couldn't offer the same comfort.

—Mum, I said. —I remember everything.

—Oh, I forgot. Photographic memory, isn't it?

—Donnie phoned up from London to tell you about being gay.

—And I put the phone down on my own daughter!

—I was eating Brussels sprouts.

Mum wiped her face and looked right at me.

—What the hell do Brussels sprouts have to do with this?

—That's what I was eating when you put the phone down on Donnie.

—Sometimes I wonder about you, Walter.

Placing her hand on top of the urn, Mum suddenly seemed decades older. In that moment, I was confronted by her mortality, the foresight that she wouldn't be around forever. One day, I'd have my hand on her urn.

I didn't care.

Death was a door I'd often thought about opening, just like Kurt in Seattle.

—I wish things had been different.

Normally, I'd tell her something about regret being a weight you had to shift. Something profound about looking forward, not backwards. But I couldn't. Because I couldn't follow my own advice; my past was very much in my present. Donnie

241

recognised that that last day we met in The Kopper Kettle when I told her about Baby C. I carried him, the memory, around with me the way Mum did her daughter's ashes.

If I said anything, I'd be a hypocrite.

But when had that stopped me in the past?

—This isn't healthy, Mum.

—I just wanted to take her out for the day.

—I know.

We sat in silence while the bingo hall emptied. It took some time, because all the pensioners walked slowly towards the exit. But I was glad to just sit in silence with Mum. Eventually, the room was empty and we had to leave. I stood up first. Then I scooped up my sister's urn in both hands, clutching it tightly against my chest.

—I don't want to go home just yet, said Mum.

—It's Donnie's birthday, I said. —We should do something.

We got outside and stood in the sun for a few moments.

I hated the heat. It made me sweat and my hands slippery.

—What do you want to do?

Mum took me off guard, but it turned out she hadn't asked me.

She'd asked the urn in my arms.

—Let's go for something to eat, I suggested.

Donnie and I were grubbers, which was something else that ran in the family along with heart arrythmia and rampant insanity. Going for dinner on her birthday made sense.

—I haven't eaten all day, admitted Mum.

—We'll go to the Kopper Kettle. I'll pay for it.

Mum suddenly remembered something important.

—Wait. You still owe me rent money!

We passed an ATM, at which point I handed my sister over to Mum so I could take money out of the machine. Reluctantly, I paid my rent for the month.

It wasn't all bad. Mum paid for dinner.

Chapter 51

A Change In Fortune

My life changed forever during a trip to the bank. I made a quick stop after a shift in the library. I was braced for a tiny amount, if only because of all the books and clothes I'd bought during my last trip into Glasgow. This was a real problem for me. It was pure habit to spend and not keep an eye on the actual amount left in my account. I'd learned quickly that you can only disappoint yourself when your self-worth is connected to how much you earn. My bank balance had always been low, so there was little point in punishing myself by watching the money dwindle to zeroes. I preferred to spend until my cash card stopped. By the time I got paid, I usually only had a few quid left in the bank.

Money never stayed in my account for long.

Life savings? At eighteen years old?

Don't be daft.

Checking to see no-one was nearby, I inserted my card.

Tapping out four digits, I waited.

Then I pressed CHECK YOUR BALANCE.

Just like watching a horror movie, I peered out from between my fingers.

There was money in my account.

The total started with three and ended in five zeroes.

I rubbed my eyes.

It couldn't be.

I looked down, then back up at the screen again.

The number hadn't changed.

I had more money in my account than I'd ever had in my life, would ever have again.

There was more money in my bank than most people had ever seen in a lifetime.

My sister had transferred all of her cash into my account.

But she was gone and the money remained.

Looking around, I saw no-one suspicious. No men from London were following me. Why would they? The woman who took their money was dead. There was no way for them to recover the cash. They had no way of knowing what she'd done with it.

With a trembling hand, I pressed WITHDRAW.

The words on the screen blinked back:

HOW MUCH?

Shrugging, I ordered the machine to give me £100.

The slit on the wall spewed out tens and twenties.

I pressed WITHDRAW again. And again. And again.

It didn't take long for me to reach my daily limit, but that meant nothing in the face of my newfound wealth. There was more money in my wallet than I'd ever had in my entire life. This money could last me for years and years. No-one else needed to know about it.

As I stood in the middle of the shopping centre, lost in a daze of dreams, pondering over my sudden change in fortune (literally), it occurred to me that I had to be very cautious over the next week or so. Knowing what happened when I went to live with Granny Frances, my sudden good luck could shift in seconds. The last thing I wanted to do was spend all that money – only for the sodding bank to take it off me.

Over the next few days I did what I'd always done.

I woke up.

I washed my hands.

I ate breakfast.

I went to work.

I washed my hands.

I read books.

I ate dinner.

I washed my hands.

And so on.

And so forth.

Nothing changed. I kept living my life as I always had.

If anyone asked whether or not they'd noticed any changes in my behaviour, the response would be a clear and simple —No.

There was no point in succumbing to panic.

I could afford to be patient.

Actually, I could afford everything.

Chapter 52

Goodbye Cumbernauld

Money only left my bank account when I took it out.

No-one was coming for my cash.

Donnie's death had ensured it would be mine forever.

Obviously I could have been honest and handed it back to the bank, explained that my sister stole it when she lived in London. But why would I do that? Why the hell would I deprive myself of my only means of escape?

I knew exactly what I needed to do with the money.

It was my way out of Cumbernauld.

No-one noticed me packing all my things away. But then, my family had never really noticed anything I did anyway. They'd spent years discussing their private business right in front of me while I sat on the couch reading. They never ever considered me in the slightest. My feelings were insignificant. I was a glorified barista when everyone needed a cuppa. I was rent money and someone to take the bins out. But my power to be invisible finally proved useful as I got ready to leave town. I was frightened. Of course I was. I'd never really left Cumbernauld. Any time I got away, something always dragged me back. All of that, however, was about to change. My money could take me far away, lead me to a place with nice buildings and good people. White picket fences. Freshly mown lawns. Free parking. Uncracked pavements. A place where babies weren't shoved into boxes, dumped like trash for kids to find. I'd spent my entire life dreaming of another world. Now, thanks to my sister, I had the power to make my dream a reality.

Leaving town meant saying goodbye to my family. Also, I'd be abandoning all of my precious books. Everything I'd ever known would be lost to me.

Weirdly, it was far easier than I thought it would be.

I left a note for my family in the one place I knew Mum would find it. I stuck it underneath her spare packet of cigarettes. Apparently, she'd switched brands without me knowing. Instead of smoking 20 Club King Size, she now enjoyed Mayfair. How posh!

With luck, my family wouldn't send the police to find me. It seemed unlikely. I was an adult, capable of making my own decisions. Besides, I specifically requested they not phone the police. If anyone asked where I got my money from, everything might unravel.

My reasons for leaving were deliberately vague.

I wrote about trying to *find myself*.

I wrote about needing to see the world.

I even wrote some nonsense about taking a year out from society.

Really, I just wanted to escape this shithole.

I called a taxi..

Then I headed outside and stood impatiently by the front door.

How did I feel?

Scared. Excited. Nauseous.

Free.

Finally!

The taxi arrived and I loaded it with my ugly green tartan suitcase. It always looked easier on *EastEnders* when characters left The Square; aptly this usually happened in the back of a taxi. But there was less drama in my departure, which was just the way I liked it.

—Where to? The driver asked pleasantly.

Actually, I hadn't considered where I wanted to go.

—Somewhere nice, I said.

—What?

—I want you to take me somewhere nice. Anywhere but here.

The poor driver probably thought he'd picked up a nutter, but he played along in hopes of getting a nice tip. He seemed to consider what I'd asked of him.

Then, finally, he came out with it.

—Do you know what's nice this time of year?

—Surprise me.

—Have you ever been to Blackpool?

I hadn't.

—I could drive you down to Blackpool.

—Blackpool?

—Oh yes, said the driver as he warmed to his subject.

—Blackpool, I repeated.

—If I take the M6, it'll be a three hour drive there and another three hour drive back.

—I'm not coming back.

—Yes, but mate...I *am*. Look, if you want to go somewhere nice, then Blackpool's for you. It's great this time of year. It's sunny. The water's good. Go to Blackpool.

—Does it have a library?

—Yes, it does.

—Okay, take me to Blackpool.

Guess what?

He took me to Blackpool.

Chapter 53

My Fabulous Life In Blackpool

I stayed in Blackpool for three years and it rained every second day. Rain didn't bother me, in fact I found the sound of it on my window soothing, the soft tapping gave me nice background music whilst I read my books. I read an average of twenty books a year while in Blackpool, really thick books with hundreds and hundreds of pages. Also, I chose not to buy a flat, preferring instead to hop around different B&Bs. Suffice to say, some were better than others. My favourite was The Pier, a nice little villa owned by a gay couple who were (pardon the pun) anal about everything. However, Frank and Larry kept clean skirting boards, nice carpets and they ensured I had a nice vegetarian breakfast waiting for me in the dining room downstairs every morning. There was only one problem with The Pier. Frank, it seemed, had aspirations of being a famous drag queen. Every Friday to Sunday, he would become 'Betty Poofroyd' and entertain us with his energetic cabaret performances. Personally, I loathed cabaret. It seemed to be the domain of middle-aged men with too-tight waistcoats and hairlines that receded all the way to their ankles. Blackpool was full of these 'entertainers'. They told jokes about their mothers-in-law and women drivers. It was a time-warp of weirdness, a strange hangover from the eighties. However, none of this really impacted on me. Whenever I felt slightly down, I simply spent my way back to happiness, going wherever I wanted, staying in any house that accepted credit cards. My bank account was crammed with cash. Literally, I could spend and spend and spend – and there would always be more than enough money left to spend and spend and spend the next day.

Sometimes, I couldn't believe my good luck.

If I ever needed a change of surroundings, I'd take a bus to Preston and go shopping. There were some really good shops in Preston. They had a Woolworths, some burger bars for whenever I stopped being vegetarian and there were also some really good clothes shops. Oh, and Elsie's Bakery. They made the best scones.

What initially struck me about the people of Preston was that they knew how to have a good time, which explained why I never moved there fulltime. Frank and Larry often jealously joked that I kept the economy of Preston afloat.

It was in Preston that I learned two planes had dropped from the sky, both of them smashing into the Twin Towers. Not even in my secluded little Blackpool bubble could I force out the real world. Truthfully, I'd never actually heard of the Twin Towers before the 11th of September, but by the 12th such ignorance was an impossibility. Everything suddenly felt much darker in the world, even in Blackpool or Preston.

This was also one of the few times I thought about my family back in Cumbernauld.

The thought, however, was a fleeting one.

There was simply too much money to spend and not enough time to spend it.

Three years I spent in Blackpool. Three years of birthdays, books and bags of shopping.

My peaceful new life in Blackpool came to an abrupt end thanks to an encounter with Larry, one of the owners of The Pier. It was a warm day, the sort that would bring out revellers with ice-cream cones – not the sort that came laced with LSD, thankfully. I'd popped out to get some books from the Blackpool Library, my trip taking just shy of an hour. My book borrowing technique was simple and effective: I just grabbed books with the nicest cover art. Life was too short to read books with ugly cover art. Anyway, upon my return to The Pier, I passed Larry in the hall. He was polishing the front desk, using some sort of cloying, perfumed spray. It went for my lungs, but being terribly polite, I didn't say anything to him. Instead, I suffered in silence, only breaking the silence with a cough or two.

Larry, in his peach-coloured pinny, noticed me.

—Ah. Just the man!

—Good afternoon, Larry.

—You too. You too. Listen…

I'd already climbed the staircase, but I stopped, waiting for him to finish.

—Someone was here looking for you.

—What?

—He came by about twenty minutes ago.

—Did he give his name?

Larry thought about it, then said:

—No.

—What did he look like?

—Tall, tall. Black hair. A white tracksuit and white trainers.

—I don't know anyone like that!

—He asked for you by name, Walter.

—But no-one knows I'm here.

—There's one other thing…

I waited, but my patience was already started to evaporate.

—He spoke in a London accent.

My legs nearly gave way, but I managed to steady myself on the bannister.

This couldn't be happening.

Not to me!

Oblivious to my distress, Larry continued wittering away in the background.

—Or should I say a 'Lahn-dahn' accent?

—Is he coming back?

—Probably. I told him you'd be back in an hour.

My mind reeled with ideas and plans, devious schemes that would keep me safe. There had to be a way to turn this in my favour, or at least keep me out of harm's way.

—You told him an hour?

—Yes. Did I do something wrong?

—How long ago was that?

—He came in about one-ish, so I'd say fifty minutes ago.

I tore up the staircase in the direction of my rented room just as a small family of four were leaving theirs. Without giving them right of way, I literally bolted through them, causing the mother to curse. It didn't matter. I had to get out of The Pier and Blackpool as quickly as possible. Throwing the door of my room open, I snatched my ugly old suitcase and started cramming all of my worldly belongings into it. However, because I'd spent the last three years shopping in Preston for snazzy gear, I'd bought too much. Hats, outfits, shoes, boots, accessories. I couldn't fit it all in! Frustration made me scream. I tried desperately to get my clothes in my suitcase. I sat on it. I stood on it.

Goodness, I even *lay* on it.

Eventually, I took what I could and headed off downstairs.

Larry was still there. He smiled, and asked:

—Are you going?

—I'm going insane, maybe.

—I know the feeling, honey. I know the feeling.

After paying him for his hospitality with all the notes in my pocket, I found myself roaming the street looking for a taxi. Eventually, one stopped for me. Ten minutes later, I was in Blackpool Bus Station, desperately looking around for the right bus. I only felt safe when I made it onto a Citylink stagecoach.

It took me back to Scotland.

Chapter 54

My New Neighbour

My life was starting to mirror my sister's just a little too much for my liking. She'd moved from Cumbernauld to London in a bid to find herself. Instead, she'd swindled some crooks for their £££££ before making her way back home. She didn't quite reach it though, opting instead to live in Glasgow, her expensive apartment a monument to her newfound power and status. In a bid to break the narrative my sister had earlier created, I decided to do things in a slightly different way. Instead of moving to Glasgow, I headed for Edinburgh. Rightly or wrongly, I'd always regarded Edinburgh as a cosmopolitan mecca for the middle-classes. It was classy, not trashy. Edinburgh seemed like a good fit for my pretensions.

It would be my new home!

I'd be safe there!

It was everything Cumbernauld wasn't!

Except…

My next-door neighbour turned out to be a shrieking crackhead named Harry. I'd swapped a Larry for a Harry. His surname and life were a mystery. All I knew was that he loved drugs and hated Catholics. I didn't meet Harry for the first few weeks into my new lease until the night he knocked on my door, surprising me with a box of toothpaste. No amount of Colgate could shift the tea-coloured tint from my teeth, but not wanting to have those teeth knocked out, I stood and listened while he attempted to hawk his wares. Wearing a suspiciously clean tracksuit, holding a shoebox full of guff, he gave me his pitch.

There was just one problem.

I couldn't understand a word he said.

We were born in the same country, but it might as well have been separate planets.

—Ya wan' toothpaste?

I seized on a word I thought I'd understood, though he pronounced it 'tooth pissed'.

—Toothpaste? No, that's okay. I've got my own toothpaste.

I paused.

—And my own teeth.

—Awrit. Ya wan' som' tea?

He had loose teabags in his shoebox, which was practically his version of a window display. Actually, I did need some more tea but I always bought my own whenever I popped down into Waverley Mall. Besides, I didn't want teabags that had been stored next to his supply of crack. The very idea made my hands feel the need for boiling water and soap.

—Awrit. Ya lik' cock?

—Excuse me?

—Ya lik' cock? Ah goat cock. I lik' cock loads.

—What you do in your spare time is none of my business!

My only recourse was to edge away from Harry, back off into my flat and hope against all odds I could get the door closed and locked before his foot managed to wedge it open.

—Ah stik cock up ma nose every day.

—Fuck off and leave me alone, you depraved druggie slag! I screamed.

Before Harry could say anything else, I slammed the door shut and locked it. Quickly, I lifted the spare baseball bat I'd stashed by the door in case of emergency trespassers. It was an old trick Mum had taught me in order to scare TV License men away from the house.

—Ah sell ma cock cheap!

—Get to the Job Centre and get some work, I wailed from behind the door.

Harry wasn't sure what to make of me and my bat. In the following months, he remained in the background, a baleful presence in my life. Normally, I'd call the police and have him dealt with, but that wasn't possible now because I didn't want to draw attention to myself. Worse, I'd paid rent in advance, more than enough to cover me for the foreseeable future, using money my sister had robbed from some shady men in London. I could afford to be wasteful, of course. But a part of me (a major part) resented throwing good money away. So I chose to remain in Edinburgh, stuck inside my flat, trying desperately to avoid Harry and his cracked-out commentary. He'd holler through the walls in the early hours of the morning, waking me out of my fragile sleep-state, bothering me with his problems. His drug-infused mood swings were extreme. He'd kick the wall, scream obscenities about the Pope, or wail and weep about someone named Claire.

Okay, so the twist in this sordid tale is that Harry hadn't uttered the word 'cock' when he first approached me with his tube of toothpaste. Actually, like any connoisseur of drugs, he was offering me 'coke' because obviously (in his mind) it seemed like a good deal.

He took *coke* up his nose, not cock.

He sold his *coke* cheap, not his cock.

None of this detracted from an important and fundamental fact: my next-door neighbour was violent, frightening, unpredictable and obnoxiously loud. As a result, I locked my door religiously, each turn of the key a reassuring pat on the back that no-one could get to me. But Harry could just wait at his door, ambush me when I returned from the supermarket. Even I needed to get out from time to time: I needed library books, milk, and teabags to live. All it would take to reach me was a bit of luck on his part.

He was my next-door neighbour and only a wall kept him away from me.

As I sat in my living room, sprawled out on the black leather suite, I considered my options. They were limited, but I knew one thing above all else:

No matter what happened, no matter how bad life became in Edinburgh with my crazy next-door neighbour, I would endure it all with style and grace.

Nothing would drag me back to Cumbernauld.

Nothing!

Chapter 55

The Front Page

The case broke overnight and newspapers put it on their front pages the next morning.

One headline caught my attention while I was out buying milk and teabags:

ARREST MADE IN CARDBOARD BOX BABY DEATH.

I almost dropped my carton of Fresh' n' Lo.

No, I thought. It *couldn't* be. Not after all this time.

My heart thumping hard, I lifted the paper from the stack on the shelf and read as my past finally caught up with me.

According to the story, a break in the case had happened because the DNA of Baby C had been matched to that of a forty-three-year-old woman. The exact details were vague, but according to a story in *The Scotsman*, she'd been brought in for questioning by police and arrested on suspicion of negligence and manslaughter. The article didn't say much else about the woman in custody. I knew her age and the fact she lived in Cumbernauld, but very little else. Who was she? Did I know her? Had I passed her on the street?

There was something else in the story. An unsettling fact.

The police had unearthed a recording of the phone call that led them to Baby C.

A recording of *my* voice.

Before I could finish reading the story, something remarkable happened:

Without thinking about it, I found myself shredding the newspaper with my hands. Literally, I ripped it into tiny paper pieces, my teeth gritted with effort as I used muscles I hadn't used in years, if ever. Eventually, the newspaper was a bundle of scraps between my fingers, shredded slices. For the grand finale, I threw my hands up and let paper rain down on me. In the middle of the little newsagents in Edinburgh, I danced in a self-made blizzard. The other shoppers stood by, watching in amazement.

Clearly, I wasn't over what had happened in 1992.

What I'd found that day still exerted a malignant influence in my life.

Then...

All of a sudden...

An audacious idea formed in my head, a hopeful thought:

That woman in custody was the only person who could make sense of what happened that day. Only she could make sense out of senselessness. She held the secret of Baby C.

Maybe, just maybe, I could finally put it all behind me.

Looking down at my hands, the skin pink as a result of a violent scrubbing, I knew something had to give. I needed to make peace with my past once and for all.

That's when I decided to go back home.

Goodbye Edinburgh.

Hello Cumbernauld!

Chapter 56

Welcome Home

The journey back home from Edinburgh took approximately three hours. It should only have taken two hours, but the bus broke down in the middle of the M9 during rush hour traffic. Thankfully, I still had a paperback copy of *Marabou Stork Nightmares*. I got through two chapters by the time a replacement bus arrived. Fortunately, I managed to get a seat in the very centre of the bus. I always took the middle seat. It felt like the safest spot on the bus to survive a motorway smash. Sadly, I wasn't alone in preferring the middle seats. A pensioner decided to alleviate her loneliness by sitting next to me. I considered telling her to sod off, that I wanted to sit alone, but instead, I smiled as she got comfortable beside me. It made sense to just…be…nice.

—Tell me, young man…do you believe in the power of The Lord?

Immediately, I regretted my decision.

—No, I said coldly.

She looked surprised. I started to suspect she'd been working this routine on innocent bus passengers for years. If that really were the case, I was to be her latest victim.

—You don't believe angels are watching over us, guiding us to the gates of Heaven?

—Look, love. I just want the bus driver to guide me back home.

—Oh, where is that?

—Cumbernauld, near Glasgow.

She pulled a face that suggested someone had taken a shit on her morning muesli.

259

—A ghastly shithole, she said.

—Do you think the angels are watching over it?

She shot me a filthy look. I smirked slightly, triumphant in my petty little victory. However, the old dear wasn't quite ready to give up. Worse. In telling her where I was headed, I'd given her ammunition to continue our conversation, taking it in a morbid new direction that I wasn't keen to follow.

—Did you see the news?

—Yes, I said.

—Someone was arrested for that poor baby's death.

—Yes.

—What kind of a mother would do that to her child?

It was a question I'd asked myself many times over the years, albeit one I'd never been able to answer. In my own mind, I'd come to the conclusion it was someone very frightened. Or mentally unstable. I veered between the two theories.

The pensioner half-heartedly attempted to start up another conversation, but I had no desire to talk anymore. The rest of the journey was spent in silence.

By the time the bus pulled into Cumbernauld Bus Station, I'd turned the last page.

Nothing much had changed in the three years since last I'd last been to my house. Minor cosmetic differences marked the rest of the street though. Most of the windows now had Venetian blinds, a fact I found strangely hilarious. As I gripped the handle to open the front door to my house, a fearful apprehension made me stop. Some sort of déjà voodoo. Truthfully, I didn't know if I'd be welcomed back, certainly not enough to simply walk through the door as though nothing had changed. Three years *was* a long time. How would my family react? Would they be happy to see me? But really, it wasn't as though I'd vanished without a trace. They knew I was down in Blackpool. They didn't know where exactly. I'd also avoided telling them

I'd moved back to Scotland. They had no idea I was only a train and a bus trip away from them.

Taking a deep steadying breath, I twisted the door handle – and stepped inside.

The carpet was different. The walls had been painted. But Donnie's shrine was still in the hallway, her urn the centrepiece of the memorial. I reached out and touched it, my way of saying hello to my sister again. That's when I noticed the new addition to the shrine.

An enormous life-sized portrait of my sister dominated the wall.

It had been painted from a photograph that Mum particularly liked.

—Mum got someone to paint that using Donnie's ashes.

I turned around slowly and found Laddie standing in the kitchen doorway.

—Where have you been, Walter?

He looked older, of course. His hair thicker and longer. Actually, he looked like a masculine version of Mum and Lorna. His skin was slightly weathered, traces of acne remaining to tell the tale of an eternal battle fought between a boy and his hormones.

—I had to get away, I said.

—You're a selfish tosser, he replied.

—Totally.

He got upset. We hugged. It seemed to make him feel better.

—Where's Mum?

—Upstairs with Davy Death watching *Dad's Army*.

—Go up and tell her I'm here.

Laddie passed me and headed upstairs.

I heard his voice telling them they had a visitor.

Actually, he told Mum the debt collector was waiting downstairs to collect payment for unpaid catalogue bills. The screech of rage she gave drowned out Captain Mainwaring.

I snickered, but said nothing.
Mum bounded downstairs and burst into the kitchen.
When she saw me, she froze.
Then something odd took place between us:
Mum burst into tears before hugging me.
This was followed by a hard slap across the face.
—You should have phoned, she said over and over again.

Chapter 57

Home Truths

Mum and Davy ordered takeaway from the Dragon Palace and we had dinner together for the first time since I fled over three years ago. It was a special dinner, if only because Laddie actually stopped playing his PlayStation for an hour to come and sit with me. Lorna came over too. She didn't slap me, but I knew she was in a bad mood. She barely said anything to me as we ate our Chow Mein and chips. It was apparent (at least to me) that she wanted to talk without the others being around. She got her chance later on when I offered to do the dishes. Everyone headed upstairs; everyone with the exception of Lorna.

She leaned in close while I was scrubbing a plate with a wire brush.

—How did you survive in Blackpool?

—I told you. I got a job.

That was my official story and I knew every little detail of my lie.

—Doing what?

—I worked at a candyfloss stall.

—You paid your rent by spinning candyfloss?

—It's obscene how much candyfloss the English eat. No wonder they have bad teeth.

—And there was me thinking you had Donnie's money all along.

This confirmed my suspicions. Donnie had eventually told Lorna about her embezzlement scheme from her stint in London. They'd lived together for a while, so it made sense for them to talk into the early hours of the morning, the way

I used to with Donnie when we lived together in Craigieburn Road, during Fishtank's reign.

—I don't know what you're talking about, I said.

I must have been convincing, because Lorna suddenly seemed less certain.

—Remember that day when you came over to see my flat when I first moved in?

—That lovely pensioner flat?

—Yes. Donnie asked about your bank account.

—So she did! But I refused. Don't you remember?

God, I was good. Slowly, I started scrubbing another plate with the sponge.

—I just thought…because you suddenly left…nah, never mind. It's just me.

For a moment I wanted to spill my guts, tell my sister everything, explain why I'd run off: the feelings of terrifying stagnation that smothered me in this town. But I couldn't. Why? Well, I told myself that the men from London might undertake reprisals. But even as I held that thought, I knew it was a lot of shite. The truth is this: I didn't want to tell Lorna about the money because I wanted to keep it all. The idea of being poor frightened me.

—Walter, said Lorna suddenly.

—What?

—You're scrubbing too hard.

—I can't get the dirt off.

—But…you finished washing the plates five minutes ago.

She was right. I looked down to discover that instead of washing our plates, I'd been scrubbing my hands with the wire brush. My skin was shredded and bloody. I almost passed out at the sight of the blood, but kept myself together.

—You're a loony, said Lorna as she went into a nearby cupboard in search of a First Aid box. She actually found one too. A new addition since I'd last been home. Davy Death was a hypochondriac, so it made sense for him to have vitamins and bandages.

As Lorna wrapped my hand up into a mummy's mitten, she looked right at me and said:

—What happened to you?

—Honestly?

—Honestly.

I took a deep breath and told her everything. I explained how I'd found a dead baby in the undergrowth behind the flats in Sandyknowes Road. I even admitted to calling the police anonymously. Lorna didn't watch the news, but she knew about Baby C.

Everyone knew about Baby C.

—Was he really dumped in a cardboard box?

—It was a cardboard box for a brand new microwave.

—Why didn't you tell anyone?

—I told Donnie.

—But she would have told me! She told me *everything*.

—She died literally days after we talked about it.

Lorna suddenly understood why I'd returned. I could see it in her eyes.

—The police got someone for it. You've come back to go to the trial.

—I want to speak to her, I said quietly.

—Why would you want to speak to a baby-basher?

—I just want to see her for myself…

—This isn't some Nancy Drew bullshit. This is murder, Walter. *Real* murder. It's the worst kind of murder too. A baby, for fuck sake.

The bite in Lorna's tone annoyed me slightly, because it implied I was playing a role in some sort of make-believe fantasy. I didn't think I'd solve the mystery, crack the case. The culprit had already been caught, her DNA matching her to the corpse.

But I needed to look in her eyes.

I had to hear her voice.

How could I make my sister understand that?

Actually, I didn't understand it myself. But I knew I wanted it to happen.

Lorna suddenly softened, probably in response to my wounded expression.

—Look, Walter. You might be able to see her after the trial. I don't think she'll go to prison. I bet she's on her way to a padded cell in Carstairs.

Carstairs was the state psychiatric hospital and a place I didn't really want to visit.

Yet I knew Lorna was right. Sensible, thoughtful, but most of all she was smart.

If I couldn't talk to Baby C's mother before or during the trial, then I'd have to be a little bit patient and wait for the verdict. Then I'd make my move. No matter what happened, I'd find a way to get to her, even if I had to throw a hook up onto the roof of Carstairs and climb the wall until I reached her window.

—It's funny, said Lorna suddenly.

I couldn't think of anything about this situation that might make me laugh.

—What's funny?

—Mum wanted to know why you'd run off to Blackpool.

I smiled. I could only imagine what she'd said in my absence.

—She thought you'd gone down there with a man.

—Why would I do that?

—She even hired…*laughter*…a private detective.

—What? An actual detective?

—Yes!

Lorna stopped laughing and gave me a hug.

—She got some wanker from an agency to track you down.

—What? No way. An actual detective agency?

—Yes. From London.

I whizzed back to that last day in Blackpool when I had returned to the news that a stranger with a London accent had been looking for me. I'd assumed he was there looking for Donnie's money, that he was part of the group she'd robbed. Instead, he was in fact...

Lorna couldn't understand why I burst into laughter.

Chapter 58

The Trial

The trial of Baby C's mother was held at The High Court in Edinburgh. Only the most severe crimes were tried at the High Court. Unlike most court cases, the trial was closed to the public. This was very rare, apparently. No-one seemed to care except me. But I couldn't make a fuss because I didn't want to draw unnecessary attention to myself. The only witness the police had was the boy who found the box. They had his voice on tape. They didn't have him, though. And I wouldn't come forward. I couldn't. The last thing I wanted to do was utter one word in front of a policeman. Knowing my luck, they'd look into my finances and have both me and my 'wages' arrested.

Patiently, I waited.

It felt a long wait.

The trial lasted nearly a fortnight.

A fortnight!

I decided to take my mind off the trial until the verdict was reached.

And to that end, I reached out to an old friend.

Two, actually.

They weren't difficult to track down. Actually, I managed it on my first attempt. A lot had changed over the years, but their contact details remained the same. I simply picked up the phone, jabbed the buttons on the keypad (*bleep, bleep, blippity, bleep*), and hummed an off-tune rendition of *Freak Like Me* until…

At last, someone answered.

—Hello?

—Hello, I said.

The sound of silence at the other end wasn't encouraging, so I tried again.

—Can we meet up for lunch? Both of you should be there, if that's okay.

—Okay.

—Tomorrow at 12 o'clock?

—That's fine. Where?

I froze. I wasn't sure where to go in Cumbernauld for food. Not anymore.

—The Dovecoat, I said in hope.

The Dovecoat was a Beefeater restaurant that had been around in Cumbernauld for years and, with luck, still existed.

—See you tomorrow at The Dovecoat.

The call ended abruptly.

The next day I arrived at The Dovecoat dressed in a tartan suit I'd bought down in Preston. The print was bold and bright and beautiful. Red and green, it felt a bit punk, especially in a town that didn't just forget style – it didn't know style in the first place.

Taking a loud breath, I entered the restaurant.

They were at a table at the far side of the room, waiting for me to arrive.

Poppy. Moo. My old friends.

They *mostly* looked the same, just taller. Poppy's hair was the colour of candy floss, the sort sold in Blackpool, packed full of artificial colours and flavourings. When she stood up to greet me, I noticed she had a key-chain hanging limply from her pocket to her belt. Her nails were black, like her outfit. Yes, Poppy had gone goth.

Moo was dressed in a white tracksuit, the sort I could never ever wear in public, but it was casual. As I headed over, I immediately noticed that Moo didn't stand. He seemed reluctant to acknowledge any of my attempts at being polite, which wasn't a surprise. For a brief moment I wondered whether this had been a good idea, but somehow it seemed important. In all honesty, I just wanted to make amends with my old friends.

Poppy spoke first.

—You look...

—Different? I suggested.

—No, the exact same.

—Oh.

Moo still hadn't said anything, opting to let his cousin do all the talking.

—How are you doing?

—I'm getting used to being back home. It's surreal, to be honest.

The waiter came over and unfortunately we made him wait.

—And how about the two of you? How are you doing?

That was my attempt at bringing Moo into the conversation. He wasn't quite ready yet. But I knew he'd break. I could almost see his resolve to remain an arsehole crumbling. Moo wasn't a bad person, just a bit stubborn. It was good to know I could still read him.

—A lot has changed since you left, said Poppy with a light smile on her face.

—Oh?

—I've got a daughter, she said.

—Oh.

—Her name is Lily, which I really like. It sounds a bit classy, doesn't it?

I suddenly noticed the waiter.

—I'm ready to order, I said (much to his relief).

—Me too, agreed Poppy.

Moo continued to give me the silent treatment.

Once we'd ordered, I leaned over and asked what I hoped wasn't a personal question.

—So who's the dad then?

Poppy gave me an expression of mock shock, but went to answer…

Moo got in there first.

—Gary Dowds, he blurted.

It was a name I hadn't heard in years.

—He used to give Walter a hard time when they were kids, said Moo as though Poppy was completely unaware of that fact.

—That wouldn't happen now, I said.

And it wouldn't. I'd changed so much over the last few years. Maybe it was Donnie's death or the fact I'd lived away from Cumbernauld, but my confidence was unshakeable. Nothing could stand in my way. I knew what I wanted to do and I had the funds to make it happen. No-one would ever belittle me again. Not Gary. Not Fishtank. Not even Moo.

—What *is* your problem? I demanded.

—You dumped us, snapped Moo. —You walked away from us. Your best friends!

—Can't you see he's trying to apologise?

I smiled appreciatively at Poppy for helping me out.

—I just wanted to make sure we were all good.

Moo suddenly seemed embarrassed by his outburst.

—Do you still hear from Becca?

—No. And I don't want to hear from her either.

Poppy sensed scandal. She homed in on it.

—Why?

—She shagged my brother.

Both Moo and Poppy howled with laughter. I kept quiet, at first. But I soon joined in and we all laughed together as friends again. The ice broken, it suddenly felt like old times, before Becca and high school. Our food arrived and we ate and chatted away until it was dark outside. We vowed to keep in touch, though I wasn't sure it would happen.

Before I left, there was one thing I needed to know.

I turned to Moo and asked a question.

—Was Billy The Squid a real person?

—Only in our hearts, he said.

That…made no sense to me.

—It's better you don't know, added Poppy.

I waved goodbye and headed out of The Dovecoat in the direction of home.

The rain hissed down onto the pavement and soaked through my clothes, but I didn't care. What had happened that day felt quietly important to me; making up with Moo and Poppy was something I had had to do for the sake of my soul. There was something else I had to do. A very important personal thing for me.

As soon as I got into the house, I immediately checked the local news on Ceefax.

The trial was over. The verdict was in!

NOT GUILTY, it read. BY REASON OF INSANITY.

Finally, Baby C's mother had a name.

Elsa Norrington.

Baby C also had a name.

Kevin Norrington.

—Kevin Norrington, I said aloud in the living room.

—Who's Kevin Norrington? Mum asked.

—Someone who didn't get a chance to be anyone, I said to myself.

Chapter 59

Carstairs

Carstairs was built to keep a lot of mentally unstable people within its walls. A high security hospital, it had strict security protocols in order to protect the staff, the public and the patients themselves. Upon arrival, all visitors had to report to a secure reception area where appropriate ID would be presented. The visitor would then have their photograph taken and used for a special hospital-issued badge. Certain items weren't allowed past the reception area. Visitors were routinely vetted by security, who would remove any items that might injure patients – or aid them in escaping the hospital.

Getting into Carstairs was nearly as difficult as getting out.

Nearly, but not quite.

After an entire week of planning different ways to reach the elusive Elsa Norrington, I finally came up with a plan that would get me past the hospital doors. It took a little preparation and some false ID, but I had the funds to make it happen. My plan of action in place, I finally worked out the quickest route to Carstairs. Finally, I chose the day. A few phone calls sorted everything out. Oh, and I bribed three security guards too.

I had the funds to make that happen as well.

The trip to the hospital wasn't nearly as bad as I'd expected. Rare rays of sunshine warmed me as I left the house to begin my journey into South Lanarkshire. It would take just shy of an hour if I managed to stick to the timetable I'd created in my bedroom. I'd always felt safe in my bedroom, secure and comfortable. But where once my bedroom had seemed spacious, it now felt pokey and claustrophobic. I'd changed too much to be confined. After doing what needed to be done, I would look for somewhere to live.

Maybe I'd buy a home somewhere on Byres Road and have lots of full bins.

The train I needed to get me to Carstairs was late and I found myself standing at Cumbernauld train station far longer than I'd expected. The train eventually arrived just as rain started. I hurried onboard, thankful to be out of the downpour. After sitting down, I spent the journey tutting and glowering at everyone. Eventually, I got bored of being mean and relaxed a little. I had brought a book with me, a well-thumbed old paperback edition of McIlvanney's *Laidlaw*; a few chapters made the noise fade into the background and the journey feel faster.

—We are now approaching Carstairs Rail Station, said a pleasant voice over the tannoy.

I got out of my seat, though I'd only really had half of it due to the passenger beside me being a rather large man who'd spent the journey in a constant state of discomfort, shifting his weight, pressing his legs against my legs, his knees sharp and knobbly. Once free of the cramped compartment, I headed outside and found a waiting taxi by the station entrance. Thank goodness. I hadn't planned to walk, so getting a taxi that easily was a pleasant bonus. Breathing a sigh of relief, I opened the door and climbed inside.

—I'd like to go to Carstairs Hospital. If you make it fast, I'll give you a tenner tip.

The driver put his foot on the pedal and tore down the road at speeds so illegal that if I had had a wig, I'd have been holding onto it for dear life. It didn't matter. I still got there on time.

*

Though I walked confidently through the entrance to Carstairs' reception area, in reality I felt anything but. A nervy twinge at the bottom of my belly manifested in the form of a loud gurgle. As a result, I felt slightly nauseous. It was the sort of feeling you'd get before a really important exam, job interview, or a severe bout of diarrhoea. But I pushed through the discomfort and went ahead as planned. I'd come all the way from Cumbernauld and I wasn't going to leave until I came face to face with Elsa Norrington.

Nothing would stop me.

At least that's what I kept telling myself whilst waiting to have my ID checked.

Mercifully, it didn't take long.

The man doing the check was small, yet seemed to tower over everyone else in the room.

He was in charge, clearly.

—Your identification checks out, he informed me.

Of course it did. I'd paid enough to have the best fake ID money could buy. One of the few perks of being related to Jake was the fact I knew some really good fraudsters.

—Follow me, said the little man in charge.

A few minutes later, I was posing for my temporary Carstairs Hospital visitor's pass.

—Stop posing, barked the man behind the camera.

I did. As a result, my photo looked really dull, but that was the point, wasn't it?

—You're here to speak to Elsa Norrington?

The little man seemed mildly surprised when he read the visitors' schedule. He checked my credentials again.

—You're a journalist?

—Yes, I said.

Did it count if I hadn't actually stuck around long enough to complete my HND?

—You're on to plums there, he told me confidentially.

I didn't understand.

—Elsa doesn't speak. We've been trying to get her to say something, anything, but no-one's managed it yet.

—She'll talk to me.

He assumed what I took to be a sympathetic expression. Clearly, he didn't expect me to succeed – but he clearly had no idea how determined I was when it came to getting what I wanted. Also, I'd just outsmarted him. He'd never know that, of course. It was a powerful feeling, knowing that I'd managed to get past the gates and guards at a state hospital. Nothing stood between me and Elsa Norrington. Finally, we would meet.

But would she listen when I spoke?

The room we met in was functional and featureless. Literally a room with a table and two chairs. A uniformed guard stood by the door, constantly vigilant, mindful of my safety. I sat and waited for someone to bring Elsa so we could get this over and done with.

She entered the room and gazed blankly at me.

All the anger simply vanished from me the moment our eyes met.

Elsa Norrington was a wreck of a woman. Her legs were wide and unwieldly. She struggled to walk, huffing and heaving loud gasps of breath with each step she took. Her hair was a shock of silver frizz, which offset her dark facial hair. Her eyes were wet and sad. This was someone close to the end of her life. For some reason, I suddenly felt a tremendous rush of compassion for her, the woman who killed her own baby.

Navigating her bulky body onto the chair took a few arduous seconds, but she managed it in the end. I peered around at the guard, then turned my full attention to Elsa.

—Hello, I said.

Elsa said nothing.

—I've come to see you. To talk. Is that okay?

The sound of her chest painfully heaving out air was the only reply I received

—Actually, you can sit there and listen to me in silence for all I care.

I leaned over the table and lowered my voice.

—You put your baby inside a cardboard box that came with a cheap microwave oven.

She frowned, but said nothing.

—What sort of a person does that? I asked.

Elsa looked away, as though I'd simply vanish if she couldn't see me.

No such luck for her. Leaning closer, I whispered:

—I found him.

She looked back at me.

—The box was wet, stuck half in the ground, covered in muck and dirt. I found him by accident, but I've never been able to forget. I have a feeling you're the same. Or maybe you're desperate to forget about your baby. The one you killed.

—I didn't kill him.

A triumphant smile spread across my face. I knew she'd talk. I knew it! For some reason, I'd guessed she'd open up to me when I told her I'd found her child, that I was the one who led the police to his makeshift grave. But once the excitement of Elsa actually saying something wore off, I realised what she'd said in her quiet little voice.

—What?

—I didn't kill him.

—Of course you did.

—No. I'm telling you the truth. I didn't kill him. It wasn't me. I'm a good girl.

She was nuts, of course.

—If you didn't kill him, who did?

Elsa covered her face like a weird game of peek-a-boo, then opened her two hands up so that I could see her again.

—Jimmy.

Now we were getting somewhere. Where that actually was, I didn't know.

—Who is Jimmy?

Elsa looked at me as though I were insane and not her.

—Jimmy? He's Jimmy, obviously.

—Do you live with Jimmy?

Elsa sighed dramatically.

—No, I don't live with Jimmy.

She paused, before adding:

—Jimmy lives with *me*.

—You're taking the piss, I told her plainly.

Everything changed the moment I raised my voice.

The guard reacted with a burst of speed and yanked me away to safety.

Elsa launched the table at me, but it missed, instead crashing into the wall.

I spun around and fled the hospital, not stopping until I reached the train station.

Chapter 60

Failure

I spent the next few days in my bedroom, lamenting my terrible failure and eating boxes of cookies. The worst thing in the world for a dreamer is for reality to intrude on their dream. This happened quite often with me. I'd expected to confront the woman I associated with the darkest moment in my life, breaking her down gradually with the truth like a lawyer in an American crime movie. Then, finally, I'd be able to walk out of Carstairs with my head held high, the soft sunlight diffusing my skin, the last shot of a movie before the final roll of the credits, which *of course* would have been soundtracked by an optimistic pop bop. Instead, I'd run out the gates as fast as my feet could take me (not that fast) and found myself none the wiser as to what had gone wrong in my dream scenario.

Really, what did I expect from a woman who had killed her own baby?

Or had she?

Something wasn't right.

I knew it. I *felt* it.

It wasn't until my fifth box of cookies that I came to a startling conclusion.

Elsa was telling the truth.

Someone else killed her baby.

Munching the last cookie in the box, I looked down at my bed. Books (and crumbs) were strewn across the bedcover, each novel selected for my pleasure. I looked at them, taking in each cover, wondering which one would make me feel better. But the book I really wanted to read wasn't there. It was the BT Phone Book and it was in the hall under some unopened debt letters. Slowly, cautiously, I poked my head out of my bedroom door.

A parody of David Attenborough's familiar voice came at me from the staircase.

—At certain times of the day, he leaves his natural habitat to find sustenance.

It was Laddie. He was dressed in a white Lacoste tracksuit with socks pulled over the legs of his trousers, making him look like Little Jimmy Krankie dressed as a football hooligan. I scowled at him, but said nothing. His joke, like the best comedy, scraped close to the bone (not the funny bone). I wouldn't give him the satisfaction of knowing he'd upset me.

—I haven't been in my room that much, I protested.

—I thought you'd gone into hibernation, he said.

In a brilliant example of multitasking, I gave my brother a two-fingered salute and managed to grab the phone book with my other hand. Sometimes I amazed myself. Then, without uttering another word, I headed back into my bedroom.

—Happy hibernation, said Laddie as I shut the door behind me.

But hibernation was the last thing on my mind.

Quickly, I flicked through the pages until I reached N.

Then I ran my finger down the list of names and numbers until I got to NO.

Norman.

Normington.

Norrington.

My finger froze.

My eyes widened and my heart quickened.

Elsa Norrington   54 Sandyknowes Road   01236 239839.

I immediately picked up my mobile telephone (a gift to myself during my three year stint in Blackpool) and dialled the number. The sound of the dialling tone was mercifully brief. I remembered to keep the phone slightly away from my head for fear of being poisoned by gamma radiation. I only needed to rule out what Elsa had told me.

If no-one answered, I could assume there was no such person as Jimmy.

Suddenly a guttural, rasping voice filled the space between the speaker and my ear.

—Who is it? Who's there?

My heart fluttered in fear.

—Hello. I'm looking for Jimmy.

—I'm Jimmy.

That was all I needed to know. I ended the call and fell back onto my springy mattress, my chest tight with tension. Flat on my back, staring up at the ceiling, trying hard to lose myself in the Artex swirls, I finally came to a decision. There was no way I could just stay in my bedroom. Not now. I had to know the truth. It was the only way to finally leave this weird state I'd found myself in ever since returning to Cumbernauld. After all, wasn't that why I'd come back in the first place?

With a sudden spurt of energy, I threw on my tweed riding cape and matching bowler hat, before heading out into the rain, walking, walking, walking, until finally I found myself walking towards the place that had always repelled me until now.

The last time I'd ventured this far into Sandyknowes Road was a week or so after I'd found Baby C. I'd made another attempt years later, the same day I went to visit my sisters at their new flat for the first time. This time I wouldn't turn away. It wasn't easy, of course. Something invisible pushed at me until I finally decided to push back and I found myself standing outside the familiar blocks of flats. Taking a deep breath, I came to the main entrance. I found number *54*. Elsa's name wasn't there, but most of the names had been crossed out and replaced by other names, hastily rewritten in ink.

This confirmed to me that Elsa had literally lived in the flats overlooking the forest where I'd found her baby. The forest. I still had to go there. One final time.

I skirted around the block and found myself headed towards the grass verge, the same place I'd been all those years ago, retracing my steps with size ten feet. My first emotion was an overwhelming sense of crushing disappointment. The forest, the dark forest, looked exactly the same as I remembered. My photographic memory had preserved it perfectly, but I hadn't taken into account the difference in my size and height. To my adult eyes, the forest looked like some trees and a bit of grass. Not so much a forest but woods, or a stand of trees.

—Hmph, I said.

The patch where the box had been buried was still there.

Mentally, I superimposed where the box had been, with the dead baby inside.

Something snapped in me. Finally, a strong emotion!

I turned and headed to the back entrance of the block of flats where Elsa lived.

The entrance was open to all – someone had snapped the lock.

So far, so good.

I climbed the steps, looking at the doors, most of them bland red council doors. One was brown, well-kept, a door belonging to someone who'd taken full advantage of Maggie Thatcher's Right To Buy policy. It wasn't the door I was looking for, though.

That was the next floor up.

Number 54.

Why was I here? What was I doing?

Before I could stop myself, I was peering under the doormat, hoping to find a key. Instead I found some little creepy crawlies, little beasties overwhelmed by the sudden surge of light around them. Recoiling, I dropped the mat and pushed myself away. Okay, there wasn't a convenient key waiting for me beneath a mat.

What next?

I placed my hand on the handle of Number 54.

It turned and the door fell open.

What idiot in Cumbernauld didn't lock their front door?

Stepping into the flat, I laughed out loud at my good luck.

But luck, like laughter, only comes in short bursts.

Chapter 61

17th October 2002

There's an old saying Fishtank particularly liked. It went like this: In Cumbernauld, all roads lead to Cumbernauld. Our town was built so that you could reach every part of it without leaving the safety of the path. The idea was that kids would never need to cross a road, risk being hit by cars. But that silly old phrase meant something else to me. It told me that everything was connected. The planners of Cumbernauld had simply acknowledged this as a universal truth and built the town accordingly. As I stood in the dark hallway of Elsa's flat, my eyes adjusting to the gloom, a notion that perhaps I was meant to be here gripped me. Stupid, maybe, but true. I felt like I was hurtling towards something massive and I'd either smash through it or be pulverised in the wreckage.

There were no wrong turns in Cumbernauld. Just different directions to the same places.

Slowly, I took a step forward. I stood on something hard and brittle.

I backed away, listening for movement in the flat. Nope. Nothing.

Looking down, I saw what I'd stepped on. It was an empty margarine tub, now completely flattened by my Dr Marten boot. The floor was covered in clutter. If there was a carpet under the trash, I couldn't see it. Then there was the smell. It was horrific. An unholy mixture of mildew and nicotine. The walls, yellow, were smeared in dirt and grime. It made my skin crawl. Or was that the dust mites wafting in the air? My hands twitched with the familiar sensation that could only be calmed with soap and water.

Not now. It wasn't the time. Fight the feeling!

At the end of the hall, I turned and found myself standing in something like a kitchen.

There was no table, just two chairs and a box.

—Bloody hell, I said.

I'd been raised in council accommodation and we'd not had much in the way of money, but we were clean. My mother would have cracked up if we'd allowed our house to get into as bad a mess as this flat in Sandyknowes Road. The floor had old newspapers across it, a cheap and easy substitute for lino or tiles. One front page faced upwards: an exclusive from The Sun, with Liz Hurley's face looking slightly quizzical alongside bold letters that read HATE MOB STUN LIZ. Stepping on Liz's face, I crossed the kitchen to the window which had net curtains. The glass was grimy, flecked in bird shit and green mould. The edge of the sink pressed hard against my belly as I leaned over. The sink was full of dirty dishes, flies divebombing the plates over and over again. Sitting alongside the pile of dishes was a large green glass ashtray and some mugs, all of which used to be white, but were now tinted a shade of tea-stained brown. The walls were the same colour, as was the ceiling.

Even though the window was filthy, I could still see what was happening outside. Kids with skateboards zipped down the concrete path, then back the other way. They were next to the patch of grass I'd been on ten years ago, the day I found the box.

The box.

I suddenly thought of something else.

The past returned in full colour, the way it always did with me.

There had been something on the surface of the box.

I remembered...

A logo. Faded, difficult to read. But there.

AMSUNG MICR WAV OV N

Samsung Microwave Oven.

I didn't want to look behind me, but I made myself turn around until I faced the microwave I knew would be on the worktop. Peering closer, I saw the logo. It was Samsung. The packaging for this microwave, this actual microwave in front of me, had been used to hide a dead baby – and not very well, because the box had only been taken a few metres away from the block. Regardless, I felt excited. The police had arrested Elsa because her DNA matched the baby's and she'd failed to report her baby's death. Yet I'd found my way to a different conclusion through my own persistence. If Elsa was telling the truth, someone else was responsible, at least partially. Someone by the name of Jimmy, who'd kept out of sight. He couldn't be allowed to get away with murder. No way. I was his karma in a pair of Dr Martens.

I had to leave as quickly as possible so I could contact the police.

Something moved.

It wasn't me.

Frantically, I ran out into the hall, giving no thought to the clatter my boots made. I reached the door and yanked it open. Except it didn't open. It remained fixed in place. Desperately, I tried again and again to get out of the flat.

The door was locked.

Laughter filled the flat. Demonic, vile laughter. Suddenly, a voice from nearby (I couldn't quite fix its location except that it was coming from somewhere in the flat) started singing a single sentence over and over again.

—There's somebody at the door! There's somebody at the door!

I didn't reply, opting instead to find a way out of the flat. There *had* to be a way out.

—There's somebody at the door! There's somebody at the door!

Where was that voice coming from? It felt close. Too close.

—There's some...body...at the door!

I rushed into the living room, but it was empty. The television was on but the screen was just grey static, which caused a disconcerting background buzzing. Leaving the living room, I headed towards what I assumed was a bathroom. I kicked the door open, almost causing it to fly off its hinges. But the bathroom was empty, the toilet unflushed. Fuck!

More laughter followed. I started to panic. Backtracking into the kitchen, I leaned over the sink towards the window and looked outside. To my relief, the skateboarding kids were still there, grinding on the ground next to the grass and trees. My first attempt at opening the window was met with almost impossible resistance. The window in 54 Sandyknowes Road hadn't been opened in years. My plan was to get a message out to the kids, tell them to go and get help. The window refused to budge. I tried desperately, but it wasn't shifting.

A voice, closer than before, addressed me.

—I knew you were coming. What took you so long?

Cautiously, I looked around, hoping to find the source.

It seemed to be coming from inside the walls themselves.

There had to be a way of drawing the voice's owner into the open.

Finally, I spoke up.

—You must be Jimmy, I said.

He didn't reply. I pressed on, hoping to find – and follow – the voice.

—Elsa told me about you, I said.

He laughed, but I still couldn't find him.

—Elsa told me about *you*.

There was a cupboard in the kitchen, the door of which wasn't completely shut.

I opened it and looked into the darkness.

The darkness blinked back at me.

I screamed and fell away in fright.

He emerged from the cupboard on all fours, moving like a dog until he found his footing. Then, like the evolution of man, he climbed onto two legs and towered over me.

In my haste I found myself backed against the worktop, trapped in the corner.

The man from the cupboard loomed large. He was dirtier than the walls and floor of the rubbish-infested flat. He wore a shirt and tie, though they were tatty and torn. He stunk of piss and shit and packets of fags.

He didn't need to introduce himself. I already knew his name.

—Jimmy, I said quietly.

He nodded in the affirmative, smiling darkly while his head bobbed up and down.

—What are you doing here in my flat?

—Actually, I was trying to get out of your flat.

—You asked Elsa about me. Didn't you?

His eyes widened as he spoke, getting impossibly bigger with each word.

—DIDN'T YOU?

I didn't flinch. Actually, I wanted him to talk. I was safe while he talked. While he talked, I could plan a way to escape 54 Sandyknowes Road with my life intact. Despite my fear (I was terrified beyond all measure) I wouldn't just stand around helpless. I'd never been helpless, just unprepared. If I'd learned anything from a childhood with Fishtank and the rest of my family, it was how to survive craziness.

—Yes, I went to see Elsa. I asked her why she killed her baby.

—She told me you found it.

Ah. Elsa had been on the phone to Jimmy.

—It? I said.

—I didn't want it. I said to her not to have it. I didn't want to pay for it.

—He was your baby?

—Do you think someone else was the father?

—No! That's not what I meant. I just wanted to know.

Jimmy squinted at me, a sharp line of sunlight from the window behind us cut his face in half. I knew literally nothing about this man other than his name. I had no idea what his motivations were. Why he seemed so feral. I wanted to know everything.

I gave him silence so he'd fill it with words. My plan worked.

—I didn't mean to kill him. It was an accident. Just a stupid accident.

—How did it happen?

I didn't want to hear this, but I'd put myself in this position.

—It wouldn't stop crying, so I put a cushion over its face until it shut up.

On seeing my horrified reaction, Jimmy shrugged apathetically.

—I was trying to get some sleep but it kept crying and crying. So I shut it up. But you can't keep a dead thing in the house. Flies kept buzzing around. BZZZZZZ! That's the sound flies make. I had to get it out the flat, so I put it in a box and buried it outside. No-one saw me. No-one even knows about me. No-one except Elsa…and you.

A weird notion occurred to me.

—Is Elsa your wife, girlfriend, or mother?

—She's my girlfriend.

I sighed in relief.

—And she's my ma too.

It was official. I was trapped in an episode of *The X-Files*.

—Let me out of here, I demanded.

Jimmy laughed. It sounded like a choked coughing fit.

—That's not going to happen.

He lifted a knife from the worktop, the kind used to cut steak. It had an old, serrated, rusted blade set in a plastic handle. It looked like it could do me a lot of damage.

I stood still, waiting for Jimmy to get closer.

Once he was close enough…

I introduced his left foot to my right Dr Marten. Stamping down as hard as possible, I felt something crack underneath the sole of my boot. The pain on Jimmy's face brought me wicked joy. He gasped in agony, his throat trying to form a scream too large for his mouth. Then, weeping and wailing, he dropped to the floor and rolled around in the dirt.

I wasn't quite finished yet.

Acting quickly, I reached into the cluttered sink and grabbed the first object at hand.

A large green glass ashtray. It felt satisfyingly heavy in my hand.

I raised the ashtray above my head.

Then, summoning all the strength I had in me, I brought the ashtray down on the top of Jimmy's skull. He fell onto the floor without making a sound. Breathing hard and heavy, I looked at the body at my feet. At first, I worried he was pretending to be unconscious, but the stream of blood onto the newspaper-covered floor convinced me otherwise.

The ashtray went out the window, taking the glass with it.

The kids on skateboards looked startled as I yelled down for help.

—Phone the police and tell them I'm in danger!

They didn't do anything.

For fuck sake.

I only had one chance. I had to make it count. Praying that stories still mattered, that children passed legends around, I leaned out the window and shouted:

—I'm stuck in here with Billy The Squid! You know who that is? He's trying to kill me!

That caused the reaction I needed. The kids got on their boards and sped off to find help. However, I couldn't just stand around and wait for the police. I had to find a way out of the flat. There had to be a key for the front door somewhere in the flat.

That's when I felt something long and thin against my throat.

Hot breath invaded my ear, followed by a cold voice that said only one word:

—Die.

I realised there was something underneath my chin.

The blade of a blunt and rusty kitchen knife.

The blade suddenly disappeared out of sight, slicing fast across my throat.

A slit opened on my neck, letting out a rush of air and blood.

I uttered a sigh of pain as everything from the neck down suddenly dripped red. Clutching my neck with a corner of the cape I was wearing, I pressed as though my life depended on it – actually, it did. With supreme effort, I looked across at Jimmy. He'd dropped to the floor again, the knife in his hand now by his side. He'd managed to force enough life into his bones to get up and stab me. Now we were both on the filthy floor of his flat. Horrible thoughts came and went, sharp and short, just like my breathing. Would I get tetanus from the knife wound? Was there asbestos in this flat? Could I get Hep C from a dusty floor? How would I be able to wash my hands if I had one hand against my throat? But in the moments before I blacked out from the loss of blood, I had other thoughts: genuine questions that would probably never be answered. How would my family cope without me? Would Mum wander the bingo with an urn full of my ashes? Had I done enough for the little baby I found in a cardboard box ten years ago? Would Fishtank care I was dead? However, my last thought before everything slipped into darkness wasn't a question or a paranoid notion. It was something far more mundane: on the floor of that filthy flat, I suddenly realised I really didn't want to die.

—Bugger, I thought as everything went dark.

Chapter 62

The Next Chapter

There was no white tunnel. No old man with a beard. No angels. No gates. I got the sense of weightlessness, a sensation of floating away. When I opened my eyes again, the room had changed completely. It was painfully bright and the air had a faint whiff of chemical, an antiseptic tinge that my brain immediately associated with hospitals. I was on a bed in a weird little gown that I wouldn't have worn by choice. My first instinct was to get out of bed. To this end, I sat up, or rather I tried getting myself into a position where I could hoist myself out of bed.

Someone screamed in my ear:

—HE'S AWAKE!

Then I remembered.

My fingers immediately went to my throat and brushed against the bandages.

—No, don't touch those! I'll get a doctor.

It was Lorna. She was already pulling my hands away from my neck, slapping them aside. The message was completely understood: don't touch the bandages. I opened my mouth to say something, but the voice that came out wasn't my voice. Except it was, just deeper.

Oh, I liked it. I sounded really manly.

—How...did I...get here?

My brain felt fuzzy, like someone had taken it out of my skull, wrapped it in cotton wool and stuck it back again.

—GET HIM SOME WATER, Lorna bawled.

—Tea, I said in my new voice. Tea!

Mum came into the room with Davy Death by her side.

—Is he alright?

—He just asked for tea, said Lorna.

—Yeah, he's alright.

Despite being twenty-one-years-old, I had my family fussing over me as though I were a child. Actually, I enjoyed it a little. I hadn't had this much attention from my family since…well, ever. A nurse came by to check me out, then she summoned a doctor. They looked at my vitals (apparently not finding anything too discomforting) and the nurse headed off, leaving me with my family and a doctor. The doctor seemed pleasant enough. Tall, dark-haired, with bags under his eyes big enough to be charged as extra luggage on holiday – if he ever actually managed to get a holiday. While my family watched nervously, he examined my neck with his fingers, gently checking the bandages, manoeuvring my head backwards and then forwards. It was a disconcerting experience to have someone control you like a dummy, making you move in his direction.

—Your wound seems to be healing nicely, he said.

I let out a deep, grateful sigh of relief.

It wouldn't last. Too many people wanted an explanation.

—What the fuck were you doing in a flat in Sandyknowes Road?

I looked over at my mother and raised an eyebrow.

—You could have died, she added.

Lorna tried to explain everything as quickly as possible.

I got the sense she wanted to say more, but didn't dare.

—A bunch of kids called the police. They said you called to them from a broken window. By the time the police arrived, you were in a puddle of blood, not all of it yours.

Mum shivered. Lorna continued.

—The other guy is in intensive care. He's got a blood clot in his head.

—That's Jimmy. I hit him with an ashtray.

Mum looked alarmed.

—Shhh. Don't say anything until we get you a lawyer.

I didn't care anymore. Life looked slightly different from a hospital bed. Having your throat cut in front of your own eyes tended to make you prioritise things.

As for the animal who cut my throat, my only regret was that I hadn't hit him harder.

—That baby-basher deserves everything he gets.

—Baby-basher? Laddie said, completely bewildered.

Lorna knew. She'd already worked it out. But then, she had the added advantage of knowing more than the others. Her mind made up, she leaned in my direction so she could readjust my bedsheet, even though it didn't needed readjusting. Of course, there was another reason for my sister's sudden interest in my sheet. As she fiddled with it, she whispered something in my ear.

—The police are on their way.

I understood. My options had suddenly narrowed down:

I could tell the truth or I could lie.

By the time the police arrived to interrogate me, I'd already decided to tell the truth, the whole truth and everything but the truth.

Chapter 63

Survival

It took me a long time to recover from my injuries. There's now a long thin line on my throat that reminds me of the day I broke into a flat in Sandyknowes Road. That scar doesn't bother me too much. Not anymore. There's always another problem to face, another battle to win. I still wash my hands too much. I don't think that'll ever change, but at least now I've got some control over it. There are some days I can go several hours without thinking about hot water and soap. Those days are usually happy ones.

I've often wondered what would have happened if I hadn't discovered little Kevin Norrington inside his cardboard coffin. I used to think life would have been much better if I hadn't found him, that maybe I could have been normal. But normal is for boring people. I know that now. How can you live your life without adversity? I pity people who navigate through their days and nights without any problems. I'm stronger because of everything I survived. I'm made of steel. I'm a fucking superhero.

If I've learned one thing over the years of living in Cumbernauld, it's this:

Normal is *not* normal.

Kevin Norrington's case went to trial on the 23rd of January 2004. I took a long black golf umbrella to the courtroom, swinging it idly as I walked down the street. It wasn't just for the rain, it was to give me something to use as a weapon if any of Jimmy's freaky friends were waiting for me. But it turned out the only people waiting for me were photographers and reporters. I remember that day as clearly as I remember everything. Perks (and problems) of having perfect recall. The photographers took their photographs and I nearly posed for them. I'd dressed for the occasion, of course. My coat was genuine Burberry and didn't I make sure everyone knew it! None of that Kappa shit, thank you very much. After passing and posing for the throng of reporters gathered outside the main entrance of the courthouse, I entered and waited to be taken before the judge and the jury.

I floated into the courtroom in a haze.

Was this really happening to me?

The trial lasted eight days. I wasn't there for most of it, preferring to observe from a safe distance, which has always been my default mode. Besides, I'd already provided my testimony on the first day of proceedings. In the end, I had to be honest. After years and years of keeping secrets, I told the jury word for word what I told my lawyer:

I found a box with a baby inside it. I called the police anonymously.

The recording of the call was played in court for the benefit of the jury.

—*Operator. Could you please state your emergency?*

—*I found a dead body.*

—*Where did you find the body?*

—*Down in the forest behind the flats at Sandyknowes Road...*

I listened and my heart lurched for the little boy I used to be. My life was so different back in 1992. I had not one but two sisters and a radio mast on the rooftop of our house in Craigieburn Road. My brother wasn't in prison for murder.

I hadn't run off with a bank account full of stolen money.

Something absolutely extraordinary happened to me whilst on the stand.

I hadn't cried for Baby C.

I hadn't cried at my sister's funeral.

Yet the moment I heard my voice from over ten years ago…

I felt tears in my eyes.

Real tears. The kind that run free and fall far.

—*Thank God,* I thought. —*I'm human after all.*

I don't actually know why I cried.

I'm still trying to work it out for myself.

I went to court to see Jimmy being sentenced to life in prison for the murder of Kevin, the attempted murder of me and perverting the course of justice. He smirked at me as police led him out of the dock, but I knew it would be wiped from his face as soon as he reached his cell.

Jimmy was to be taken away to start his sentence in Barlinnie.

The same prison my brother was currently serving a life sentence in.

Though I didn't know for sure, I had a suspicion Jimmy would be dead within a week.

It took two weeks, actually. During his first day on the job, one prison officer found Jimmy twisted and broken at the bottom of a staircase. He'd tumbled to his death, or so the official story claimed. An accident, said the investigation. A preventable yet unfortunate mishap. Shortly after being informed of Jimmy's death, I received a birthday card in the post. It was a card meant for an old lady, but I suppose it was the only one available at the time. I knew Jake had sent it, because his handwriting looked a lot like mine, except that I knew to put a capital letter at the start of a sentence and a full stop at the end of one.

HAPPY BIRTHDAY, said the card.

I appreciated the gesture, but my birthday wasn't actually due for another nine months.

It didn't matter. I understood exactly what Jake was trying to tell me.

Suddenly grateful for him, I found myself silently thanking my brother.

He cared in his own way. Really, I would have visited him in Barlinnie except...

I was too busy packing my stuff to leave Cumbernauld.

Things would be different this time. I was moving away, not running away. Last time I had to escape, I wanted to find another way of life, something else better than Cumbernauld. This time would be different. I chose to leave because I wanted to, not because I had to. And this time I didn't intend to stay away forever.

I broke the news to Mum while we were in our garden. She was sunbathing on the grass with a towel under her. It was one of those infrequent hot summer days when every man in Scotland walked around shirtless. Every man except me. I didn't want to give anyone nightmares. Besides, my pale skin was a constant reminder of my aversion to the sun. I belonged with the rain.

—You don't need to move out, son.

—I can't stay here forever.

—Why not? You left before and you came back. Home is here with your family.

—Look. I won't be moving too far away. I've already got a flat. You can help me decorate it. Doesn't that sound good? I'm going to paint it fuchsia.

—You've got a flat? Whereabouts?

—Have a guess, I said mischievously.

—Byres Road?

I gave her two thumbs up for getting it right.

—I'm going to have more bin bags than anyone else in the street.

Mum didn't seem to mind my choice of home. She'd come a long way, because a few years ago she'd have torn me to shreds for even thinking about moving to a place like Byres Road. Too middle-class. Too pretentious. Not working-class enough.

—That's not too bad. Byres Road is just a bus ride away.

—A bus ride and then a trip through the subway, actually.

—You never liked this place, she said sadly.

—You never liked it either, I replied.

—Maybe we'll move away too.

—Would Davy be okay with that?

Mum paused to think it over, but I already knew the answer.

—Cumbernauld is depressing, drab, and dull.

She paused for effect. Then said:

—Davy loves it here, of course.

I laughed. How else could I react? It felt good to laugh again.

Mum suddenly became very serious, as she tended do to when we were alone together.

—I'm sorry I didn't do more for you all.

—You did great.

—I don't know why I stayed with your dad for so long. I can't believe it, really.

—You had five kids and four jobs. I get it.

—You do?

—Yes.

—At least that poor baby you found got a decent funeral, said Mum.

—Yes, I repeated.

—Apparently someone stepped in and paid for his funeral. No-one knows who.

Mum didn't see the glint in my eye or the smile on my face.

The phone rang from inside the house. Two times. Then it stopped.

It was time to leave. I'd already prepared for my departure.

—Phone me when you get to your new flat, said Mum.

We hugged awkwardly, but it still meant something.

Mum had no idea I wasn't going to my new flat.

Not yet. I needed a holiday. Somewhere to chill out and enjoy myself.

I headed outside and made my way down the street towards a waiting cab. My suitcases were so large they'd probably need a separate car. The driver of the cab jumped out, rushing to my aid. I smiled and waited as he loaded the boot. A few moments later, I was in the back with my seatbelt safely buckled around my chest.

The driver, a lean older man with a beard, craned his head towards me.

—Where to?

Honestly. I had no idea.

—Somewhere exciting, I said.

—You need to be more specific than that, mate.

I readjusted my weight and pulled a map out of my back pocket. It was my little map of the UK I'd bought from the Scan Bookshop earlier that morning. Unfolding it until the paper was smooth, I looked over the country from the back seat of my taxi. After a few moments, something caught my eye. A location. Somewhere I'd never visited.

—Is Scunthorpe a good place for a vacation?

—Oh God. You're that Blackpool guy, aren't you? I've heard about you.

—The rumours are all true.

—Do you know the drivers fight over who gets to pick you up? Your tips are legendary.

I barely listened as he spoke from the front of the car, his hands tight on the wheel. I was thinking about the past, remembering the sharp parts of my life, all the events that had brought me to this point in time. As the world whizzed by the windows of the cab, my life flashed before my eyes, memories served up in small portions. I'd survived it all.

Now it was time to replace those horrible old memories with bright new ones. I'd spent my life on the outside, peering in from the cold. Sometimes I had felt like I wasn't there at all, just a ghost, watching and commenting. It was time to change that, but I couldn't do anything while I lived in Cumbernauld. I'd miss my mad, crazy, ridiculous family. Of course I would. But they were only a phone call away; lines and cables and space junk keeping us close even when we were far apart.

Soon enough, my thoughts turned to the future. I didn't know what was going to happen. Somehow I knew I wasn't going to get married and settle down with anyone. No girlfriends. No boyfriends. No wives. No husbands. I would never start a family like everyone else, because I wasn't like everyone else. At long last I'd come to realise that being me wasn't a bad thing at all. But who was that? A weirdo. A lover of books. Asexual. A minor sufferer of OCD. I ate too many packets of cookies and drank too much tea. I also had a brain that took in everything and discarded nothing.

I'm all those things and more.
Mostly, I'm a survivor.

It was getting dark outside. I found myself looking out of the window at the streetlights as all the bulbs switched on one by one. Not all of them worked, some flickered erratically, giving out garbled messages in their own crazy Morse Code.

Eventually the flickering lamplight became less and less frequent.

The stars, however, lasted the whole night.

Like me, they'd come a long way.

Follow me on Twitter. Follow me on Instagram. Don't follow me home.

Twitter.com/KirklandCiccone
Instagram.com/KirklandCiccone
www.KirklandCiccone.co.uk

Thank you